Achilles' Helmet

A Commissaire Pierre Rousseau
Mystery

Graham Bishop

The Vidocq Press

This print edition published 2023
by
The Vidocq Press

By the same author

Joker in the Pack

Le Grand Mystère de Gornac
(in French)
A Local French Affair
(English trans)

Pierre Rousseau Mysteries

Achilles' Helmet

The Athenian Connection

The Crusader's Chronicle

Return to the Parthenon

The Walking Man

The Moroccan Connection

For Stephanie and Caroline who challenged me to write a novel 'instead of all those boring French text books.'

Main Characters

The rival collectors: Lord Glenbrae and Le Comte Alexandre de Villeneuve

The dealers: Charles Everidge and Ed Robson. Their boat is the **Artemis.**

The Italian tombaroli: Vincenzo Samborini, Giovanni Lucca, his right hand man, and others.

The International Art Fraud Squad team for Interpol: Commissaire Pierre Rousseau from France, Inspector Antonia Antoniarchis from Greece, supported by Major Soliman Kahn of the Turkish army. Their boat is the **Pericles.**

The smugglers helping Everidge and Robson: Martin Handley (English) and Dominique Krevine (French). Their yacht is the **Phalaris.**

The rival gang working for the Comte de Villeneuve: Paul Sondheim (South African), Alain Tremblay (French Canadian), Natalie Marceau (French). Their boat is the **Edelweiss.**

Prologue

The marble figures of Patroclus, Ajax and Hector looked down on them with sightless grey eyes. The two men were standing side by side in the Aegina Marbles room in the Glyptothek Museum in Munich gazing spell-bound at the figures in the frieze. Charles opened the guide book and read, while his companion continued to stare at the carvings.

'The god Apollo, losing patience, strikes first. The helmet takes most of the blow, but Patroclus still staggers and falls back under the sheer force of the contact. The mark on his helmet is clearly visible and the clash of metal on metal has momentarily amazed his senses. He vainly struggles to regain his feet, to get some purchase in the wet sand, in order to fend off the next assault. But he is too late; Hector is already standing over him, gleaming sword raised, a dark silhouette against the sun dazzling his victim. He strikes, easily avoiding Patroclus' vainly held up shield. He disdainfully drops his own shield to better deliver the final blow two-handedly. Patroclus' helmet flops heavily onto the sand, the head inside gives out a rasping sigh, the eyes lose their shine and grow pale. The helmet rolls slowly to a stop in a pool of blood; darkness closes in.

'When Prince Achilles is told the news his tormented cry can be heard all over the battle ground, reaching even inside the very walls of Troy itself, striking fear into the hearts of friend and foe alike. His vengeance will be terrible and many must die to ease his soul. Hector is slain and his body dragged round the city walls for all to see. Twelve young Trojans are

sacrificed on Patroclus' funeral pyre. But Achilles too must die young as his mother Thetis foretold. He will not live to see the fall of Troy.'

Charles snapped shut the guidebook and, turning his attention to his companion, continued in his own words:

"Then legend has it the two of them were buried together under a mound overlooking the Hellespont close to the walls of Troy. Their ashes were mingled and placed in a single urn. Their armour and other effects were buried beside them. The tomb has never been discovered as far as is known."

Charles did not dare interrupt the silence which fell as he finished his account. The older man stood as if rooted to the spot, his eyes fixed on the frieze. Half a head shorter than Charles and stockier, he had that air of natural authority and confidence that comes with real wealth and status.

"Will ye just take a look at that helmet, Charles," he barely whispered, unable to take his eyes off the figure of Patroclus. "Achilles wore that helmet before he fatefully lent it to Patroclus. Just think of that, man - over three thousand years ago."

He tore his eyes away and turned towards Charles.

"It might still be there somewhere, Charles. Will ye find it for me? Do whatever ye have to, but find it for me."

Slowly, as if in a trance, he moved away from the frieze and walked unsteadily towards the entrance to the gallery, head down, unable to contain his emotions any longer. He had just seen the missing centrepiece to his whole private collection. He could already picture the helmet in his mind's eye taking pride of place in his secret gallery, which very few besides Charles and a few trusted friends had ever been allowed to see.

Charles Everidge watched him walk across the room, the older man's words echoing round in his head. The collector turned at the door just before he left the gallery and looked across the room to him again. His eyes alone repeated his request: Prince Achilles' battle helmet. The real thing. Find it for me.

Chapter 1

Hidden amongst the hills of Tuscany behind the towered village
of San Gimignano the old stone shepherd's cottage merged into
the surrounding terrain. From a distance it was visible only to
the most practised eye. The walls were constructed from the
local stone which lay strewn around on the barren ground; the
sun had basted the roof tiles to the same pale brown of the
parched vegetation of this heat-wave-scorched landscape.

Outside, the lookout sat motionless, conserving energy in
the meagre shade of a gnarled olive tree. A small troop of goats
kept him company, swishing their tails to ward off the irritating
flies and occasionally scratching their flanks against the trunk of
the tree which at that height had been rubbed smooth and
shiny, completely devoid of bark. Every few seconds the
lookout fanned himself with his dust-covered beret, causing the
flies to rise momentarily in a black cloud above his head, before
settling back to where they had been previously the instant he
replaced it. The sun hung high in the cloudless sky, any early
morning mist having long been burned off. His eyes only
narrow slits, his gaze never left the winding road far below.

Inside the old cottage the walls were bare and rough – the
way the outside must have looked before the sun and the wind
had weathered them. They were empty of ornament, only those
tools necessary for the shepherd's living hung on wooden hooks
around the room. Blackened pots, pans and ladles surrounded

the open fireplace. On one side of the hearth a low bunk was covered by a coarse wool blanket.

Four men sat around the wooden table in front of the hearth playing cards. They played with the offhand concentration and silent commitment of well-honed habit. Hardly a word passed between them during each hand – each knew the characteristics of the others' tactics. The bluff and counter bluff going on in their minds excluded all superfluous talk. Grunts and gestures took the place of words. They showed no outward sign of listening for the expected visitors from outside, but there was an almost imperceptible hesitation from all four half way through what was to be the final hand as each picked up the sound of the distant engine.

The hand reached its natural end with no quickening of pace. Without a word the dealer calmly collected the cards and placed the pack in the centre of the table. The others pushed back their chairs and turned to face the door. The lookout entered and, with a scarcely perceptible nod, took his seat beside the others. Five pairs of eyes focussed on the door.

An old truck drew up in the yard outside, doors slammed and Charles Everidge and his partner at their London gallery, Ed Robson, entered the cottage, stooping to avoid the low doorway. They hesitated on the threshold, temporarily blinded, until their eyes adjusted to the gloom of the interior. Both were wearing jeans and open shirts, but, clearly unused to the heat, were perspiring heavily, their red faces streaked with the dust blown in through the open windows of the truck from the drive up the track.

The leader of the tombaroli, Vincenzo Samborini, stood as they entered. He was not a tall man, French in appearance rather than Italian; his face full and weather-tanned, hair greying, but with sharp piercing eyes and a way of staring at strangers which immediately disconcerted them as they realised they were being summed up. Charles and Ed were no exception, growing more uncomfortable by the second as they stood waiting for Samborini to pass silent judgement. At last he held out his hand and smiled with his lips. Both Englishmen relaxed a little when they saw they had passed whatever test it was that was being applied. They would not have been so pleased if they had known that Samborini had been deciding whether they were clever enough to lie to him or double-cross him. His firm verdict was that they were not.

The atmosphere lightened and Charles and Ed took their seats at the table. A bottle appeared and glasses followed. Samborini filled each with the local *eau de vie*. Ed made a slight movement to pick up his glass, but quickly suppressed it at a glance from Charles. The five tombaroli listened as the visitors described what they wanted and the sum they were offering. When the sum offered had been doubled and all the arrangements for the transfer to Turkey agreed, the first payment changed hands. At a nod from Samborini the glasses were raised and the deal was sealed.

*

"That went well. Odd bunch of blokes, though," remarked Ed as Charles put the truck into gear and edged across the yard trying to avoid the rocks strewn around. Ed Robson was shorter than his partner, slightly thinner with that pale freckled skin which goes with ginger hair, but with an expansive face which broke easily into a smile. Years in the art business had given him the habit of narrowing his eyes when he was thinking, as if he was concentrating on the details of a work of art in front of him and gauging its value on the market. He had said little in the cottage, content to leave the bargaining to Charles while he studied the faces of the tombaroli. He had come away from the meeting convinced that they were dealing with an experienced gang, but disconcerted by the feeling he had not been able to get behind their mask-like expressions and that they had controlled the bidding more than he would have liked.

Charles on the other hand had been too occupied with the negotiating to take in much about Samborini's partners. He was more a planner of ways and means than a student of character. Not that it would have been much help to him to know more about the Italians – their lives were so far removed from his own that he would not have been able to make use of the knowledge – apart from the fact they were considered by those who knew, to be the best professional tomb robbers in Italy.

If Prince Achilles' helmet did still exist and the legends and historical facts which he and Ed had spent months researching in the UK were accurate, this gang would find it. The success or failure of the mission was now up to the experience and flair of this band of illiterate peasants. Ed chuckled to himself at the irony of it.

Chapter 2

On the hills above the Bosphorus the last walkers of the day were watching the setting sun and the dying glimmers of fiery light sparkling on the white-flecked surface of the sea in the narrows. Even the presence of modern shipping could not banish the ghosts of the distant past for those who were ready to see them.

Some could see the Dardanelles and the catastrophe of the Gallipoli landings in 1915. Others could imagine the Persian armies of Xerxes, his soldiers crossing on a bridge of 800 boats in their thousands two and a half millennia before, as they massed on the far side and prepared to march into Greece to take on the Spartans at Thermopile; or perhaps the ghosts of Alexander the Great's Macedonian warriors caught their attention, crossing in the other direction a century and a half later to assert their power over the Persians by taking Persepolis – the magnificent city of light – only to burn it to the ground.

The more romantically inclined could make out Leander fighting against the waves in the Hellespont as he swam strongly from Abydos to Sestus. They could make out the priestess Hero on the far shore as she anxiously watched her lover's progress, beseeching the goddess Aphrodite to look favourably upon him and to protect him from the monstrous creatures of the deep.

Perhaps a few, looking up, caught the last rays of the sun glinting on the Golden Fleece of the Ram as he winged his way across the narrows taking Helle and her brother to safety.

Perhaps they could even hear Helle scream as she lost her precarious grip on the Ram's back and plunged to her death in the sea which ever since has born her name.

Others imagined Lord Byron proving to himself, and demonstrating in his vanity to admiring others, that the Hellespont could indeed be swum, romantically determined as he was to prove that the legend of Hero and Leander was true.

Observing the tourists warily through dark, piercing Italian eyes, as night quickly fell, was a group of watchers in a very different frame of mind. For two months the tombaroli too had roamed the hills above the Hellespont near the ancient city of Troy. Many times they had found tombs and burial sites and carried off what they found inside. The hills had been good to them – even better than their home ground in Tuscany - and none begrudged the time spent. There was always a ready market in Turkey for what they looted and they had grown used to the meetings and hard bargaining with the rapacious local middle men, who were only too pleased to relieve them of their haul each evening, accepting nonetheless that the Italians were keeping back the choice pieces for themselves.

As the days went by, the tombaroli had developed an eye for spotting likely signs on the ground which would lead them to their spoils. A hollow here, where the ground had settled; a slight rise where there should have been nothing but bare soil. A collapsed heap of stones or just a patch of stony ground, where there was no reason for there to be any stones at all; each sign told its own tale to their expert eyes and alert minds focussed on discerning the slightest clue over the long weeks. But not once had they come close to finding the specific tomb they were seeking, the one which would bring them the greatest reward.

It was time to move down onto the edge of the plain.

*

Commissaire Pierre Rousseau was stiff and uncomfortable. Lying on hard ground watching for hours at a time, day after day, was not his idea of action. Restless by nature, it was more his habit to get up and walk about, or stalk about, as his ex-wife would have put it. The best he could do here was to wriggle back from the edge of the ridge until he was far enough away to be able to sit up and reach for his cigarettes. Now that he no longer played tennis or indeed any sport, he had resumed the habit after only six months, partly because, he excused himself, he had become more desk bound after promotion at the young age of 37 to the rank of Commissaire. His work for the *Office central de répression du trafic des biens culturels* had involved more sitting down than he would have liked and he regretted having lost his former fitness.

His Greek colleague attached to the Greek Art Fraud Squad, Inspector Antonia Antoniarchis, was if anything even less patient and even more restless. She joined him in the hollow behind their observation point, leaving their Turkish liaison officer Major Soliman Khan to take over and to post soldiers to watch the Italians at work in the plain below the remains of ancient Troy.

Antonia Antoniarchis had begun her career as an academic at the university in Athens and then as a visiting professor at Berkeley, California. On her return to Athens after four years away, she had soon been granted a full professorship in her home university as she rose to prominence through her research, largely funded by the National Archaeological Museum of Athens.

Her youth and striking looks, combined with a bubbly personality not often associated with serious academics, had brought offers to present television documentaries both in Greece and in the United States. She had several times been consulted as an expert witness by the Greek Fine Art police to identify stolen artefacts they had seized.

Eventually she had decided that joining them would add some excitement to her life and enable her to combine her love of research with the practical side of tracking the perpetrators of what she considered to be crimes on a par with murder. Human beings regenerate themselves, but the antiquities they stole and sold purely for personal profit were irreplaceable, she reasoned. Sharing the stony ground here with her colleague from France was a natural consequence of the job.

Major Kahn's men had rigged up a low shelter for Pierre and Antonia at their base camp to give protection against the searing heat of the day which reached the low 40s in the afternoons. Particularly for the French northerner the temperature was close to being unbearable.

Later as each day drew to a close, a welcome land breeze would spring up, being pulled down from the higher ground behind, drawn down and across the plain by the rising heat from the sea as it cooled. Only then did the two of them feel more comfortable and able to talk more easily.

The extensive and not very discreet researches undertaken by two London art dealers, Charles Everidge and Ed Robson concerning the possible site of the burial ground for the fallen Greek heroes of the siege of Troy had attracted the attention of the specialist New Scotland Yard Fine Art Unit. The two dealers had contacted high profile classical scholars and archaeologists in university departments all over the country and even outside the UK, some of whom had grown curious about such intense interest in a legend that had been far from proven to be true.

However, interest had recently been renewed in the claims of the German archaeologist Schliemann who, a century and a half ago, had excavated a site overlooking the Bosphorus which he was convinced was the seaport of Troy.

More recent research had shown that the site, now four miles inland, could indeed have been a port as described by Homer. Centuries ago the plain now separating it from the coast had been under the sea, which had reached as far as the walls of the present remains of the city.

Try as they might however the specialist Fine Art Unit had been unable to discover whether the two dealers were acting on their own behalf or for an anonymous private collector. With the help of the Italian Fine Art police Everidge and Robson had been tracked to Tuscany. Their meeting with a gang of tombaroli known to have broken into countless Etruscan tombs confirmed that they must have a specific job in mind as a result of their researches.

Interpol had taken over and Commissaire Pierre Rousseau had been appointed to head a team to discover what the Italians had been tasked to find. Rumour had it there might also be a French collector involved, possibly based in London. So Pierre and his Greek and Turkish colleagues had spent the best part of a month staking out the Italians near the site of the ruins of ancient Troy.

The Turkish soldier they had left on watch scrambled his way up to the edge of the outcrop for the nth time that day. He had lost count of time and no longer had any real sense of why he was observing the men below scratching around amongst the rocks, as he put it to himself. He felt hot and sweaty, dirty, sore and dehydrated. This was not what he had joined the army for.

"Allah belasini versin!" he muttered as he caught his hand yet again on a jagged shard of rock and watched the blood running between his fingers. He rolled over onto his back to reach more easily into his pocket for his handkerchief. The side pocket of his uniform was already stained with blood from the

previous times he had snagged his hand. At that moment he
knew from the muffled shouts below that he may have missed
the very event he had been ordered to watch out for so long.

"Allah kahretsin!"

He squirmed quickly back up the slope to peer down
again at the animated huddle of men not far below. The
tombaroli were crowding round one of their number in a small
hollow only about 100 metres below to his right.

They were showing more excitement over this find than
over their many earlier discoveries during the previous
interminable weeks. The soldier himself was wary of being too
optimistic that at last the long watch might be over – there had
been too many false hopes raised already. However he worked
his way down below the ridge with a lighter heart than usual and
went back to report what he had seen, forgetting the dust
covered sticky blood still oozing from the wound on his hand.

"Probably nothing again, but we'd better check."

Pierre prepared himself to worm his way carefully back to
the ridge.

"I'll come with you," Antonia said.

As they moved gingerly across the stony ground, Antonia
was grateful for the thick army trousers she was wearing to
protect her legs. Hot and not flattering, she mused as she led
Pierre up the slope, but practical. It irritated her that her French
opposite number refused to wear such practical clothing and
maintained a sort of Parisian chic despite the heat.

Once they reached the ridge and could see the tombaroli
below, Pierre wiped the sweat from his eyes and surveyed the
scene through his binoculars.

"Mm, this time they do seem very excited. They are
Italians, so it could be nothing, but this time is different, I
think."

He turned to look at Antonia, who was smiling, despite her annoyance at his stereotyping.

She stretched out alongside him peering down onto the plain, binoculars glued to her eyes. She made no comment, but continued to watch. The Italians were indeed working more intensely than usual. Two of them had gone back to their camp at the foot of the outcrop just out of sight of the watchers. When they reappeared they were carrying a pot-holer's climbing ladder, which they set down beside the opening in the ground which the other two had by then enlarged. They struggled in the hard ground to peg one end firmly down and then unrolled the ladder into the hole.

"Tomb more large than before," whispered Kahn, who had joined them on their narrow vantage point, as more and more of the climbing ladder disappeared into the hole.

"We'll get a better idea how much bigger, if we go along the ridge to that point over there just above them," Pierre said. "Leave your man here, Major. Make sure he misses nothing, while we move over."

The three of them worked their way back from the vantage point and, once they were below the line of sight, they covered the hundred metres or so in a crouching run. Carefully crawling back up to the edge, they were just in time to see one of the tombaroli emerge from the hole and say something to the other three. He climbed out and helped up the fifth man. They pulled up the ladder, laid short planks across the hole they had made to the tomb and covered them over with the earth and stones they had dislodged when they began to dig. Three of them headed off along the foot of the cliffs while the remaining two finished the job of removing all trace of activity round the site as far as they could. They knew rival tomb robbers were about and they were taking no chances on anyone poaching their find.

Having retreated to some rocks about 20 metres away, they settled down to guard the spot. Darkness had fallen and they pulled their shepherd's cloaks around them against the drop in temperature. Within a few minutes all that the watchers on the ridge above could make out were the soft glows of two cigarettes in the gloom.

"No more action tonight I think," Kahn said. "It cause a lot too much attention. Time to go to bed. I make a watch with the men – they wake us as soon as something happens. The guys who left come back early tomorrow, I think so."

He disappeared into the darkness behind them. Pierre and Antonia followed him down more slowly. When they reached their base camp, Antonia wished Pierre good night and he watched her walk over to her tent. She lit the lamp inside and Pierre could see her shadow through the canvas as she prepared to settle down for the night.

Despite the cold Pierre remained outside. Fetching a blanket from his own tent, he pulled it around him and sat warming himself in the heat of the braziers Major Kahn's men had lit by the large tent they used as a canteen. Watching the stars in the clear night sky, he thought about the events of the last few weeks and realised he had grown close to his Greek colleague and knew that when this operation was over he would miss her alert mind.

He laughed at himself – it was more than that, he knew. Genuine attraction or desire or both, which was it, he wondered? At no point had she flirted with him or given any sign that she saw him as anything more than a colleague. They had not talked much on a personal level and, realising he knew little about her private life he wondered if she had a partner. As the light in her tent went out, he shook himself and forced his mind back to review the present situation.

He had worked in the department for ten years fighting the illegal trade in stolen art and artefacts in France. During this time the struggle had been all uphill and he had seen France become, with Italy, the most pillaged country in the world – thefts from châteaux all over France had become endemic. The dealers had become more and more adept at spiriting paintings and artefacts of all sorts out of the country at an alarming rate to Switzerland, Belgium or Holland from where they were quickly 'laundered' and passed on until the paper trail was so complex passing from one national justice system to another in quick succession.

To make matters even worse there are 16 canton jurisdictions in Switzerland alone, such that moving goods from one to another made it well nigh impossible to trace their origins. At each stage the buyer becomes more and more removed from the original transaction and less and less guilty of being responsible for the acquiring of stolen goods. Even governments were culpable of turning a blind eye to the sale of illegally acquired artefacts and of being slow to sign the UNESCO convention banning the illicit trade in cultural property.

Unscrupulous dealers and auction houses were complicit in giving antiquities a false saleroom history. The resources of the agencies charged with tracking the movement of illicitly obtained antiquities were kept pitifully low. Gradually however some progress was being made and the great national museums and collections of Britain, the US and Switzerland were beginning to show embarrassment at acquiring such artefacts. Much of this embarrassment stemmed more from the fact that they had fallen victim in the past to purchasing fakes and it was this fear of being publicly shown to have been duped rather than having suddenly acquired a higher moral conscience that caused them to look more closely at the origins of the works they were buying.

Pierre mulled over the chances of successfully tracking the transporting of whatever the tombaroli had found back to the paymaster-collector at the top of the chain. His thoughts were interrupted when he spotted a soldier reporting back to Major Kahn.

Kahn moved over to where Pierre was sitting:

"My men think we not the only ones to watch the Italians. They see three guys behind the hill over there on the right. Could be rival gang, could just be just young ones sleeping out under the stars."

"How likely is that? We're a long way from a major city," asked Pierre.

"Not so likely."

"So, it's probably another gang. That we do not need. OK. What do you suggest?"

"I send two men to look round and they find out more."

"Good. But no moves before they report to us. If it is a rival group, there must be someone financing them – another private collector in the hunt perhaps. This job is too specialised for an ordinary tomb robber. And fencing the finds ..." he looked at Kahn, "... selling the finds, will be almost impossible. I'll let Inspector Antoniarchis know what's happening."

Kahn silently slipped away to brief his men. Pierre rose stiffly, feeling the cold despite his blanket and walked over to Antonia's tent. He stood awkwardly outside unsure how best to attract Antonia's attention. He called softly and, after a moment, Antonia opened the flap and looked out.

When Kahn returned, the early dawn was beginning to show and they would soon lose the cover of darkness. Pierre and Antonia were preparing coffee on a small stove at the front of the tents. The soldiers were waking and stamping their feet to shake off the cold in their limbs. Kahn sat down and reported:

"Sure, we get close enough to hear them speaking on mobiles. They speak to someone, maybe in Switzerland, maybe in Belgium possibly. Three guys, as my men say - two men and a woman. No others come when we watch."

He gratefully accepted the cup of coffee Antonia handed to him.

"One man, he speak in English, but is American or South African I think. The other two, they speak in French. The lady, she speak the most on the phone and tells what is going on below. "

"You're certain they're connected in some way with this business and are not just tourists?" asked Pierre, stirring his coffee thoughtfully.

"I am certain, yes. They have lots of things for long wait – sleeping bags, things to cook with, binoculars and more. I do not understand why we do not see them before this. Perhaps they only just arrive on the hills."

"OK. Well, we'll have to be extra careful. I don't want them to know we are on to them. But now we have two gangs to watch; that complicates matters."

Antonia looked at the other two.

"Major Kahn, can you ask in the next village if these three have been staying there before coming up here? I can't believe we wouldn't have spotted them if they've been here for long. We'll need to follow both gangs so please post soldiers to watch them and the Italians. If the tombaroli have found what they've been looking for all this time, then they'll be moving on pretty soon."

Major Kahn got up as Pierre nodded his agreement to Antonia's plan.

"Sure – I phone you on mobile. If they stay nearby it will be in the downtown Çanakkale, certainly – we ask there in hotels. Not long job, I think," he laughed, "not too many hotels. Maybe they also have boat there too."

He drained his coffee, saluted and was gone.

Chapter 3

Charles and Ed were sitting at what had become over the past few days their usual table outside a café by the tiny harbour of Yükyeri Iskelesi watching the ferry nose up to the dock with its cargo of tourists, just back from the mysterious offshore island of Bozcaada. In such a small place the arrival of the ferry was a major, if regular, event and attracted the attention of the locals as well as the visitors. For the shops and cafés beside the harbour it meant that business would perk up for an hour. Some of the passengers would even stay overnight, but most would depart quickly and head inland in the waiting tourist coaches. The ring on Charles' mobile was an alien intrusion into the surroundings – a modern interloper on an ancient scene. He picked it up and listened intently, his expression betraying nothing to Ed who was anxiously studying his face. When Charles switched his phone off, he asked:

"Glenbrae or …?"

"No names, Ed, not even here," Charles interrupted quickly. He glanced around him:

"No, it was the Italians. This might be it. They've found something promising."

His face was alight with scarcely suppressed excitement.

"We mustn't get our hopes up too much, but there is a single urn which they say is larger than usual. That could be a good sign – remember the legend. The tomb is also bigger than normal with enough room inside for two of the tombaroli to move about easily, but the floor is covered in debris and stones which have fallen from the roof. It may take some time before they're sure and there may be nothing else there."

"Has it been broken into before?"

"They don't think so, but it's difficult to tell yet."

"Let's hope to god they're careful if this is the right tomb. I'm sick of waiting around on this wild goose chase. We need to get back to London to the gallery."

"Be patient and think of the prize. It might not be long now. Just keep your voice down. We'll have plenty enough to do soon. I'll contact Martin Handley. It's time they left Crete, if they are to rendezvous with us in Skiáthos."

"Are you dead sure Samborini will bring the helmet here – that is, if there's anything left of it? They might just go off with everything and sell it to the highest bidder."

"You're getting jumpy, Ed! No way. For a start there are no other bidders and we've offered him a price he simply can't refuse. Why run the risk of starting another deal with someone else? News would quickly spread there's something special on the market and the police would soon catch on. Samborini is smart enough to know that."

"Let's hope you're right."

Charles left the money for the drinks on the table with a nod to the barman and strolled across the road towards the harbour, mingling with the tourists as they disembarked from the ferry. Ed picked up his hat and dark glasses and followed him, glancing around as he went. When they reached their boat moored at the quayside, Charles pulled out his mobile again and made several calls.

*

On the hills above the plain, dusk was falling. Pierre and Antonia sensed their long wait in the heat was finally going to bear fruit. Nothing had stirred below all day. The two tombaroli on guard had not moved and those who had gone off the previous evening had not returned. The soldiers Major Kahn had posted to help the two Interpol officers organised watches throughout the day and Pierre and Antonia visited the look out spot regularly. The only movement had been the occasional tourist, guide book in hand, walking round the ruins of the site of Troy in the distance. The three watchers on the other side of the hill had also remained at the same spot all day taking it in turns to keep an eye on the events below them. It had been a long and exhausting wait in the hot sun.

But finally, in the failing light, there were signs of movement. The three missing tombaroli returned wearing backpacks and carrying something bulky between them. At the same time Major Kahn reported to Pierre and Antonia that a 4 x 4 was parked about 100 metres back from the site in a hollow, well out of sight of the road to Çanakkale. The new arrivals disappeared from view joining the other two tombaroli right up against the cliff face.

Crouching low all five moved swiftly out to the entrance of the tomb and began to remove the covering they had placed there the night before. They unrolled the wire climbing ladder and fed it into the opening. Two of them climbed down into the tomb. From above on the cliff in the growing darkness, Pierre and Antonia and Major Kahn could just see the lights on their heads bobbing about. Those outside the tomb let down a net and after what seemed like an age, began to haul it back up again. The contents were taken off and taken back of sight under the cliff. The net was let down again and again into the tomb.

After two hours of this routine, carried out in absolute silence, lit only by heavily hooded torches, the two inside climbed out, dusted themselves down and wiped the dirt and sweat from their eyes. They covered over the entrance again and rejoined the rest of the group. The sound of a car's engine in the distance signalled to the watchers that it was all over at least for that night.

The soldier Major Kahn had posted to watch the 4 x 4 reported that the Italians arrived at the vehicle carrying three heavy crates which they loaded into the vehicle. It drove along the track for a short distance with all five of the tombaroli on board, but up where the track joined the road to Çanakkale, two of the men got out and, carefully carrying a separate package, transferred to a car parked at the side of the road. The car did not follow the 4 x 4, but turned off and took the road south towards Geyikli.

"*Merde!* OK Major, you follow the main group to Çanakkale and we'll follow the other two in the car. I'm sure they're heading for Yükyeri Iskelesi – that's the nearest harbour where we know Everidge and Robson are waiting for them in their boat. Keep in touch on the mobile and don't lose them whatever you do. Let's go!"

They all stood and Major Kahn was moving over to where his men were waiting for their orders, when Antonia added;

"Oh! And be sure to leave someone watching the other gang, Major. I want to know if they follow the truck or the car."

Kahn touched his cap in acknowledgement.

*

It was early in the morning and the heat of the day had not yet had a chance to build. The local fishermen, preparing their boats to go out for the day's fishing and potting, were still wearing their sweaters. No one paid any attention to the two men wearing shepherds' capes who had climbed stiffly out of their old car and were making their way along the quay. They stopped by a modern fast motor yacht moored alongside. The name on the stern read Artemis. In the cockpit Charles and Ed had quietly watched the Italians' progress towards them, waiting until they reached the gangplank before they stirred and stood up to receive their visitors. Treading carefully – perhaps because they were not used to being on the water – the two Italians clambered unsteadily aboard and stepped into the cockpit. Without a word all four went down into the cabin out of sight of prying eyes. Ed started to speak, but a touch on his arm from Charles silenced him. Small talk was no part of the deal.

Samborini reached under his cape and brought out a package wrapped in what looked like a whole sheepskin. The Golden Fleece thought Charles to himself; quite appropriate really. He nodded to Ed who began to unwrap the object inside. It was larger than he had thought. What finally was revealed made the two art dealers gasp with wonder, despite their well practised technique of never looking too excited at what people brought them to view for fear of causing the price to rise.

Their first emotion was one of amazement at the way the gold still shone after three thousand years. Rationally they knew it was normal. They had seen gold on the body armour and shield of King Philip II, Alexander the Great's father, displayed at Vergina, but even that was not as impressive as this huge gilded helmet with its high crest, whose brilliant shine reached out to them, bridging a gap of over thirty centuries. Neither of them said a word for what seemed like several minutes. They just stood transfixed by the sight, lost in imagining what sights the helmet had witnessed.

"And the rest?" Charles said at last, not taking his eyes off the helmet.

"On its way to the boat in Çanakkale as instructed," replied Samborini, who was scrutinising the reactions of the two dealers, calculating whether he could make further demands of them.

Charles's brain was on fire as he continued to gaze at the helmet and weigh the odds of getting it safely to its final destination. If anyone else found out about it … He didn't even want to contemplate the dangers they would run. He quickly made up his mind.

"Exceptional work, Signor Samborini. I'm doubling the first payment. The rest will be paid as agreed when we see the other goods delivered to the church in Volos."

Samborini placed a finger on the envelope which Charles slid across the cabin table, pinning it down in front of him, but making no move to pick it up. Apart from this gesture neither Italian moved. Ed wrapped up the helmet again in the sheepskin and removed it to the forward cabin, while Ed reached behind him for a bottle of the best raki he had been able to buy. The glasses were filled, raised and a silent toast drunk.

Then without a word Samborini picked up the envelope, which disappeared beneath his voluminous cape as if he had palmed it like a magician, and the Italians got to their feet. They nodded briefly to the two Englishmen, climbed out of the cabin, negotiated the gangplank and walked back along the quay.

"Why did you do that?" Ed called out from the forward cabin, where he was unwrapping the helmet again this time on the bunk with the curtains drawn. Charles watched from the cabin doorway as he did it.

"Do what?"

"You know very well what – double the first payment."

Ed was staring at the helmet, mesmerised again by the brilliance of the gold. It never ceased to impress him that gold doesn't tarnish, and on an object this ancient it was as if the helmet had come alive and was ready to do battle again. He looked closely at it with that eyes-half-closed expression he always adopted when assessing a work of art. Had the large dent on the side happened during the battle itself or was that just his imagination working overtime?

"Hell, Ed! I'd no idea they would have gilded it after the battle. It's even more magnificent than we thought. Granted Samborini may have realised when he saw it that it was too hot to handle, whatever plans he might have had before, but he could still have held out on us and taken it with him, or even said it wasn't there."

He reached out to touch the helmet, brushing it lightly with his fingertips.

"But now he won't tell the others about the double payment and the man with him will share in the extra. That way you've caused a split in the gang and destroyed some trust. You're a clever bastard, Charles," Ed said smiling.

"OK, enough! Put it away. We need to get back to Skiáthos quickly to meet Martin and the girl."

"I reckon about 10 hours for the crossing if we push it, so let's get going as soon as it gets dark. But I need to work at the chart first," Ed replied, proud of his navigating skills. "It won't be easy crossing overnight even using the GPS."

"Right, but I've an idea. We'll stop off briefly at Skópelos first."

Ed looked at him questioningly, eyebrows raised.

"Tell you later, Eddy boy! Right now we need to hide that thing and get some food aboard. Then we stay up top on deck as much as possible and maybe do a spot of fishing from the boat as innocent as you like."

*

In the same small café where, the previous day, Charles and Ed had sat watching the ferry arrive, Pierre and Antonia were keeping themselves awake with cups of coffee. They had spent an uncomfortable morning , keeping watch on the Italians. They had watched Everidge greet them on board and seen them go below.

Now they observed the two men shambling back along the quay to where they had parked their car. They had taken off their capes, now that the sun had seen off the cool of the morning and were carrying them over their shoulders. They stood for a moment by their car with the doors wide open, apparently just allowing the trapped warm air to escape, but at the same time scanning the port for signs of danger. Neither man moved his head much, rather they swept the harbour with sharp eyes darting here and there, much as they would when out hunting or searching for missing goats from their flocks on the Etruscan hillsides. For a second, Samborini's eyes held those of Antonia sitting at the café not fifty metres away from them. She held his gaze steadily and saw him take in the rest of her body before moving on. His eyes hovered longer on two young tourists sitting by their backpacks sporting the Swiss flag on the harbour wall munching on souvláki pittas and licking their fingers as the juice dripped out of the bread.

Finally satisfied, the two men got back into the car and drove off noisily in the direction of Çanakkale, leaving behind them a cloud of exhaust and the smell of burning oil from worn out piston rings as the car struggled up the hill out of town.

"Kahn will tell us if the two of them go back to join the other tombaroli in Çanakkale," Pierre said. "They've done a deal and probably made a delivery here. I'm certain they didn't come just to collect the money – not when the main finds are going by another route. This was something out of the ordinary, something special. They could have hidden anything under those capes – most likely the helmet which sparked off this whole search in the first place. I'm sure Everidge and Robson are running this bit as a separate operation from the rest. They're not interested in anything but the helmet, if our intelligence about the researches they did in London is correct."

"OK, assuming you are right; who do we follow? The Italians or the Brits?" asked Antonia.

"I say we stick with Everidge and Robson and let Major Kahn deal with Samborini and the others. We'll need a fast boat though to follow them. I'll get Kahn to arrange it."

He reached for his mobile. After a few minutes, Pierre ended the call and looked across at Antonia.

"It's done. He'll have a boat brought over for us. What is it?" he asked, sensing that an idea was forming in her mind.

"All we really want is to catch the private collector who is financing all this, Pierre. If you're right and the main piece is here with the London dealers, why don't we let Kahn seize whatever else the tombaroli found in the tomb and have taken to Çanakkale before it all leaves Turkey? The main piece alone will lead us to the collector. We don't need the rest and Kahn will be over the moon at being able to grab a load of artefacts. It will be a great payback for him. He's a nice guy and we owe him."

Pierre hesitated for a moment.

"*D'accord.* OK – you phone him, but off the record. He'll have to act fast."

*

One of the two young Swiss tourists, sitting on the harbour wall, feet dangling close to the water, reached for his phone when the

Italians left the port. They had only glanced up momentarily when they passed by them to walk along the quay, but Antonia's attention was caught by the way the girl, wearing a wide brimmed hat and sunglasses, her long blond shoulder-length hair partially covering her face, had turned slightly to observe them all the way to the British boat and until they disappeared from view below. After that Antonia noticed that the girl hardly moved, her eyes stayed glued to the boat until the tombaroli reappeared and came back along the quay. She then turned to her companion and appeared to take no further interest in them.

Once the car was out of sight, her companion continued to talk on his phone as he and the girl got up and made their way towards the small rocky area in the corner of the harbour not far from where the British boat, Artemis, was moored. There they settled down to sunbathe, spreading out towels and shedding clothes. They both leaned back against the rocks, hats over their faces to protect their eyes, or was it to make it less obvious what they were watching? wondered Antonia.

She touched Pierre's foot with her own and nodded towards them.

"Perhaps it's nothing," Pierre said. "Many tourists come here."

His phone went.

"Kahn says it's all set up. The military on Bozcaada Island opposite will bring a boat over for us in an hour. Divers will put a bug on the 'Artemis' – to enable us to track them. He's an efficient man with connections, the Major Kahn."

"Artemis – goddess of the hunt," Antonia said quietly.

*

The Swiss couple had not moved from the rocks when Pierre and Antonia made their way past them an hour later to reach their rendezvous point with the boat provided by the military from the island. It was a modern fast looking motor yacht; nothing militaristic looking about it from the outside, though they knew there would be arms aboard. Smuggling was a major industry on this coast. The Turkish customs and military were used to shadowing smugglers in unmarked boats and boarding them when necessary.

For that they needed to be well prepared as the smugglers were not averse to defending themselves if the odds looked good. Pierre and Antonia climbed aboard and were led down into the cabin to be briefed. Antonia noted with satisfaction the name on the stern – 'Pericles', the democrat who built up the Greek navy in the fifth century B.C. And built the Parthenon.

On the rocks, the girl sat up and made her way down to the water's edge. She was wearing a dark blue bikini, her blond hair tied back this time revealing more of her face, and round her waist a belt with a small water-proof pouch attached – the sort tourists can put their money and passports in for safe keeping when they are swimming. She waded slowly into the water and then swam lazily out towards the Artemis. Everidge and Robson were not on deck.

Carefully keeping a fishing boat moored nearby between her and any line of sight from the Artemis she approached to within ten metres or so. Anyone watching would have seen her dive and resurface near the bow of the boat. Treading water, she opened the pouch on her belt and took out a small device. She reached up above her head, attached it under the lip of the deck and sank soundlessly below the water again.

*

Later that afternoon, Antonia was at the helm of the Pericles when she and Pierre left the harbour to take up a position behind Bozcaada Island, from where they would be able to observe the London dealers in the Artemis when they set off with whatever the two tombaroli had brought them. Pierre sensed that Antonia was gripping the wheel lightly as they cleared the entrance.

"You're thinking how beautiful it all is?"

"Sure – and I was also thinking that we're doing exactly what my Greek ancestors did all those centuries ago. They tricked the Trojans into thinking they were finally giving up the siege and leaving, but really they were massing for an attack and hid their whole fleet in this same bay, while they waited for the Wooden Horse to be dragged into the city and for the gates to be opened from the inside. It's enough to send shivers down my spine."

Coming in the other way, a motor yacht flying the Swiss flag nosed in through the entrance to the port. Pierre picked up his binoculars and turned to watch it make for a clear mooring position on the quay, where it tied up stern first not far from the Artemis. A short, stocky figure came onto the deck to take care of the mooring lines. Pierre judged him to be in his forties. His hair was greying and was tied back in a pig-tail. As soon as the yacht was secured, he went up on the foredeck and searched the shore for a few moments, before waving briefly to the couple now sitting on the harbour wall, who immediately packed up their things and walked along the quay to go aboard, passing by the Artemis without a glance.

"You were right, Antonia," he said, taking the binoculars away from his eyes and turning towards her. "There's more to that young Swiss pair than I thought. Just who, I wonder, is the man on the boat they have gone to join? It's called the 'Edelweiss', by the way."

"Not very original for a Swiss boat," replied Antonia. "But, wait. I have an idea."

She picked up her phone and spoke to Major Kahn for several minutes.

"Kahn confirms the descriptions fit the other group who were watching the tombaroli from the cliff. The man who piloted the boat in is probably the South African. Kahn's men saw him board the Edelweiss in the harbour in Çanakkale."

"So, now we know how they reached Troy and where their base was."

"The other two are the ones who were speaking in French – a younger bearded man with untidy dark hair in his thirties and a tall, blond girl with style. The descriptions fit."

"And that confirms they suspect, like us, that there was a separate deal going on here. They must be after the same item – Achilles' helmet. Word must have got around in London. I suspect another collector is funding them."

"Or they're working for themselves," Antonia said.

Chapter 4

The British registered yacht Phalaris was approaching the harbour on the island of Skiáthos. Martin Handley and his French partner Dominique Krevine guided the gleaming white ketch watchfully in over the blue-green water keeping a sharp eye out for small local fishing boats and the larger round-the-islands tourist boats. They were heading for the island's old port with its narrow entrance. To their right, as the Phalaris crept in, lay the small pine-covered promontory of Bourtzi, which separates the fishing port from the larger main harbour. Dominique could see a few swimmers and sunbathers on the tiny beach at the outer end of the Bourtzi and, further round within the harbour area proper, men and boys fishing off the rocks.

        To their left on the main island, the land rose more steeply, towering above them and giving the small harbour protection from the winds. The sides of the partially wooded slopes were tiered with the traditional white-washed houses, their shutters painted that shade of sea-blue found nowhere else but in Greece, the colour a proud symbol of resistance to the Turkish invader. As they approached, the waterfront stretched out ahead of them, lined with multi-decked tourist boats, their sterns to the quay, taking on the visitors who boarded over precarious gangplanks.

        Behind the boats they could see more tourists, sipping cold drinks or spooning up huge helpings of ice cream from tall glasses topped with paper umbrellas. All were watching the comings and goings from the seamless row of cafés lining the harbour, their tables and chairs invading the quayside. In the left corner of the harbour the smaller gaily coloured boats of the local fishermen swung on their moorings, their patch of the quay a mess of nets and buoys, upturned dinghies and gulls looking for discarded bits of fish.

Martin and Dominique dropped the sails and edged in cautiously on the engine. Dominique stood on the foredeck watching for hazards and ready to drop the anchor. A hundred metres or so off shore Martin put the engine into reverse for a few seconds and when the yacht had slowed completely Dominique released the anchor. The chain rattled out noisily sending a clutch of seagulls, which had settled on a nearby fishing boat, screaming into the air.

Dominique peered down into the blue-green water searching to see where the anchor lay on the bottom, but the light breeze had rippled the surface making it opaque for the moment. When the chain stopped running out she secured it round the chain post on the foredeck and remained standing there as the boat swung round to the wind. Lining up landmarks on the shore, she checked there was no drag. Satisfied, she turned to survey the busy quayside for a moment and returned to the cockpit, where Martin had already fixed the awning over the boom and poured them both a cold beer. With his feet on the seat, he was leaning back against the cabin and surveying the scene all around from behind his sunglasses.

"The anchor's holding", she said as she joined him and took up a similar position on the other side of the cockpit. She followed the direction of his gaze and saw that he was focussed on the approach of the fast passenger hydrofoil from Volos.

The hydrofoils were converted former Russian military torpedo boats with an impressive turn of speed. Now painted dark blue, the ferries brought locals and tourists out to the islands from the mainland port of Volos. Just off the headland it slowed down and descended from its hydrofoil stilts almost disappearing into its own dazzling white spray as it sank sluggishly low into the water – a swan suddenly transformed into an ugly duckling. It went out of sight round the Bourtzi promontory to reappear minutes later slowly approaching the long jetty on the other side in the deep-water harbour which they could just see from their mooring.

It docked against the jetty not far from the regular rusty car ferry which was finalising its loading and preparing to leave for the final crossing that day back to Volos. Last minute foot passengers were scrambling across the car ramp, many laden with goods to sell in the market there the next day.

"I 'ope this is going to be worth it – we were making good money chartering in Crete. It seems a shame to stop when we were doing so well."

"Don't worry, Dom. Charles is paying us a good bonus. I couldn't resist it when he phoned and told me what they were doing."

"If it's so good, it has to be illegal! Per'aps it's drugs, Martin, I won't do that, you know it."

"Relax! I've told you, it's not drugs – it's artefacts. Charles is an art dealer, not a drug dealer. "

"If you're sure, but it make me nervous all the same. So we do what now?" Dominique said, calming down and settling back on her seat, sipping her beer.

"We just wait. Charles'll contact us tonight up there."

Martin pointed in the direction of the upper town where the houses and restaurants scrambled over one another on the slopes of the hillside overlooking the harbour.

"Why this name Phalaris?" Dominique had asked him when he first brought the ketch into St. Malo and she came aboard for the first time.

"It's Greek for coot," he had replied, smiling. "When I was younger and sailed with my dad, it was the name of our first boat. The class name was Coot - just an open deck racing dinghy – and the owner before us must have had a classical education! I just decided to keep the name."

"The owner was a pompous ass, according to me."

"Perhaps, but he also had a sense of humour. I found out later that Phalaris was also the name of a Greek tyrant with a very different idea of education. He had a cauldron cast in the shape of a bull. Whenever anyone annoyed him, he used to fill the cauldron with oil, light a fire underneath its belly and pop his victims in."

"Don't tell me. 'E used to boil them and enjoy listening to their screams which come out of the bull's mouth. A lovely man."
"How did you guess?"

Now hundreds of nautical miles from St. Malo as they swung gently at anchor in the little Greek port surrounded by the myths and legends of the ancient world, Dominique was reminded of this strange story.

"So, which are we? A silly 'armless coot bird or a nasty Greek tyrant with a sense of 'umour?"

"I'll tell you after tonight. It may depend on what exactly we have to do."

Both fell silent as they continued to observe the scene around them. They knew their arrival would not have gone unnoticed, not least by the Greek Coast Guard. Martin was sure Charles and Ed would contact them that evening in the restaurant and not before. If, as Martin suspected, their offer was on the dodgy side of the law, they would not want to attract attention either to themselves or to the yacht by rowing out in broad daylight.

Skiáthos is much further north than Crete and the scene was bathed in different colours Martin noticed, as he took in the surroundings with his keen eye for the architecture. Though the port was animated by similar activities as at their base in Chaniá, the houses and churches here are almost all painted white. In Chaniá the Venetian occupiers of old had given the buildings a greater variety of styles and range of colours which made the town look more Italian than Greek.

The three-day and night non-stop passage from Crete to Skiáthos had been long and tiring. Now the growing heat of the day was taking its toll. The two of them were content to rest and to move about as little as possible, grateful for the shade of the cockpit cover and the slight breeze off the water. Soon the motion of the boat caused them to doze off into the traditional siesta of the afternoon.

Later, when their dinghy bumped against the hull in the wash from a tourist boat as it passed close by, the noise brought them back to the woken world. As they drowsily took in where they were, Martin murmured:

"Time I fixed the radar housing."

Dominique raised her eyebrows.

"No, it's OK, you stay here, Dom – it shouldn't take me long."

He disappeared down into the cabin and soon emerged with a tool kit belt strapped round his waist and carrying a harness. He made his way along the deck to the main mast, strapped on the harness, hooked himself on and winched himself up to the level of the radar scanner housing just beyond the second spreader. A good twenty feet above the deck he steadied himself with his feet on the spreader and got to work.

By the time he had finished and abseiled back down to the deck, Dominique had dozed off again in the cockpit. She woke with a start as he brushed past her to drop down into the cabin.

"You have done it?" she enquired sleepily. "Sorry, I fall asleep again."

"Fell. Yes, no problem. I'm just going to test it now," he replied, disappearing from view. After a few minutes, his head reappeared in the cabin hatchway:

"All OK," he announced. "I've done this before – we should be safe enough."

As he expected, no contact was made that afternoon. Charles and Ed would not appear until later. More visiting yachts arrived at the island, but most went on past the old harbour heading for the deep-water side where the facilities for visiting yachts were better. Martin was hardly even aware of the fast motor yacht which did enter the old port and drop anchor not far from them, close to the fish quay. It was flying the Swiss flag.

*

Ed and Charles were being paid handsomely for their search for the helmet by the Scottish collector. A chance to work in Turkey and Greece made a pleasant change from their normal routine in the gallery in London. It had taken months of careful reading and of interviews with archaeologists and academics before the most likely stretch of Turkish coastline had been narrowed down to something manageable.

Until recently it had not even been an offence to sell antiquities of doubtful provenance in the UK, even when they were known to have been illegally excavated and imported. However there had been a general tightening up after several

high-profile cases and they would have to be careful, if their
reputation as top art dealers in London was to be maintained.

They had reasoned that if the tombaroli did succeed in
finding the helmet, or even if they found other worthwhile
artefacts, then they would have to be smuggled out of Turkey
and brought back very quietly into the UK. They knew their
researches would not have gone unnoticed and that there were
several other collectors in the market who would be capable of
relieving them of their prize. They decided to split up any
artefacts found and to bring them back by different routes. This
was where Martin and Dominique became part of the plan.

Later that evening they climbed the narrow streets of
Skiáthos town up to the restaurant overlooking the harbour
where Charles had arranged to meet. The streets were crowded
with visitors looking in the shops and gathered in bunches
around the menus displayed outside the numerous cafes and
bars. They had to weave their way through,so talking was
difficult, but in a gap in the throng Ed asked:

"Tell me more about this Martin character. Can we trust
him?"

"Oh! Sure," replied Charles, "we go back a long way. We
did the same course at Southampton Uni and knocked about a
bit together. We were both studying languages, but got to know
each other better during a scuba diving course in the university
pool. We went together on a week's expedition diving off the
coast of Israel at Aqaba. After Uni Martin didn't know what to
do, but he was mad on sailing so he went to the Caribbean and
worked out of Fort Lauderdale in Florida as a yacht deliverer."

He stopped for a minute outside a gift shop to look in the
window, but really to get his breath back, after what was already
a stiff climb.

"He said it meant sitting around a lot until the agent had a client with a yacht in the wrong place who needed it moving, but he had some adventures and it wasn't such a bad place to hang out. There was so much drug smuggling and piracy going on – still is, I guess – that anyone setting off in small boat in the area had to be armed in case of hijack. I'm sure he never got involved in drugs, but he certainly had some near scrapes with pirates in speed boats who threatened to board their yacht."

"Sounds a tough character. I'm not sure I'd want to risk dangers like that."

"It goes with the territory out there – you need a good crew who will hold their nerve too."

They continued their way up, coming to some wide terracing which also served as steps on the way up to the restaurant. They threaded their way through the tables of another restaurant that spilled out across the whole width of the path. The tables were full and the lights were coming on as dusk came and went rapidly, giving way to the darkness. Down below they could see the coloured restaurant lights round the harbour and make out the Phalaris swinging at anchor with her riding light winking.

"Yes, nice bloke though," Charles continued. "He saved enough money there to buy himself a yacht – the ketch you saw in the harbour – and came back to Europe to do yacht chartering out here."

"You kept in touch while he was out there in the U.S.?"

"Only the odd postcard now and then, but he gave me a ring when he first returned to England about a year ago. He wanted me to come with him here to Greece, but by that time I was just starting up the gallery with you, so I said no."

They paused again for a moment to skirt round a group of evening browsers blocking the street.

"He had met this French girl at Uni who lived in Brittany, so he crossed the Channel to St. Malo, where apparently she was waiting on the quay when he sailed in."

"Very romantic!"

"She agreed to go to Greece with him as she's mad on sailing too. Now I come to think of it, she took up diving as well during her year in Southampton, though I think she did that more to get to know Martin than for any other reason, at least at first."

At the top of the steps they turned down an alleyway back into the street proper. Shortly afterwards they entered a restaurant and made their way to the front balcony hanging, it seemed, in mid-air over the harbour where Martin and Dominique were already sitting looking at the menu.

"Martin! Great to see you – what's it been now? Over a year? Dominique," he added turning to her. "Lovely to see you again too. I last saw you in diving gear in Southampton. Let me introduce my friend and partner in the gallery, Ed."

"Hi Charles – good to see you too. Pleased to meet you, Ed," Martin said, turning towards him and putting out his hand. "Great spot for a restaurant – what a view!"

"This is such a lovely place," Dominique said. "How did you find it, Edouard?"

"We've had a couple of days to look around and to try out the food," replied Ed. "Someone had to do it."

"Ed's always thinking of his stomach, and he has a real nose for a good restaurant," Charles said, as they drew up their chairs, sat down and picked up the menus. The meal passed without incident and the talk was mostly of when they had been in Aqaba and the adventures Martin had had in the Caribbean.

Charles had placed himself strategically from where he could see all the other tables in the restaurant and discreetly keep a check on the comings and goings of the diners. As the meal drew to its end he seemed satisfied that they were not being observed.

"The instructions are inside this brochure," he said to Martin, as he opened a tourist brochure and appeared to be showing him something. "The money has been transferred to your account in Berne and we'll hand over the goods at the rendezvous point."

"OK. When?"

"Tomorrow, on the next island. You'll need to set off at first light and we'll meet you there. There should be no bother – all the rest has been taken care of. There's nothing to worry about."

"Until you said that, I didn't think there was," Martin said. "So we've got to be careful then? Rivals somewhere out there?"

"You did sharpen up out in the Caribbean! Yes, we think there might be. I can't believe no one noticed the researches we were doing in London – it's taken a long time to get this far and word tends to get around. Nothing specific mind, but some of the people we spoke to in England got a bit curious and it caught their imagination too. So just keep an eye out."

*

On the other side of the glass wall between their restaurant and the next one along, Pierre looked across at Antonia.

"The deal's been done. Nothing bulky was passed over though, so the helmet, if they have it, is still with Everidge and Robson. There must be another meeting arranged."

"Or perhaps you're just imagining it and this was a chance meeting between friends on holiday."

Pierre smiled and said: "You don't believe that either. We've another long night of watching ahead of us, I'm afraid."

"That could be quite romantic in this harbour," she replied with a smile as she leaned back, feeling content after the meal and the wine. "And much more comfortable on the boat than on the hard ground of a Turkish cliff."

Their crossing to Skiáthos in the Pericles had passed without incident. They remained out of sight below the horizon as Major Kahn had recommended, using the electronic tracking device planted by a military diver, to follow Ed and Charles in the Artemis. The only surprise had been the brief stop the men made at the nearby island of Skópelos before heading to their final destination of Skiáthos.

Antonia had contacted the Skópelos police ahead by phone and they had followed the two Englishmen when they went ashore. They reported that the two men first breakfasted in one of the many restaurants near the harbour and then gone souvenir shopping in the town, including a visit to a well-known museum shop on the island. They then returned to their boat and left the harbour.

They continued on to Skiáthos and moored up in the main harbour. Pierre and Antonia followed them at a discreet distance, but veered off into the old port.

Pushing their chairs back, Charles and Martin got up to leave the restaurant. Ed waited while Dominique gathered her things and took her arm as they all began to make their way down the hill towards the harbour through the twinkling streets, still full of late diners and the smells of different meals being prepared every time they went past an open kitchen door.

Seeing the four of them leave, Antonia and Pierre got up too and left their restaurant to follow them back down towards the harbour. They watched the newcomers say good night to the two dealers on the quayside and row out to the Phalaris in the old port. They followed Everidge and Robson as they walked on to where they were moored against the quay in the main port.

Antonia put her arm through Pierre's as they returned to the old port and along the quay towards their dinghy watching their feet to avoid the bits of fishermen's ropes and tackle strewn about in this working section of the harbour.

"OK. They're obviously not going to hand over the helmet tonight so let's get some sleep – it'll be a long day tomorrow and nothing will happen before the dawn."

"Perhaps not," Antonia said.

They rowed out and went below. From the cabin window they had a good view of the Phalaris. Antonia touched Pierre on the arm and pointed.

"Over there. Isn't that the Swiss boat – the Edelweiss – with the other three on board?"

"Could be. I can't quite see the name from here. I'll row over. You check with Kahn to see when it left Yükyeri Iskelesi."

Just as Pierre returned in the dinghy, Kahn confirmed the Edelweiss had been seen leaving not long after Charles and Ed left in the Artemis. Antonia helped him back on board and secured the tender.

"It's them alright."

"I know. Kahn has just confirmed."

They kept watch for an hour, but there was no movement on the Edelweiss and no lights came on in the cabin.

They set the radar scanner to warn them of any movement if the Phalaris or the Edelweiss slipped their moorings.

Later, Antonia remarked:

"There's something magic about lying so close to the water and hearing it lap against the side of the hull."

Pierre turned on his side and looked at her.

"The water moved for you too then?"

Chapter 5

In the main harbour before first light Charles and Ed rose from their bunks and made the boat ready for the crossing back to Skópelos. The rendezvous with Martin and Dominique was to be in the small fishing village of Agnóntas on the south-west side of the island. Not only was this quieter and less public than Skópelos town, but also it would be more difficult for anyone following or watching them to be inconspicuous.

"Now we'll see whether I'm imagining things, Ed. If that Swiss boat does follow us over to Skópelos, then I'm right."

"You just see spies everywhere! Everyone comes to Skiáthos before heading south. It's nothing."

"Just keep an eye out when we leave – that's all I'm saying."

"OK – whatever. If it makes you feel better."

"What did you say it was called?"

"Edelweiss."

"Lousy name for a boat!"

Ed was not a morning person and all this activity and thinking before breakfast was more than he could cope with. He returned to the galley to make coffee. He could still taste the meal from the night before. Must have been the fish, he thought, as he fiddled with the coffee maker.

The previous evening Charles had noticed the Swiss boat about to enter the main harbour not long after them. But it suddenly changed course and headed for the smaller fishing harbour. He was fairly certain it was the same boat as the one he had seen arriving in Yükyeri Iskelesi harbour back in Turkey. Could be a coincidence, but then again it might not be. Perhaps Ed was right and he was just getting jumpy and irritable now that the helmet was in their possession and they had more to lose.

He could just see across into the old harbour by standing on the cabin roof of their boat, but could not see any movement on the Edelweiss at that hour, whereas he could make out a dim light in the cabin of the Phalaris. Good old reliable Martin, he thought, not going to miss the hand-over. He was shivering slightly as the morning chill worked its way through the layers of sweaters he had hastily pulled on. He climbed down from the roof and went back down below where the smell of coffee being prepared and the warmth of the cabin restored his mood and raised his morale.

"That smells great Ed, sorry I snapped at you earlier. Just nerves I guess."

"No problem. Did you have the fish last night? I can still taste it."

"You landlubber, it's just the movement of the boat that's got to you. I can see a light on in the Phalaris, so Martin and Dominique are up. No sign of activity on the Edelweiss."

"There, I told you so. Good looker, that Dominique – sweet face and I just love the accent."

"Hey! It's a bit early for that – keep your mind on the job and make the coffee. You certainly did flirt with her last night, you dirty dog. But seriously – don't go too far. I want to keep Martin on our side. We need him."

"No problem – just a bit of fun."

As the sun came up Charles cast off the lines and they nosed out into the main channel and headed across the strait towards Skópelos. The breeze was still cold and when they left the shelter of the harbour the wind, funnelling down from the north through the channel between the two main islands, hit them with unexpected force. Ed was looking even unhappier and went below to fetch a full waterproof to keep the cold out. As he entered the cabin, he glanced at the radar and noticed they were not alone; another boat was leaving the harbour behind them. He picked up the binoculars before returning to the cockpit. Standing with his back to the cabin and looking out over the stern, Ed struggled to keep his balance and to focus the binoculars on the tiny dot in the distance.

"Bloody hell! You may be right after all, Charles. That's the Swiss boat. Over there just to the left of the headland. Now why would they be out at this ungodly hour? Dolphin watching? I don't think so."

"Well, if they follow us to Agnóntas, that'll confirm it. When we're there, I want you to put that bug you found on our bow, onto a local boat. It's served its purpose now we know they're following us – so they must have planted it. It was most likely the girl. I watched her from the cabin when she went for a swim off the beach, but lost sight of her as she dived. Anyway, if they're after the helmet, they'll leave us to follow Martin and Dominique for sure if we make it obvious we're transferring a package to them."

"Shouldn't we warn Martin and Dominique?" Ed said.

"No. I gave him a general warning – he knows how to look after himself."

"Why am I not surprised you said that? You're a hard bastard at times, Charles," Ed said. "All the same, isn't it a bit risky?"

Charles just smiled.

The crossing was becoming less bumpy as they left the open water and ran along under the lee of the island of Skópelos and began to follow the coastline toward the southern end.

Although they were not strictly speaking in the Sporades Marine Park, there was plenty of wild life about. The tourist boats between Skiáthos and Skópelos often slowed down in this area so the visitors could watch the dolphins in particular.

That morning Ed and Charles watched in fascination as a school of dolphins which had been feeding a hundred metres or so to their right, suddenly, as if on a signal, turned and headed at full speed towards them. In the low light of the morning sun their lithe bodies glistened as they took up position alongside, and rose and dived, riding the waves created by the bow slicing through the water. Several dolphins took up station on either side of the hull just off the bow and seemed to delight in diving below the boat to resurface on the other side moments later, criss-crossing each other as they played.

Ed went below for his camera and tried again and again to catch the creatures at that critical moment when they broke surface and were at the height of their leap before slipping back beneath the waves. Both he and Charles were so preoccupied with the magic of the sight that they almost forgot the object of their passage along the coast. Some of the dolphins were playing in the wake and when Charles glanced behind to watch them he noticed the Swiss boat was maintaining a discreet distance, despite the fact they had slowed while Ed was taking photographs.

"Ed, take a look behind again – our shadow is still with us."

"Yep. That's definitely them." Ed paused. "Hello – we have yet more company. There's another boat behind the Edelweiss. It's flying a Greek flag though, so could be anyone. And I can see a sail just leaving Skópelos. That should be Martin and Dominique. How do some blokes do it? He's no oil painting and she could have anyone."

"Forgotten your Angie already? You don't have to be apart long before your mind begins to wander! But I know what you mean. Not bad at all. But remember what I said."

"No harm in dreaming."

Charles looked up ahead as they sailed between Dasía Island and the coast. "We're well past Adrína so Agnóntas must be just after the next headland. Check the chart again to see whether there are any rocks to avoid – I don't want any slip-ups."

Ed went below and Charles eased the power up to their normal passage speed. The dolphins gradually gave up the chase and contented themselves with playing in the wake until the boat had left them far behind. The little harbour of Agnóntas appeared as they rounded the headland and they headed for the quay, which was used by the ferries and tourist boats in rough weather rather than risking going all the way round the next headland to Skópelos Town harbour on the other side of the island. Charles manoeuvred the Artemis alongside and Ed leapt ashore with the lines. When the boat was secured they strolled along the quay to the shore and took up position at a table on the beach outside a taverna from where had a good view of the entrance to the bay.

Keen as ever to make the best of the moment, Ed ordered lavráki and a bottle of Cretan red to wash it down.

"I thought you were off fish," remarked Charles.

"That was then; this is now. You can't get it fresher than here."

Charles, remaining as sharp-eyed and focussed as usual, ordered a coffee and never took his eyes off the entrance to the harbour. As Ed was starting on his sea bass, the Edelweiss entered the harbour, followed after a few minutes by the Greek motor yacht they had seen earlier. Charles watched the three Swiss, the two men and the girl, moor up and walk along the long concrete quay towards them. There was no movement from the Greek boat; Charles had not been able to see how many were on board or even who had secured the mooring lines as it was half hidden behind a large tourist ferry from Skiáthos which, due to the strong wind and swell, had arrived just after them and was off-loading its passengers into the waiting buses which would take them overland to Skópelos Town.

*

Martin and Dominique had also risen early and prepared to set sail for Agnóntas. There was plenty of breeze so they had decided to sail even though it meant they would arrive well after Charles and Ed. That way no one will connect us with them, Martin thought. They had plenty of time during the crossing to discuss what they were about to take on.

"Tell me more how you got to know this man Charlie," Dominique said, pronouncing his name the French way. "I am not sure I trust 'im. He is, how do you say, too smooth for me. Is it drugs which he wants us to take to England, do you think?"

"No, I'm sure that's not it, don't worry – I believe him when he says it's an artefact. Strictly speaking it is not even illegal to bring it into the UK, although it is illegit to take it out of Turkey. If there's anything we should be worrying about, it's whether anyone else knows and tries to take it off us."

"OK, so how did you meet and what is 'e really like?"

"We met at the Uni. He was doing the same course as me. Seemed a bit of a public school twit to me at first, but we got on well enough in a 'see you down the pub' sort of way. Then we discovered that we both had always wanted to learn to scuba dive. So we went on a course together at the local club."

"That was before I arrive in Southampton then?"

"Arrived. Yes, the year before. That summer we went to Aqaba for a week with the diving club. He'd decided to switch to an Art History course and to become an art dealer. He wanted to start his own gallery. After Southampton, he went to the Courtauld in London to do an MA, while I went to the Caribbean. He's got more of a business head than I have and definitely has a keen eye for a bargain. He's not above bending the rules a little, but he wouldn't do anything illegal – or at least I don't think so."

"So when did you see 'im again?"

"I phoned him from Southampton after I returned. I thought he might come here to Greece with me, but he had just managed to raise the finance to realise his dream and to start up his own gallery with Ed and couldn't get away." He put his arms round her to give her a kiss. "I'm glad he didn't come – I might not have gone to St. Malo to find you."

She pushed him away.

"*Alors.* I was just second choice for you? After a man! Typical Engleesh. But you 'ave changed your mind now, *n'est-ce pas*? I am worth it?"

Dominique shook out her hair and turned her face towards the warming sun with a smile.

They had made good progress in the strong breeze and had been accompanied for a good stretch of the way by a school of dolphins, probably the same ones which had danced around the Artemis an hour before, and now could see the entrance to Agnóntas harbour against the backdrop of the cliffs. The sheer rocky coastline was beginning to be dotted with houses, sparse at first and then in little bunches until they looked like a set of brilliant white steps cut into the green of the scrub and trees reaching right down to the water's edge.

"OK, best to get the sails down and motor in. We can moor up against the quay so there's no need to prepare the anchor."

"*Bien, chef!* But you go up on the deck this time and I 'elm the boat," Dominique said, taking over the wheel and turning the yacht into wind to release the pressure on the sails.

*

Charles watched the Phalaris enter the harbour. Dominique edged the ketch up to the quay while Martin stood on the bow ready to jump ashore. They were busy for a few minutes securing the mooring lines and then Dominique joined him on the quayside and, arms round each other's waist, they strolled towards the beach. Charles stood up from the table and waved to attract their attention. After a few moments Martin waved back and they quickened their pace slightly. At the end of the quay they turned and crossed onto the beach using the duckboards laid out between the cafés. As Martin and Dominique joined them at their table, Ed called for more glasses and another bottle of wine.

"Good crossing?" asked Charles.

"No problem. There was a steady breeze so we decided to sail most of the way."

Charles reached down to the ground below the table and picked up a package, which he placed gently on the table in full view of any observers. It was clearly heavy and he looked slightly flushed as he sat back in his chair and looked at them both.

"It's a bit fragile, but in surprisingly good condition. It's sealed and surrounded with protective packing, so best not to open it."

Seeing the expression on Dominique's face, he smiled reassuringly and added:

"Don't worry, Dominique – I promise it's not drugs. It's what I said it was, but it does have to be well-protected and as airtight as possible until we can get it back to be preserved properly. The ground around Troy was very humid, after the sea retreated and the coastline changed thousands of years ago. The tomb may even have been flooded at one point. The deterioration is quite advanced, but it is still magnificent."

"What a pity we can't see it," Dominique replied, still suspicious.

Martin broke in, not wanting a row to start up.

"We'll go back to Crete first and continue chartering for a while in order not to attract attention. Then, where do you suggest?"

"Probably Malta and from there to Sète. I think you should take the Canal du Midi through France to the Atlantic rather than risk going round Spain."

Ed had unrolled a chart and was looking at the possibilities. His finger traced the route and Martin looked at Dominique for her opinion.

"*Oui*, that is OK. The crossing to *Malte* is long – about five or six days per'aps, so we will need to stop for a while. From there to *la Corse* is another week and then on to Sète. It will be a nice trip, as you say."

Charles looked about him and noticed the crew of the Swiss boat leaning back in their chairs further along the beach, apparently relaxing and admiring the view. The older man glanced in their direction, but otherwise they appeared to show no interest in what was happening at their table.

Martin had placed the package in his backpack and continued to study the chart with Ed and Dominique. To any observer, they were simply working out their next port of call.

"Time to make a move, tempting as it is to stay here," Martin said with a gesture which took in the little bay and the shimmering sea before them.

"Are you sure you won't try the fish?" asked Ed. "Best I've ever tasted."

"You should let me cook for you, *mon petit* Edouard. I would soon show you how it should really be done, as we do in France."

"Thanks, Dominique – I'll take you up on that!"

"Not right now you won't, Ed," Martin said, getting to his feet. "Sorry, we'd love to stay, but it's time to get going; I want to catch the wind before the main heat of the day. We should make good time towards Crete if we leave straight away. We'll keep in touch as agreed and let you know when we arrive."

"Spoil sport," Ed and Dominique said simultaneously.

They all shook hands and Martin and Dominique walked back to the Phalaris.

"Are you sure you shouldn't have told them we think they're being tailed, Charles?"

"What difference would it make? If they don't know, they'll act more naturally and will be less likely to attract attention. I don't think the other lot will do anything other than watch and follow. Why should they? That way there's no risk to them. It is just the last leg to England where we'll have to rethink this."

"I suppose you're right, but I don't like it. Have you got that bug I found on our boat? Do you think it was that lot over there who planted it or someone else?" He nodded slightly in the direction of the Swiss.

"I'm not sure, but if it was them, they'll switch to following Martin and Dominique now they have seen us pass the package over. I just don't want them, or anyone else, to know where we are from now on."

"OK, I'm going for swim. Give me the bug and I'll put it on one of the fishing boats out there. That should confuse them for a while."

Ed left the table and moved down onto the pebbly beach. He walked straight into the water kicking off his shoes and leaving a trail of clothes as he went. He swum out fast for a hundred metres or so and then turned in a wide arc which took him behind some local fishing boats riding at their moorings. He reappeared on the other side a few moments later and struck out strongly for the beach. Shaking the water off him, he stumbled his way back up the beach, nursing his feet on the hard pebbles as he picked up his clothes and closed in gratefully on his shoes. He rejoined Charles at their table.

"Phew! That water is bloody cold; must be the wind and the current. I thought the sea in Greece was supposed to be warm."

He rubbed himself down as he spoke and turned towards the sun to soak in some warmth.

"We're quite far north and it's still early in the season. You mustn't believe everything you read in the brochures."

They both ordered a coffee and continued to wait and watch. On board the Phalaris they could see Martin and Dominique getting the boat ready. The familiar chug of the diesel engine broke into the silence as they cast off and turned the boat towards the entrance to the bay. Dominique held the bow into the wind while Martin raised the sails. He returned to the cockpit and the boat fell off the wind until the sails began to fill. On the shore, Charles and Ed heard the engine cut out and without a sound the yacht glided out of the harbour. They watched it until it was a smudge on the horizon.

For an hour there was no other movement in the harbour until the Swiss group left their table and walked back along the beach to the quay. For a few moments they were out of sight, screened off behind the tourist boat, but soon emerged on the other side. Antonia and Pierre were sunbathing on their deck and apparently asleep. They did not react as the three passed by them to reach the Edelweiss.

When they cast off and motored past, Antonia looked up and caught the name Edelweiss on the stern again. Just too twee! she thought.

Back on the beach Charles and Ed knew it was time for them to make a move.

"OK, Ed. We've seen enough, but I'm still not entirely sure about that boat. Time to go.I want to get back to Çanakkale to see how Samborini is getting on with moving the rest of the goods."

They paid the bill and left the taverna. Charles looked hard at the Greek boat as they walked by and noted the name Pericles on the canvas awning, but he could neither see nor sense anything out of the ordinary and dismissed it from his mind as he and Ed got ready to throw off the lines. When they moved out into the channel, Ed glanced back, his attention caught by a sound behind him. The woman had dived off the bow of the Pericles and was swimming out in a wide arc. She circled round quickly, no doubt finding the water as cold as he himself had and soon reached the steps at the stern. Her companion helped her up and handed her a towel.

"Those two seem harmless enough," Ed remarked, admiring Antonia's tanned figure as she stepped onto the after-deck...

"Anything in a skirt, or preferably without," sighed Charles.

He concentrated on heading out into the open water, setting a course for Turkey and raising the speed to a respectable 20 knots. As they turned north-east outside the harbour, Ed swept the expanse of sea behind them with his binoculars and could just make out the Edelweiss heading due south, moving at speed.

"Looks like they've abandoned us and are following the Phalaris, as you guessed. I hope they won't cause trouble for Martin and Dom."

*

Once he had helped Antonia climb back on board, Pierre sat back and watched her as she towelled herself down, taking in every detail of her body, which she did nothing to hide as she dried herself. She smiled back and moved to sit down beside him as she finished drying her hair, spraying drips of cold water onto him as she shook her head. Pierre only half reacted to this teasing, his mind racing, analysing the departures of the three boats they had just witnessed and considering their next move.

"OK, so which lot do we follow? Whatever it was Samborini handed over to Everidge and Robson in Yükyeri Iskelesi, I'm sure is now on the Phalaris. The ketch will be easy to catch up if they stay under sail. The rival gang on the Edelweiss will probably be following them too if we've got it right," he said. "We should soon get a response from Interpol on those photos I took of the three of them here on the beach if they have form."

Antonia spread her towel over the guardrail to dry and replied: "But I think we should check to see where the Brit dealers are going first and concentrate on them. We can catch up with the others later."

"*D'accord*, I agree. If you're ready, we'll go."

Antonia could feel her skin begin to glow as the sun burned into her back. Her hair was nearly dry already and she shook it out again.

"Seems a shame though, when there's so much else we could do – but I guess you're right," she added smiling, moving away just out of his reach, "we must concentrate on the job in hand."

"I am trying, believe me, but you're not making it easy, Inspector."

Pretending to ignore his last remark, Antonia continued:

"You're sure they did find the right tomb, aren't you, and that they've got the helmet?"

"Yes, I am almost sure of it. Kahn will show the archaeologists from Istanbul where the site is and they will be able to confirm it or otherwise. If Kahn was successful and got our message in time and has seized the rest of the finds, hell be able to tell us in detail what else the tombaroli found there. All the information sent from London indicated that the main object of the search was Achilles' helmet, which Patroclus was wearing when he was killed – that is if either of them existed in reality and are not just part of a story. So, if there's no helmet amongst the finds, that confirms that Samborini most likely handed it over to the Brits."

They were soon out in the open sea and could see Charles and Ed some way ahead clearly heading back to Turkey. Behind them the sails of the Phalaris were still just visible, but dropping below the horizon. Antonia continued looking for the Swiss boat.

"I can't see the Edelweiss. No, wait. That could be them over there to port, but I can't be sure, there are several boats about."

"No matter. Can you get on the radio to Kahn and tell him what has happened here and that we think the Brits are heading back to Turkey. Say to him that we'll follow, but that we'll keep well back. Tell him not to do anything when they arrive or let them know they've been seen. I just want to know how they will react and where they will head for next."

Antonia went below and Pierre could hear her speaking on the radio. He heard her replying excitedly to whatever Major Kahn was telling her, but his Turkish was not as good as Antonia's and he couldn't understand it all. Antonia put down the phone and reappeared in the cabin doorway.

"Heh! Guess what? Kahn says he's received a second message this time via the Turkish Art Police authorising him to intercept the tombaroli. It seems there was an anonymous tip-off which they passed on to him! Having previously received our message he already had his men in place watching the Italians load the boxes of finds from the tomb onto a fishing boat in Çanakkale harbour. He's ready to seize the boat as soon as everything and everyone is on board."

"Interesting – so who sent the tip-off? Did Samborini tell the other tombaroli about the deal he did with the Brits? Or did he double-cross them, I wonder?

"Check with Kahn to see if Samborini returned to Çanakkale and is on board the fishing boat too or whether he's disappeared with whatever money he got from the Brits."

Pierre raised the speed and, as the bow lifted, he concentrated on the helming. Antonia shouted up from below over the rising sound of the twin diesels:

"Yep, Samborini did return, but he didn't stay. He slipped away and didn't go on board. By the way, according to the military tracking device the Artemis is still in the harbour in Agnóntas."

"*Merde*! They must have found it and dumped it," Pierre said looking up ahead, his view was partially obscured by the spray thrown up by the rise in their speed.

*

Charles and Ed had passed the island of Bozcaada outside the harbour they had left only a couple of days before and were entering the narrows of the Dardanelles. As they rounded the headland protecting Çanakkale, they could immediately see there was a lot of activity up ahead just off the harbour. Turkish patrol boats swarmed everywhere surrounding a fishing boat. Through the binoculars Ed could see what looked like a boarding party of soldiers on board.

"Are you thinking what I'm thinking?" he said.

"Shit! I think Samborini has fouled up. I think we're about to lose the rest of the items in the tomb. Thank goodness we've got the helmet," Charles replied.

Ed turned to look at him sensing something in his voice. Charles was smiling.

"You bastard, Charles! You've done it again, haven't you? You set them up. Those Italians never had a chance – you meant them to be caught all along."

"Our job was to get the helmet, nothing else was mentioned. Do whatever it takes, Glenbrae said. The only way we're going to get away with this is if the Turkish authorities think we've failed and they've prevented the finds leaving Turkey, so I made a phone call. With any luck that's exactly what they're thinking at this moment. That gives us more chance of getting the helmet back to England, which is where the big money is, in case you'd forgotten."

"I should've guessed you had some such plan up your sleeve, but you might've told me," Ed replied.

"And miss the pleasure of seeing the expression on your face? No way!" Charles laughed, pleased with himself. "Seriously, I thought it best to see how things went. In fact I didn't give the tip off until I was sure we had the helmet. If Samborini had decided to double cross us and take the lot, the helmet would be with the rest of the finds and we would've lost that too."

"Makes sense, I suppose," conceded Ed.

"I bet Samborini was planning to take everything anyway, but guessed that if he gave us the helmet, we wouldn't be too bothered and he'd have one less problem to worry about. He knows the helmet itself is too hot to handle and so best got rid of."

"OK, so what now, master brain?"

"We get out of here fast. We'll go back to Volos and decide from there. We need to keep in touch with Martin and Dominique too as we need to meet them again soon," Charles replied.

"Why?"

"Tell you later."

He was already turning the boat and heading back towards the open water out of the channel. Shots could be heard in the distance.

"Sounds as if things are getting out of hand over there," Ed said, looking back again through the binoculars. "Speed it up a bit will you."

Charles was already steadily increasing the speed and it was not long before they were out of sight behind the island.

*

Antonia was back on the bridge standing beside Pierre as she scanned the sea ahead through the binoculars. Pierre could see the entrance to the Dardanelles clearly and was checking the chart for the channel in. There was a lot of merchant shipping about and this was not the moment to lose concentration.

"There, I think," Antonia said, pointing towards the Artemis in the distance. "They must have seen all the activity round the fishing boat and are heading away now. It looks as if they may be back-tracking to the islands again."

"I don't think they'll go far. They'll want to keep in contact with the Phalaris. Time we did the same."

"I'm not so sure," replied Antonia, her eyes still glued to the binoculars. "They appear to be heading back towards Skiáthos. They're not turning due south."

"We should follow the Phalaris now. It shouldn't be difficult for the Greek Coast Guard to pick up the Artemis later."

He turned the boat south and increased the speed.

"Check again with Kahn, will you, what the latest situation is?" Pierre said. "Tell him we want a complete list of what was in those cases as soon as the inventory has been done. If the helmet isn't there it all falls into place."

Chapter 6

The Agioi Apostoloi beach just down the coast from Chaniá on Crete was almost deserted when Martin and Dominique rowed ashore after the long crossing from Skiáthos. They were planning to spend the afternoon lazing in the sun and catching up on some rest, leaving the Phalaris lying safely at anchor off-shore in the bay in the company of several other yachts of different nationalities. The only people dotted about on the beach came from the other boats as it was early in the season and the mass of tourists were waiting for the sea to warm up.

The bow of their dinghy ran up the slope of the shore and ground to a halt as the keel dug deeper into the wet sand. They jumped out, pulled it further up to stop it floating off. They established their space a few metres further up where the sand was warm and dry. After fixing up the parasol and, spreading their towels out, they both stretched out gratefully, suddenly overtaken by the fatigue of the previous ten days' sailing and feeling pleasantly drowsy in the warmth of the sun.

Dominique fell asleep instantly, but Martin remained awake reflecting on their next move. Should they stay for a while and resume their yacht chartering work or could they risk heading straight on? They had done some day-hire sails on the way over to maintain their cover and it might be safer to do more chartering from the quay in Chaniá. The local authorities were used to their presence and that would attract less attention than if they moved on immediately. As he lay on his side deep in thought, watching the beach with unseeing eyes a movement caught his attention.

About twenty metres away another couple were settling down to sunbathe and his eyes were drawn to the girl who was on the side nearest to him. She lay face down, head turned away from him towards her partner. Martin idly took in the details as he watched. She was wearing a chocolate brown bikini, the lower part high cut on the hips, emphasising her long legs, the top half secured only by a thin bootlace of fabric across her back, tied in a bow; the sort he could imagine coming undone with a flick of the finger. The faintest line showed where it had rested too long on a previous day's sunbathing preventing an even tan. Her blond hair was swept back over her neck and off her shoulders, and her skin was only softly browned – probably not been in Crete long, Martin reflected.

As he watched, she raised her head and for a second he was able to glimpse her profile, before her long hair fell across her face and hid it from him. She rolled onto her side away from him and reached behind her head to gather up her hair, swirl it around and, with a practised movement, twist a hair band round it. As she rolled over this time onto her back, he took in appreciatively her flat stomach, the brown triangles of her bikini, the firm breasts and the prettiness of her profile as she lay with her eyes closed against the bright sun. He watched fascinated as she stretched, arching her back off the towel like a cat revelling in the warmth of a sun-drenched doorway.

As she settled back down again, one knee slightly bent up, her hair began to loosen from the constriction of the hair band. She was lying with her arms along her stomach, wrists raised and arched like those of a pianist. Her long fingers lazily sought and eased the edge of her bikini inside her thighs and then moved caressingly along the waistband., finally settling on her stomach, elbows resting on the sand beside her. Martin could not help himself thinking he wished those were his hands, when he sensed rather than heard a movement behind him in the final second before everything went black and he lost consciousness.

The girl in the brown bikini sat up on hearing Martin's slight grunt as he took the blow to the back of his neck and collapsed off his elbow onto his back. She looked across and nodded to the man who was kneeling by Martin's side rolling him carefully onto his front. He started to walk across towards her as she slapped her partner across the buttocks to wake him up. The three of them sat quietly together for a moment until they were satisfied the incident had gone unobserved by the other sunbathers. Then they got up and ran together, shouting and laughing, down to the water's edge.

The girl waded in immediately and began to swim out strongly towards the yachts riding at anchor off shore. Some of the owners of the other yachts were lying sunbathing on deck or just chatting together and sipping cold drinks in the shade of the cockpit awnings, which most had rigged up to keep the sun off. A few were swimming, or rather drifting slowly, round their boats, cooling off for a while.

No one took any notice as the girl reached the Phalaris and climbed aboard using the steps which reached into the water over the stern. The yacht had not been there long enough for anyone – even if they had taken any notice of this far from unusual activity – to identify whether she was the same person who had left the yacht to go ashore an hour or so before.

Her two male companions were approaching in the dinghy. She took the line and secured the dinghy while they climbed aboard. The three of them settled back in the cockpit, helping themselves to a cold beer from the fridge down below. The girl waved briefly to the nearest boat, whose occupants were lazily looking in their direction. The wave was reciprocated and each yacht settled back again into its own self-contained world in the heat of the afternoon.

"They should remain unconscious for about two hours max after the shots I gave them, so we have time, but not too much."

Paul Sondheim, the elder of the two men who spoke, had a light South African accent. In his forties, stocky but in good shape, his hair thinning and greying, was tied back in a short wispy pig-tail like a sixties hippy.

"I'll take the back cabin, Alain," he pronounced the name in the English way. "You take the deck and the main cabin, and Natalie, you take the front cabin and the sail lockers. Let's go, but quietly now."

Paul was already climbing down into the well of the main cabin, and ducked low to go into the aft cabin below the cockpit. Natalie, dried by the sun after her swim out, got up to follow him down. Alain winked at her and stretched out his hand which brushed her thigh as she went passed. He eased himself off the seat where he had been lying stretched out. He was tall for a French Canadian and had to stoop to avoid banging his head on the awning. He was used to boats, and, unlike the South African who scrambled about unsteadily when on board, moved about easily as he went up on deck and looked about him with an experienced eye.

Their searches were thorough and not kind. Everything that could be was pulled out and discarded; the floorboards were raised, the cupboards emptied, bedding thrown down, the lockers cleared, every sail bag emptied, the galley completely stripped down. Every nook and cranny probed. After an hour they returned to the cockpit, smiled across to the neighbouring yacht and took up their original positions in the cockpit.

"Shite! Excuse my French. It has to be here somewhere, unless they have seriously set us up and are just the decoy."

Alain and Natalie said nothing.

"OK guys, time to go – we'll just have to keep following them to see if they drop the helmet off anywhere. Let's get out before they wake. You two should get back to your spot on the beach."

Natalie slipped over the side, swam easily back to the shore and took up her former position on the beach lying as before about twenty metres to Martin's right. She looked across to where he and Dominique were stretched out. They had not moved, but she was relieved to see the rise and fall of their breathing. Alain and Paul pulled the dinghy carefully up to its original position using the same groove in the sand and replacing the oars exactly where they had been before. Alain joined Natalie at her side where he had been earlier and Paul went up to the taverna at the back of the beach.

Dominique stirred slightly as the effect of the drug wore off. She looked about her and saw Martin still lying on his front and beginning to show signs of sunburn. She leaned over towards him and was aware of her own skin tingling and crackling. Still drowsy, fear rising, she shook him urgently and repeated his name. He groaned and rolled over towards her, wincing as his back touched the rough towel.

"What the hell was that?" he mumbled as his head slowly cleared. Then suddenly he remembered and was instantly wide-awake. He glanced across to where the girl in the brown bikini had been lying. She was still there and didn't seem to have moved. Nothing around them had altered.

"How long have we been asleep?" he asked Dominique, searching for his watch.

"About two hours – but no way we were just asleep Martin – some bastard drugged us, for sure."

Martin sat up too quickly, rubbed the back of his neck and groaned as he touched the welling bruise.

"Shit – you're right and I was hit too. I was watching that couple over there and didn't hear a thing until the last moment; then everything went black. Whoever it was must have stuck a needle into my arm judging by how sore it feels."

"Whoever it was get to me before you – I feel a prick and the next thing I knew was when I come to just a few minutes ago and see you lying there on your front. I was afraid, Martin, you looked so still."

She looked at him anxiously. "Your back is very sore too, I think."

"No need to tell me – I know! I'm OK. No serious damage, but what about you? "

He took her hand and kissed it.

"I never wanted to put you in danger, Dom."

"Silly boy!" she said, pressing his hand against her cheek for a moment. "But let me rub some cream on to your back before you burn."

He turned slightly, his back towards her. She knelt behind him and squirted cream onto his shoulders. The coolness on his tender skin made him gasp, but the sun-screen quickly soothed the smarting of the sunburn.

"So someone was following us after all and wanted us out of the way for a while. Charles did say he thought there might be another gang, but seemed relaxed about it. Oh! Bloody hell! I bet they searched the boat, the buggers, whoever they are."

He swung round suddenly nearly knocking Dominique over in his hurry to look out into the bay to where the Phalaris should be, his heart pounding. He heaved a sigh of relief as he realised the yacht was still swinging at anchor and their dinghy was still on the beach.

"Thank god the boat's still there and seems OK," he said, glancing across again towards the girl in the brown bikini. She was sitting up and facing away from him speaking to her partner. Martin looked around him, but the beach revealed no secrets and the other sun-bathers seemed unaware that anything had happened to them. He began to turn his head to see what was going on higher up the beach, but winced in pain.

"Keep still for a minute, *chéri*, I 'ave not finished and you are not right yet. Do you think Charlie knew we were being followed? I do not trust 'im you know, 'e is, how do you say? too smoothy for me."

Dominique knelt behind him again, massaging in the sun cream across his back and gently kneading his shoulders and the back of his neck.

"Smooth. You could be right, but I'm sure he wouldn't deliberately put us in danger," replied Martin, beginning to wonder himself what they had got themselves into. How well did he really know Charles? He straightened up.

"OK, let's pack up our things and get back out to the boat. I think we're being watched – I just caught the flash of sunlight reflected in binoculars coming from up there on those cliffs at the end of the beach."

He nodded in the direction of Alain and Natalie, who were still lying not far from them, but he was looking way past them up onto the outcrop of rocks rising at the end of the beach.

"Could be nothing, but then again …"

Dominique followed his gaze. High up on the cliff she could see a twinkle of light every now and then.

"Maybe, but per'aps it is just a piece of glass or an old bottle," she said.

The effects of the drug had not completely worn off and the dinghy seemed heavy to both of them as they struggled to push it back into the water. Watching them go, Alain remarked:

"*Merde*! We didn't search the dinghy. Perhaps it was there all the time right under our noses. When they next come ashore we'd better check it out."

"Maybe. But it's too small to hide anything in and they wouldn't risk just leaving it here. But there'll be another chance to make sure later," Natalie said. "Right now it's time to go before they reach the boat and realise what has happened. I don't think he suspected me when he woke up and looked across, but there's no point in taking the risk and we need to keep following them until we're sure they do have the helmet."

"I'll swear Everidge did the switch at the beach café in Agnóntas."

"... but it's possible we were set up and the whole operation there was faked," Natalie as she began to put her things into her beach bag.

"You mean Everidge knew all about us and deliberately tricked us in order to send us off on a wild goose chase?"

"I think it's possible. Agnóntas was a small harbour and that's the third time we have coincided with them. They may well have noticed us and become suspicious."

"We searched that bloody boat from top to bottom and I don't know where they could possibly have hidden it. A war helmet isn't small and from what we could see on the beach the package they passed over was quite large. *Putain*! We even checked the water-tanks – where on earth could they have put it? It just must be in the dinghy – there's nowhere else – in the bow compartment perhaps."

"Let's hope you're right. Anyway, move yourself, we'll talk about it later, Alain. They're nearly there and going to find the mess we left. It might've been better to have left no trace. They'll be on their guard now."

"That's not Paul's style – he was so sure we'd find the helmet that it was too late to clear up by the time we realised we weren't going to."

Natalie got to her feet, wrapped a pareo round her waist, gathered up her belongings and, putting on her wide brimmed hat and sunglasses, moved swiftly up the beach near to some rocks from where they could observe what was happening on board. Alain followed her, talking to Paul on the mobile.

"Yep, I can see them from here – I'm at the taverna just behind where you're standing now."

The South African sounded edgy.

Alain looked across and could make out Paul at the back of the terrace on the edge of the beach in the taverna watching Martin and Natalie's progress towards the Phalaris.

"I see you. Natalie's not sure the exchange was made at all at Agnóntas, Paul. Maybe it was a set-up and the Phalaris is a decoy. The goods may be going by another route."

"No way, man, don't be dumb. I saw them hand over that package with my own eyes! So did you," Paul said.

"OK, OK! Calm down! But you don't think they were too obvious? There could have been anything in the package – food for example. Anyway speak to you in a minute – could be it was in the dinghy all the time."

"Oh! Shit! I didn't think of that."

Paul banged his phone down on the table in frustration and some of the tourists at the other tables looked up in surprise.

As Martin and Dominique drew near the Phalaris, they knew instantly someone had been on board. Items on the deck were not quite in their usual positions; one of the curtains in the cabin was drawn; a fender was hanging at an odd angle. Dominique pulled herself up on board, secured the tender and helped Martin as he handed up their things from the beach.

A quick glimpse inside was all that was needed.

"*Putain de merde!*"

"Shit!"

They both mouthed their expletives in unison as they forced a smile across to the people in the next yacht and waved. Martin stood on the deck and squinted up at the main mast, shading his eyes against the bright sun. Dominique went below, brought up two beers, and, toasting the onlookers, they settled back in the cockpit in the shade of the canopy, made a show of raising their glasses to each other and contemplated their next move. The crew of the next yacht were still glancing across from time to time as if they were not sure of the new arrivals on the Phalaris.

"It's OK, they didn't get it – this time."

Dominique was shaking, but nodded and then added:

"I think I'll row across to the next boat and ask if we have had any visitors or whether we missed our 'friends'. They're obviously not quite sure of us. It'll give us a clue of how many came aboard and how long ago."

"OK! Good idea. I'll go below and see what the damage is."

Still feeling unsteady from the shock of what she had seen inside the cabin, Dominique pulled the dinghy alongside and stepped down into it.

As she approached the next yacht, its British red ensign flag fluttering off the stern in the light breeze, she slewed the dinghy round and called across:

"'Allo! Did we 'ave any visitors this afternoon please? We expected some friends, but spent much time shopping in the town and per'aps we 'ave missed them."

"Ah, yes. We did see some people go aboard; two men and a woman. Very pretty woman too, light hair, brown bikini – she swam out and back," replied the man nearest to Dominique. "You've only just missed them; they left about half an hour ago. They waited for some time and helped themselves to your booze!"

"Thank you, that's definitely them! We'll see them later tonight anyway on the shore."

She hesitated. "If you would like, we 'ave an *apéritif* together on our boat in about an hour or so?"

"That would be nice, very kind of you. See you later then," the man replied smiling, after glancing round at his companions who nodded their agreement.

Dominique turned to row back to the Phalaris. Martin took the painter from her and secured the dinghy, growling:

"Oh, very clever! 'We 'ave an *apéritif* together in about an hour?'" he mimicked. "Have you seen the bloody mess in here? OK, move it! Let's get the main cabin sorted out quickly. Leave the rest."

"I just thought it would be a way of making them less suspicious of who we were. Did you hear what they said about the girl being in a brown bikini and that there were two men?" Dominique said, as they worked quickly to tidy up the cabin.

"I'm sorry. You were right to invite them over. No, I didn't! So it was a trap then. And I saw only one man with her on the beach. It must have been the other one who hit me and drugged us both, the bastard." He gingerly rubbed the back of his neck.

"So, your Charlie was right, there is another gang after the helmet."

"Yep. I just wonder how much he knew and wasn't telling us."

"So, why give us the 'elmet if there was a chance it might be stolen from us?" Dominique said.

"I don't know, but no time to think about that now – let's just get on with this. Those people will be here soon."

He gathered up some tins from the floor of the cabin and stowed them in the locker above the galley, closing the door with a sharp click.

As they worked fast to clear up the worst of the chaos they did not speak much, but the emotion they had felt on first seeing the results of the invasion of their property and privacy were allayed to some extent by the knowledge the search had been unsuccessful.

Martin recalled Charles' words in the restaurant about the possibility of a rival group, who might be after the helmet. He hadn't taken the warning too seriously at the time, but this attack changed all that and he knew they would have to be more watchful. It was no longer just a game. After an hour of frenzied activity the cabin looked presentable again, at least to a casual glance from the cockpit and they began to relax.

"Do you think we should warn Charlie and Edouard we have been attacked? They may want to take the 'elmet back, to try another way of taking it to England."

"Yes, probably. But we need time to think this out more thoroughly. I'm still puzzled as to why he would have given us the real thing if he thought there was any danger of us losing it."

"You think we do not 'ave the real 'elmet?" Dominique said. "That 'e put us in danger for a fake 'elmet? The bastard! We are just an 'ow do you say – an *appât*?"

"Decoy. I don't know, but for the moment we're safe enough. They won't try again straight away and we'll just have to be more careful where we leave the boat, Dom. This is the first time we have left it in such a vulnerable spot since we left

Skópelos. From now on we'll have to stick to more crowded harbours."

Hearing a movement outside, Dominique peered out through the cabin window and saw a dinghy approaching the Phalaris.

"Ah! 'Ere come the neighbours – put on the charm Martin and bring up the drinks. I shall be'ave very sexy with them, so they look more at me than at the yacht."

Shaking his head and smiling, Martin went below while Dominique welcomed the new arrivals on board.

Chapter 7

From up on the cliffs above the beach, Pierre and Antonia
retreated from their observation point. The day was drawing to
a close and a welcome breeze sprung up as the land cooled
more quickly than the sea giving them some relief from the heat
and restoring their energy. They had spent most of the day
under a makeshift awning rigged up to protect them from the
worst effects of the sun, but nonetheless they were feeling
dehydrated and fatigued.

Pierre drew a squashed packet of cigarettes from his
pocket, extracted a battered looking white tube of tobacco and
ran it through his fingers in a vain attempt to restore its shape.
He lit it, looked at his watch, and with a sigh, extinguished it on
a rock, grinding it to a mash in his frustration.

Antonia watched this routine with some amusement,
tinged with affection for his efforts to give up smoking. She
looked down into the small bay on the other side of the
headland from where the Phalaris had dropped anchor earlier
that day. A tourist boat was drawn up, its bow wedged in the
sand, linking it precariously to the beach by a long gangplank
like the nose bone of a narwhal. Weary passengers were
boarding the vessel, moving across the gangplank like a line of
ants along a blade of grass, to be taken back to the main
harbour after a day on the beach or walking along the cliffs.

Several had come close to where she and Pierre had spent
the day, greeting them with a nod and envying them the shade
they had set up. She and Pierre had smiled back at them and

most had soon moved off along the many paths on the cliffs, after standing for a moment to admire the view.

Not far from the tourist boat their own boat, the Pericles, lay at anchor. From the height of the cliff Antonia could even see the chain in the clear blue water as it snaked out from the bow towards where the anchor had dug itself in to the sand and rocks below. Their dinghy was drawn up on the beach, awaiting their return.

"Well, that sure was a fascinating afternoon. Neat bit of work on the beach by Paul Sondheim's lot, but they obviously came away empty handed. Did you notice how Martin Handley stood on the deck and stared up at the mast as soon as he and Dominique went back on boarded the Phalaris?" asked Antonia.

"Now that you say it, yes I did. *Eh alors* ?"

"So maybe the helmet is up there?"

"Perhaps – though the only place to hide anything in would be in the radar housing."

"Sure, but they do have another radar scanner on the mizzen mast."

"That's true, good thinking. I didn't know you were so nautical!"

"There's a lot you don't know about me yet, Pierrot!"

During the long passage from Skópelos to Crete, they had had no difficulty shadowing the slower yacht, which had remained under sail. The hardest part had been to keep just out of sight and to find safe anchorage in the little harbours and bays where the Artemis had stopped for a day or two. They had watched too while they hired out their yacht for skippered day sails keeping up their cover, if that's what it was.

Harder had been avoiding the Edelweiss, which Pierre and Antonia had soon confirmed was playing the same game as themselves. Martin and Dominique seemed unaware of their trackers, or, if they were, had taken no measures to avoid them. Fortunately the 'Swiss' in the Edelweiss had seemed only to have eyes for the Phalaris and had been oblivious to the other boats all around them, including Pierre and Antonia on the Pericles.

Shortly after leaving the harbour at Agnóntas, Antonia had sent the photographs she had taken of the crew of the Edelweiss by satellite link to Interpol. By the following morning they had all been identified and the reports were waiting on the email when they awoke. The dossiers had provided them with interesting reading, while they shadowed the two boats on the journey south to Crete.

Paul Sondheim – *matches found by Interpol, the CIA and the South African police.*
White South African citizen: born – Johannesburg, 1970
Studied art history at Cape Town University for a Masters.
Did two years in the SA navy and rose to Lieutenant.
Employed 2 years at Getty Museum, California, as researcher 1992 –1994.
Movements unknown 1994 –1996.
Moved to Rome, Italy, 1997. Extensive travelling in Europe buying and selling works of art for next 10 years. Network of contacts with dealers and buyers – all apparently legitimate.
Came to notice of Italian police in Rome in September 2011 for possible dealing in exported artefacts from protected archaeological sites and stolen works of art. Shipping through Switzerland. Nothing illegal proven.

Natalie Marceau - *match found via Interpol and Swiss police.*
Swiss citizen – born: Zurich, 1984

Rich society girl. Finishing school Geneva. Studied English and Art at Bern University 2002 – 2004. Minor drug taking offences and an official caution.

Joined small art gallery Schmidt & Bernstein as researcher. Offices in Geneva and Monaco, registered in Liechtenstein. Deals in paintings and sculptures for private buyers. Owns small property (hideaway?) in La Roquette sur Var, mountain village behind Nice, close to Italian frontier. Lives there with partner Alain Tremblay (See next report). Now working with local firm in the area.

*Swiss police believe that Schmidt & Bernstein is involved in launder***Natalie***ing money earned outside the country and possibly in illegal imports. Few works of art they deal ever reach the open market again.*

__Alain Tremblay__ – matches found via RCMP, Quebec, Interpol, US Coast Guard, Swiss police.

Canadian citizen – born Quebec City 1982.

Education: formal education ended after graduation from High School – worked on fishing boats in the Great Lakes and on the St. Lawrence. Moved to Fort Lauderdale delivering yachts in the Caribbean. Possible involvement in small-scale drug running and smuggling immigrants out of Cuba. Several clashes with US Coast Guard, but nothing ever found.

Moved to Mediterranean 2006 and worked on yacht hire out of Monaco, where he met Natalie Marceau.

Came to notice of Monegasque police for evading customs duties and for having illegal arms on board. Claimed they were for self-protection against smugglers and pirates – a habit he had acquired from working in the Caribbean. Let off with a caution.

Suspected of drug running from Sicily via Sardinia to Monaco, but nothing proven.

"So the Sondheim gang had no luck this time with their search of the Phalaris and Handley and Krevine are keeping calm, at least for the moment," Pierre said. "I'm certain they were unaware before that they were being followed. But now they do know they may change tactics."

"So you think the Brits didn't warn them – assuming they knew."

Pierre mechanically drew out another a cigarette from the battered packet. Seeing the look on Antonia's face he stubbed it out unlit, muttering *"Merde!"* and looking at his watch.

"I agree," Antonia continued, amused again at Pierre's little pantomime. "I'm sure they were drugged on the beach. So they must be angry and frightened – we should try Interpol with their photos too. Martin Handley may have some form, though I think Dominique Krevine is probably clean. They will be much more alert now. We'll have to be even more careful too – we don't want them to know Interpol are on their tail."

"Can we be sure they still have the helmet on board?" Pierre said, leafing through the documents. "It was difficult to keep a check, what with all the stops on the way here. They were very cool to hire the boat out for day sails on the way over. That was very good cover if they wanted to hand over the helmet to another set of couriers."

"If they had off-loaded it why did Handley look so anxiously up the mast? I'm sure it's still there – one of our agents on the islands would have heard something by now if they'd passed it on to anyone."

"True. OK. We should go now. I'm in need of a beer and of a seat that is comfortable."

He struggled stiffly to his feet, dusting off his trousers and rubbing his elbows.

"You Frenchies are so soft! We Greeks are used to the hard ground. I'll buy you a good meal in town tonight, with a good Greek wine," Antonia replied as she picked up her backpack and started to scramble down the path to the beach below.

"Don't look at me like that – we do have good wines here in Greece. You French don't have them all," she added, looking round at him and tossing her hair back as she laughed.

With a sigh, Pierre bundled up the awning, glanced at his watch again and set off down the steep path in her wake.

*

Later that evening, the Artemis entered the old harbour of Chaniá and Martin and Dominique went ashore to go to their favourite taverna.

They strolled along the waterfront arm in arm enjoying the warm evening breeze and watching the visitors as they tried to find the restaurant which would offer them the best value. Parents with tired young children tugging at their sleeves stood around the menus, making calculations, translating where they could, deciding, hesitating, moving on to the next or going back to the previous one. Waitresses outside each establishment were enticing tourists of all nationalities to stay and ushering them towards tables before they could move away.

In amongst all this normal evening bustle, a young woman cycled towards them along the quayside, weaving in and out of the crowds. As she swept past the wind from the sea and her speed on the bicycle moulded her light tee-shirt to her body revealing such a perfect figure that for a split second time stopped; men literally halted in their tracks, mesmerised, and waiters froze like statues. As she flew by, they were conscious too of the dazzling smile and flowing blond hair of someone fully aware of the effect she was having, and enjoying every moment of it.

The image was gone as fleetingly as it had appeared and, like a film that had momentarily snagged and then flickered back into life, the activity on the waterfront resumed its former rhythm. Tourists continued their searching; waiters resumed taking orders and serving food. Men shook their heads in disbelief first at such a manifestation of their fantasies and then with regret as the image faded as quickly as it had appeared.

Martin nudged Dominique. "Did you see that girl? I'm certain she was the one on the beach who was sun bathing not far from us …"

"… and who the people on the yacht beside us described as the one who swum out to the Phalaris and went on board."

She clutched his arm tightly.

"They're watching us all the time, Martin. Per'aps they're not the only ones."

She and Martin turned into their taverna and were distracted for a while as the patron recognised them, greeted them like long lost friends and recommended the best dishes of the day. They left the choice to him, happy to be relieved of making a decision, however trivial.

Although they had recovered from the initial shock of the assault and the search of their home, which the Phalaris surely was, they were still uncertain of how to proceed. Martin had contacted Charles and Ed, who had expressed surprise and shock at the attack, but said they were too far away at the moment to take back the package. Charles advised them to leave Crete and to make for the little harbours of Avlémonas on the island of Kýthira where they would meet them in three days' time.

"Tomorrow we stock up with food and water and check the boat over thoroughly before making our move some time after midnight. We need to slip out of the harbour under cover of darkness if we're to stand a chance of losing whoever is following us."

"*Entendu*! One of us must stay on the boat all the time tomorrow, so I'll do the shopping and you stay here on guard."

"OK – this is getting more and more like the Caribbean; I never thought I would have to fight off pirates over here in Greece," Martin said, passing his hand across his forehead in a gesture of fatigue.

"You're tired from too much thinking, *chéri*. Try not to think about it for a while and enjoy your meal. We'll soon be away from 'ere."

Their waiter arrived with the ouzo and Martin poured ice-cold water into each clouding glass, stopping at a nod from Dominique. Both of them settled back into their chairs, exchanged glances and sipped their drinks. However hard they tried this was not going to be the relaxing evening they had hoped for. There had been something not quite convincing about Charles' reaction to the attack, when they contacted him. He didn't show enough surprise. Had he known all along they were being followed?

Now they were faced with a crossing to Kýthira not knowing whether they would be attacked again at sea this time. In low voices they weighed up the dangers together. Perhaps it would be safer to arrange a diversion of their own for the benefit of the watchers. Dominique could take the ferry from Crete to Kythira, and Martin could hire a local boy to help him crew the Phalaris. That might split up any followers. On the other hand, Dominique on her own would be more vulnerable to another attack whether or not she took the package with her and could be held as a hostage. They decided it would be safer if they stayed together after all.

"Fuck you, Charles," Martin said aloud. "I'll make you pay for this."

*

Antonia and Pierre had picked a table in the next restaurant. It was a perfect evening and Pierre's first reaction as they took their seats and ordered a beer each was to breathe a sigh of satisfaction as he sunk into the deep soft cushions of the basket chairs. Antonia read his thoughts:

"Just as I thought – as soon as it becomes comfortable you go off duty. Not this evening you don't though – we still have lots to do."

"Thank you for reminding me, Detective Inspector, but this is my first decent meal all day and I intend to enjoy it. So, you must wait until we have chosen from the menu before we discuss business again."

"Food before business! Is that French or what?"

He studied the menu intently, pretending to ignore Antonia's efforts to distract him.

"*Psária plaki, kléftiko* and a *baklavá, parakaló*" he announced to her in his best Greek, settling back again in the cushions.

"*Marides, choriátiki salata e ena giaourti kai méli*," she responded. "And I promised you a good wine, so a *Gentilini* from Crete.

"Nothing quite like being on duty!"

Pierre sipped his beer and glanced across again to where Martin and Dominique were sitting, heads down, talking seriously.

"I think our friends are too edgy to relax. So what will they decide to do now?"

"That may depend on the how the Sondheim gang react. Maybe they are watching even now. It may only be a matter of time before they catch on to us too."

Their waiter approached and Antonia ordered quickly for them both, responding to the waiter's questions and discussing the wine in particular, anxious to prove her defence of her country's viticultural reputation. The waiter took the order, noting Antonia's slight American accent even when she spoke Greek. Pierre looked carefully around, scanning the tables to see if Paul Sondheim and the others were anywhere in sight. Just as Antonia finished giving the order and the waiter moved away, Pierre stiffened slightly. He had spotted the girl – Natalie Marceau – sitting at the back of the restaurant on the other side.

"There's your answer. Marceau is at the back over there. I can't see the others, but they won't be far away, I'm sure."

"Well, at least we know roughly where everyone is for the moment, so let's enjoy our meal. There won't be any more action before tonight," Antonia said, seeing the waiter approach with their first course and the wine. He poured the wine and she took an appreciative sip.

Pierre swirled it round in his glass, sniffed it suspiciously and wetted his lips. He made as if to spit it out, but then turned to her with a grin:

"So! *Un petit vin* – but quite drinkable all the same."

He winced as her kick hit its target.

They had received the reports from Interpol on Martin and Dominique before they came ashore earlier that evening. There was nothing noteworthy on Dominique, but Martin's made more interesting reading. They knew he had spent time in the Caribbean, but there was no evidence he had been involved in anything illegal. The most that could be said was that he had gained a certain amount of experience in being watchful and was prepared to fight off pirates if the need arose. He knew how to handle guns and he may have used his skills as a diver to hide or pick up drugs, but he had never been seen in the wrong company. His activities had all appeared to be legitimate yacht delivery for rich clients, mainly operating out of Fort Lauderdale – a coincidence with Alain Tremblay, but probably nothing more – using agents to hire the delivery crews for him.

The meal was excellent and they felt themselves relaxing in the warm evening sun. The fishy smells from the harbour, the wine – a second bottle had seemed necessary – and the good food all combined to favour intimate conversation rather than watchfulness. The noise-world around them gradually reduced to a low hum as Pierre and Antonia talked on a more personal level.

The sound of chairs being pushed back and voices rising brought them sharply back into the present. Martin and Dominique had already left their table and were walking slowly along the promenade, arms around each other's waists, towards the harbour. Pierre looked round quickly to where he had seen Natalie Marceau earlier. She was no longer at her table. Sensing danger, his eyes darted around the scene. Then he spotted her following about fifty metres behind them, speaking into her mobile.

"Time to go," he said to Antonia as he stood up, put money on the table and grabbed the remains of the second bottle. "Things are happening."

Chapter 8

Martin and Dominique walked back to where they had moored the Phalaris. Neither was as relaxed as they had hoped after their evening ashore. Their heads were buzzing with the anxieties they felt about the next stage of their journey and the threat of another attack hanging over them, possibly during the crossing to Kýthira island. Assuming they did arrive safely, the meeting there with Charles and Ed would be the sort of confrontation which left a nasty taste in the mouth, a feeling of having been betrayed by someone you trusted.

In the meantime they would have to remain vigilant and guard against a second attack by the 'Swiss' until they were ready to leave Chaniá harbour. As they walked close together, as much for unspoken protection as by affection, Martin scanned the dozens of visiting boats which filled the harbour at that time of the year, but there was little chance of spotting the Edelweiss amongst the forest of masts and flags in the half light of the evening. Under any other circumstances the scene would have been a delight – the last glimmers of daylight in the sky, the play of harbour lights of many colours dimpling the water in ever changing rippling patterns, the smell of the sea mingling with wafts of fish cooking as they passed the restaurants on the water front – but that evening neither of them was any longer in a mood to register such appeals to the senses.

They reached the Phalaris, relieved to find that nothing had been disturbed. Martin immediately began to wind cotton lines across the decks and over the guardrails, attaching small bells concealed behind cleats, riding lights and handrails.

"Just a little trick I learned in the Caribbean," he said to Dominique as she watched him at work. "It gives us a slight chance of a warning if anyone boards in the night."

*

Lying flat on the cabin top protected by two lines of yachts between them and the Phalaris, Antonia watched through night vision binoculars the ghostly green images of Martin's comings and goings on the deck.

"Handley definitely is a professional. Must have learned to do that in the Caribbean," she said. "We should have a quiet night – they're certainly not preparing to leave straight away. I don't think Sondheim will try anything tonight either. It's a well lit area and close to those taverna. The local fishermen would notice anything suspicious. It's far too public for any rough stuff."

"Perfect! I shall sleep well tonight – your Greek wine has finished me off completely," replied Pierre.

*

Early the next morning, Martin was on deck again clearing the trip lines, while Dominique finished the list of stores they needed for the crossing. Neither of them had slept well that night, tossing and turning in their bunk, disturbed by dreams of possible attack.

Martin went down below and poured himself a coffee, warming his hands round the cup against the early morning cold. Preoccupied with making a list of the stores they would need for the passage to Kýthira, Dominique hardly looked up as he set down another cup in front of her on the table.

"We can eat in the taverna opposite and still keep an eye on the boat, so just get what we need for the crossing," Martin said.

Dominique said nothing as she stood up to go to the companionway up into the cockpit. He reached out to catch and squeeze her hand, turning her back towards him.

"Come here, Dom," he said, giving her a hug. "Don't look so worried, they won't try anything today. Just keep an eye out to see if you're being followed. That girl we saw on the bicycle is one of them, I'm sure. While you are away I might go for a stroll along the pontoons in the marina and see if I can spot their boat this time – it should be easier in the daylight and I'll be able to keep the Phalaris in sight."

"Just be careful, *chéri*. *À bientôt!*"

She ran her hand down his cheek, broke free and left the cabin.

Martin finished his coffee, looked for his dark glasses and, pulling on an old Fort Lauderdale baseball cap, locked the cabin door and went out onto the pontoon and along the gangway onto the quay. Out of habit he gave a quick look back to check the mooring lines were secure and sauntered off towards the rows of visiting boats. He caught sight of Dominique in the distance, on her way to the nearby covered market, her face partly hidden by a wide brimmed sun hat.

*

Sitting in a taverna over coffee, Paul Sondheim watched them leave the Phalaris and turned to Alain and Natalie.

"Quite a sharp cookie, Handley. Trouble is, they're all fired up now. They know someone is after them and we'll have to watch them constantly to work out their next move."

"I'll follow the girl – she won't recognise me, I don't think," Natalie said, getting up to go, while Dominique was still in sight.

"And I'll follow Handley. Perhaps he's looking for us," Alain said.

"OK, you guys. But don't let them see you. No foul-ups this time. Low profile and keep your heads down. Clear?"

Both of them turned sharply at the tone of Sondheim's voice, but suppressed their reactions and abruptly left the table. Alain brushed against a chair, steadying it as he passed, glancing across at Natalie. At the door of the restaurant, they whispered briefly to each other before separating. Alain crossed the road towards the quayside. Natalie continued up the street to the covered market, catching sight of Dominique's hat just as she entered the market halls.

Inside the market area a symphony of smells assailed Dominique – fresh fruit, vegetables, fish, local cheeses, honey and above all the smell of baking bread, mingled with that of huge round gýros of souvláki lamb turning slowly on their vertical spits. She concentrated on her list and moved from stall to stall, her mood improving as she eyed the quality of the local produce on display. For a welcome half hour she was lost in the pleasurable business of choosing and buying food. It was as if she was back in the market in Nice, sampling cheeses, pressing fruit and scrutinising vegetables for freshness.

Only when she turned to find her way out of the market did it come back to her that she might be being followed. She slipped out of a side entrance into the Stivanádika with its bustle of small shops and early crowds of tourists picking over the displays of sandals and leather goods. She sat down at a café from where she could watch the entrance to the market. The waiter automatically set down a glass of ice cold water in front of her and she ordered an ouzo, knowing it was earlier than usual for her.

She picked up a local newspaper discarded by a previous customer and settled back, making as if to read it. She scarcely noticed the print as she scanned the street looking for the girl on the bicycle of the previous evening. It did not take her long. Over on the far side sitting towards the back of another café an elegant looking tourist wearing a cream coloured dress and dark glasses was watching the people go by. The drink on the table in front of her had hardly been touched and she was occupied with brushing off an over-friendly local young would-be gigolo, who was offering to keep her company, despite the fact there were plenty of spare tables at that hour.

Time to give her the run around, Dominique thought, feeling quite light-headed after the ouzo on an empty stomach. She gathered her things, paid the bill and started to saunter along the street.

She wandered in and out of the shops entering by one door and leaving by another, weaved her way in and out of the stalls, sometimes half hidden by the hanging garments and bags of all sorts, sometimes out in the open simply mingling with the tourists. All the time behind her, the girl in the cream dress tried to anticipate her movements and to keep her in sight. Finally tiring of the baiting and growing weary herself in the heat, Dominique dodged back into the shade of the covered market, bought a take away souvláki pitta and headed back towards the Phalaris.

*

Martin searched for the Edelweiss amongst the pontoons. He hadn't much to go on – Charles' description had been vague, but then again there were not too many boats of any sort flying a Swiss flag. He climbed down the access ladders onto the floating pontoons and strolled along to the end, retracing his steps back to the quayside and starting again on the next. He avoided pausing in front of any particular boat and to any observer appeared to concentrate more on boats flying a French flag than on any others.

On the third pontoon he passed the stern of a Swiss motor yacht with the name 'Edelweiss' in gold lettering on the stern. In the cockpit in the shade of the awning lounged a short, stocky man with a pig-tail, his eyes invisible behind dark glasses. As Martin went by, he nodded to the man and acknowledged his presence with a passing 'kaliméra.' The man muttered a reply in English, but Martin caught the South African accent.

He continued along the pontoon without checking his step, surveyed the harbour from the furthest point of the pontoon and turned to head back to the quay. Meanwhile the man had gone below and Martin studied the boats on the other side of the pontoon, keeping his head turned well away as he passed the Edelweiss.

Back on the quay he crossed the road to a souvlatzídiko stall, waited while the vendor filled the pitta bread with the selection of lamb and the salad he wanted and then returned to the quayside where he sat on a bollard fifty metres further on. Now what is a South African doing on a Swiss motor yacht, a South African who doesn't want to draw attention to himself? he said to himself. And why am I being watched by another man sitting on top of the cabin of a boat three or four pontoons away on the other side? As he got up to go, he saw the girl on the bicycle from the previous evening jump down onto the pontoon and board the Edelweiss. She looked hot and frazzled and not pleased with herself.

*

Pierre watched Martin and Dominique return to the Phalaris.

"They're both back now. The girl's been shopping in the market and Handley's been searching the pontoons," he reported to Antonia, who had just returned on board herself carrying food and flowers.

"Yes, I followed Dominique to the market and outside in the shopping district. She is not as naïve as we thought. She was clearly aware she had a tail."

Pierre looked up.

"Not me," she added. "I meant she had spotted Natalie Marceau. After she'd bought what she needed, she led Marceau a merry little dance through the shops and the stalls. I had a job myself to keep up with her. I'm certain she didn't spot me but she wanted to take revenge on Marceau for what happened on the beach. The frustration on Marceau's face was comical, especially when it dawned on her she had been sussed and the trail being laid was a false one which would only lead back to where she started, but she still couldn't risk breaking off just in case."

"Yes, I saw her return to the Edelweiss not looking too pleased. They're moored over there about four pontoons away, beside that large French yacht. I'm sure Handley spotted them."

"So what will he do?"

"No idea – it's possible he'll try and make a deal, but I think he's too angry to do that."

The satellite phone sounded in the cabin and Antonia went below to answer it. When she emerged she burst out the news:

"Interpol have intercepted a call Martin Handley made to Charles Everidge. It seems they have agreed to meet on Kýthira in Avlémonas harbour, in three days time. Martin was furious with Everidge."

"That should make an interesting reunion!"

"How long do you think it'll take them to do the crossing under sail?"

"About a day and a half non-stop, maybe more," Pierre replied, after looking at the chart.

"So they'll probably leave tonight," Antonia said.

That afternoon all activity on the three boats came to a halt. There was no movement above deck. Antonia and Pierre took it in turns to keep watch on the other two, but there was nothing to report from either boat. In the heat of the afternoon indeed the whole port seemed to have gone to sleep. Even the local fishing boats lay idle under a breathless blue sky.

Over on the waterfront side a few very pink looking British tourists emerged from the hotels to take their children down to the beach and the cafés were doing a fair trade in the tall glasses full of coloured ice-cream with little umbrellas on top, but generally the atmosphere was strangely out of season. Thunder clouds were gathering low on the horizon and the air was languid and still. Even the seagulls were quiet and there was an air of expectancy about the port.

Dusk came early and was brief. Antonia watched the three of them from the Edelweiss go ashore to eat. The Phalaris maintained a ghost-like silence.

Pierre took over the watch after they had eaten on board. The light had gone from the sky and it was difficult to see against the flare of the lamps around the water-front. There were dark shadows everywhere between the boats.

"I see movement," he whispered. "Handley is on deck. It looks as if he's wearing a wet suit – the full gear. He's got a bag on his belt. He's going over the side now. I can't see him any more, but I can guess where he's going."

"You mean the Edelweiss ?"

"Nowhere else he'd want to go – can you get over to the pontoon and watch from there?"

Antonia slipped away quickly and was soon in a position to see the boat. She saw it rock slightly, but otherwise there was no sign of Handley. Five minutes later the Edelweiss rocked gently again and she spotted him slowly swimming back to the Phalaris.

"Whatever he did, it was under water," she reported back to Pierre. "I couldn't see what, but it took five minutes or so."

"To keep the rendezvous with Everidge and Robson, they will have to leave tonight or early tomorrow, so we have a long watch ahead again."

Antonia joined him on the cabin roof carrying a rug against the chill of the evening, which came earlier and more quickly than usual off the water. The threatened storm when it finally came was sudden and violent and they rapidly retreated to the cabin. The thunder echoed around the bay, lightening cracked and the downpour drummed deafeningly on the cabin roof. Just as quickly as it had started, the storm moved on and the sky cleared.

It was not until the early hours of the morning that they heard and then saw movement on the Phalaris. She had slipped her moorings and Handley and Krevine were quietly using paddles to move the yacht out towards the harbour entrance. She was showing no navigation lights and her sails were ready, but still furled. As she reached the lee of the old Venetian Firkás fort, Pierre and Antonia could just hear the throb of the diesel engine starting up, helping the yacht on her way. They lost sight of her as she turned and headed north-west.

*

On board, Martin and Dominique were busy setting the sails to take advantage of the stiff breeze in the aftermath of the earlier storm. Both were dressed warmly against the cold and moved about stiffly as they forced their bodies to wake up and to generate enough warmth to function smoothly. Once the sails were up Martin returned to the cockpit, cut the engine and headed the boat round to catch the wind. The yacht responded immediately, heeled slightly and bounded forward into the waves. The spray came over the bow and caught him at the wheel. He grinned as he wiped the water from his face and pushed back his hair. The first dowsing of the day had completed the waking up process.

The challenge of what lay ahead seemed a long way off for the moment and he was exhilarated by the movement of the boat and harmony with the elements. His mood lift further as he and the boat worked as one to make passage away from the dangers in the harbour behind them. Dominique appeared in the cabin doorway, carrying mugs of steaming hot chocolate, dodged back under cover as he shouted out a warning, and waited for the spray to subside before venturing forward again. Martin set the auto pilot, took his mug, and put his arm round her as she came to sit beside him. Neither said a word as they enjoyed the warming effect of the liquid. Draining his mug before the next shower of spray shot up from the bow, he went forward to raise the spray shield to give them more protection.

"We need to get out over the horizon as fast as possible and then I'll set the course. I don't think they saw us go and that gives us a head start."

"Dawn will be with us soon and they'll see we've gone."

"True, but they don't know which way we're heading and it'll take a while for them to find us out here. They'll have to be lucky to catch us on the radar as I've taken the reflectors down. I also prepared a little surprise for them on the dock."

"What will happen when we arrive in Avlemonas harbour?"

"Don't even think about it – just enjoy the moment. Anyway we'll have time to stop for the night in the harbour at Kapsáli first. What about some breakfast? Fried fish sandwich do you?"

She smiled in reply and Martin went below to the galley.

"Just keep a good look out," he called over his shoulder. "We don't want to ram a fishing boat."

Twenty minutes later he reappeared. They retreated into the shelter of the spray shield again and munched two-handedly at the morale boosting fish sandwiches, still hot from the frying pan. Dawn was breaking and the wind easing as the yacht made steady progress across the open water towards Kýthira, the island birthplace of the goddess Aphrodite, and their stop-over at Kapsáli. For a while at least they could savour the release from tension.

*

It was six in the morning before Antonia tapped on the cabin top to alert Pierre. When he came up from the cabin he was carrying a mug of hot coffee which he passed to her without a word. She gratefully took a sip and gestured towards the Edelweiss. He could see the lights on in the cabin. A figure emerged on deck, still not fully awake. The younger man – Pierre identified him as the French Canadian, Alain Tremblay – looked around and immediately saw the gap between the boats on the quayside further down where the Phalaris had been, and darted back into the cabin.

"That should wake them up. Now we're going to see some action," Pierre said.

"This should be fun – let's watch from below. They might wonder why there are two people lying stretched out on a cabin top at this hour of the morning," Antonia said. "Anyway, I'm freezing."

*

"I told you Handley had spotted us yesterday – now we don't know where the hell they're going," Alain said to the other two.

"Aw, come on man, we'll soon catch them up. They can't have got far. Natalie shift your arse and get the coffee on, we gotta go," Paul said.

"Get your own fucking coffee, Paul, and stop ordering me about. I am not your maid!"

"OK you two, that's enough. Let's get out of here or we'll never find them," Alain said.

 Alain moved up to the helm and switched on the diesels. The reassuring throb of the powerful engines settled all their nerves. Paul went up on deck to throw off the lines and Alain put the boat into first gear to move off from the pontoon. The boat strained for a few seconds, the pontoon seemed to move with them and then the engines choked and died.

"What the hell … !" Paul could be heard stumbling across the deck to the stern, which was still glued to the pontoon. He jumped off the boat and lay full length on the pontoon hanging over the side and looking down into the water.

"The bastard!" Alain said, also peering into the water, learning over from the cockpit. "He's wired us to the pontoon – it's a complete nightmare down there. We probably screwed up the prop shaft when we revved up too – there's cable everywhere."

*

Pierre and Antonia watched the Edelweiss attempting to leave the harbour with some amusement. Voices carry easily across water and they smiled at the angry comments from the two men.

"Shafted you might say!" Antonia said.

"We French say a *jeu de mots* is the lowest form of wit!"

Pierre replied with a smile: "That was Oscar Wilde, a Brit, but never mind. I wondered what exactly Handley was doing under water – now we know. That should delay them for a while."

"Maybe we should leave now, while they're too busy to notice. We can get out in front of them – lucky we know where the Phalaris is going. They've created a head start on the others of about four hours, plus the time it will take to fix the propeller. That's good thinking."

He looked at the chart in front of him.

"I think we should circle round ahead of the Phalaris. We will wait for them on the other side of this smaller island of Antikýthira, in the channel between it and the main island. About here."

He pointed to the chart.

"Sounds a good plan," Antonia said looking over his shoulder. "We might even see Everidge and Robson coming down to meet them from Volos too."

"OK, let's do it. Now's a good time," he added, as he saw the regular tourist boat between Chaniá and Diakófti coming in to dock at the passenger quay.

They slipped the lines and, picking a moment when the ferry covered their line of sight to the Edelweiss and when two other boats were also making for the harbour entrance, Pierre took the Pericles out at a slow two knots to attract as little attention as possible. Once they were clear of the fort, Pierre open up the throttle, the boat picked up speed, headed north-west. Standing behind him, Antonia put her arms round his waist and let her hair blow out free in the wind created by their speed. Pierre sensed her mood and said nothing, just enjoying the closeness and the relaxation after a long night of watching. When they had rounded the Spátha headland, he set the autopilot on the new heading for the north of Antikýthira island and they went below to make a belated breakfast.

As Pierre sipped his coffee, Antonia produced the results of her shopping the night before. She placed on the cabin table a selection of koulourákia, olive rolls and fresh figs. As she did so her face was wreathed in an anticipatory smile, waiting for the predictable reaction of her French colleague.

"You're joking!"

She pretended to look hurt and said:

"But they are a real treat – I got them specially."

Pierre reached behind him and delved into the large bag on the galley. His hand emerged triumphantly holding a squashed croissant.

"It is not from this morning, but at least it's real food," he mumbled as he bit into it.

"So it's true what they say – you French don't like going abroad because you don't trust foreign food!"

Pierre mumbled something about barbarians with his mouth full and turned towards the radar screen.

"There's a boat coming up behind at speed. Could be the Edelweiss."

He looked out through the cockpit door and continued:

"That's them OK, but now they've swung round and are heading the other way. They're like a headless chicken and it's obvious they don't know where to look exactly – that's Handley's best chance of avoiding them. Let's hope for his sake his gamble pays off. They should be well over the horizon now and safe for a while from their radar."

It had taken them a good hour to free the propellers. Paul and Alain took it in turns to dive down with the wire cutters and to clear the tangle from the twin props. They inspected the shafts for possible distortion and gently revved the engines. There seemed to be no damage and they returned to the cabin to towel down. Natalie took the boat out while they dressed. The wind was dying even more as the heat of the day began to burn off the early clouds and as soon as they had cleared the entrance to the harbour they scanned the horizon for any sign of the Phalaris.

Chapter 9

Martin was lying on the top deck searching the expanse of sea astern between them and Crete through his binoculars. There was still a strong breeze that far from the land and they had made good progress after their early start. He calculated they were already about forty miles out from Chaniá and well over the horizon. There was no sign of the Edelweiss.

"It looks as if we've given them the slip for a while at least."

"Per'aps our luck will stay – look, the dolphins are with us again. I could watch them for hours – they are so graceful. Surely that's a good omen – they will look after us."

"You'll sound like the oracle at Delphi if you go on like that. Don't worry – Sondheim won't attempt anything at sea. We're safe until we arrive at Avlemonas. At this rate we'll make it OK to Kapsáli for tonight and can hide up in the harbour. Even Charles won't know where we are then."

"I don't like your Charlie. "He is a – how do you say – a filthy rat. Why did he not say to us that these people were following us? I am sure it was 'im who set us up, not *le petit* Edouard."

Martin, his eyes still glued to his binoculars, stiffened.

"Hang on. No, it's OK – that isn't them. It's flying the Greek flag and heading north of us."

"I think you're not quite relaxed yourself, *mon petit chou*. Come below – I make you a good dinner and then we can make a sieste together and listen to the sound of the water."

"Sounds fun! OK, I'll just check the autopilot and you're on, Dom."

He checked the chart for the nth time and reset the compass.

"We'll keep to the west of the island of Antikýthira, that way we'll get some shelter from the wind," but he was talking to himself now as Dominique had already dropped down into the cabin and his last remarks were addressed to the sea and the dolphins.

*

"What the hell are we doing rushing about all over the place like jack rabbits? It's time we made a proper plan and searched more logically," Paul said.

The Edelweiss had surged out of Chaniá harbour and headed west. The radar had picked up a boat going north, but it was moving too fast for a yacht. After a quick search of the bay, they had changed direction sharply to head towards the east. The scanner picked up some yachts ahead and they had spent the best part of the morning overtaking them, circling and charging off again usually accompanied by shouts and raised fists from the crews as their boats rocked in the wash of the powerful motor yacht.

They searched the whole of the northern coastline, checking the harbours and the small bays, but with no success. They went as far as Siteía almost on the eastern tip of the island, before it was obvious the Phalaris had not had time to cover such a distance.

"Decision time, Paully," called Alain.

"Don't you ever call me that again, Frenchy. But I reckon you're right," he added calming down. "OK, so they didn't head east. Must have gone north — but where the hell have the bastards gone?"

"Well, they have to get the helmet back to England sometime, so perhaps they are heading north-west, rather than due north," Natalie said. "They're more likely to go back via the Canal du Midi through France than risk the long way round Gibraltar and Spain."

Alain was looking at the charts spread out on the cabin table.

"Let's say they're making 6-7 knots in this wind and going towards … ," he hesitated, "Kýthira, which would be the nearest stop-over unless they're going straight on to Malta. They've got nearly ten hours start on us by now so they could be half way. That'd be the next best place to search."

"OK, let's hope you're right."

Paul swung the boat round in a tight turn and Alain had to steady himself to keep his footing. A nearby yacht rocked alarmingly as the wake hit them and the crew raised two fingers again at him. He laughed, as he eased open the throttle. The bow began to rise and soon they were making 25 knots into the wind and waves. As the boat slammed into every breaker it threw up a shower burst of spray and Paul's mood continued to lighten as he wrestled with the wheel to keep the boat on a straight line. He was beginning to enjoy himself again after the frustrations of the morning.

"Give me a heading, Alain."

"280 degrees northwest should do it for a while."

Paul glanced at the compass, adjusted his course slightly and settled back in the high helmsman's chair to savour the steering.

"Sorry I've been like a bear with a sore arse these last few days. You guys don't deserve it. It's just that all this chasing about doesn't suit me and I was pissed off at not finding the helmet when we searched their boat."

They took it in turns at the wheel for the next four hours or so, no one saying much, too intent on maintaining their speed to make up for the time they had spent searching that morning. In the late afternoon Antikýthira hove into sight.

"The island is all rocks with very little shelter and no beaches according to the description in the Pilot book," Natalie said. "I doubt they would have stopped here."

"OK, we'll go on."

As they passed to the north and could see the main island more clearly ahead, Natalie exclaimed:

"I can see a sail over there to the left. It could be them."

Picking up his binoculars, Paul scanned the area Natalie was pointing to.

"OK – let's take a closer look."

He swung the wheel and the Edelweiss leaned into the speed, settled back on an even keel as the wheel centred and closed the gap between the two boats.

"That's them alright. This time we're going to make them tell us where they've hidden the damned helmet. No messing after what those bastards did to us this morning."

"No rough stuff, Paul, you're not in the Navy now. We can't afford to have the police after us if we do take the helmet. After all they are only doing what they are paid to do – like us."

Alain was only too aware of Paul's temper and feared the worst if Handley and the girl put up much resistance. He had secretly admired the way Handley had nearly succeeded in sabotaging the Edelweiss in Chaniá. With just a little more luck the cable round the propeller would have caused much more damage when he put the engine into gear. That would have given them another couple of hours start, and dusk would have fallen. They might have made it to a small bay on Kýthira, where they could have hidden up for the night.

The Edelweiss was closing in fast and they could see Martin Handley on the deck watching their approach. Paul slowed the boat when they got within a few metres and they circled the Phalaris, which was still under full sail and making 8-10 knots in the breeze. Alain picked up the ship's phone and radioed across.

"Take your sails down – we're coming aboard," he ordered Dominique, who had picked up the receiver.

"Piss off!"

"*Non, chérie*, it is you who must fuck off. We're coming aboard whether you like it or not."

Martin was at her side by the chart table and she looked at him for advice on what to do. He took the microphone from her.

"This is Martin Handley. Who am I speaking to?"

"You don't need to know that, Handley. Just do as we say and I promise no harm will come to you."

"Oldest and most clichéd line in the book. What do you want?"

"You know what we want. Why don't you just heave to and we can talk? Your friends have let you down, so this may be the best deal you're going to get."

As Alain finished speaking, Martin and Dominique looked up and were just in time to see the Edelweiss almost on them, its bow high in the water, before they were thrown across the cabin by the force of the collision. The motor yacht had hit them a glancing blow at speed. The force was enough to buckle the stanchions of the guardrail and to cause the Phalaris to heel dangerously. Martin picked himself up, checked to see Dominique was not badly hurt and crawled out into the cockpit to assess the damage and take the helm. Apart from the bent stanchions and split wooden gunwale strip, there was no serious damage. Back inside Dominique was screaming down the microphone at Alain.

"What the 'ell was that for, you bastard?"

"What a delicious accent you have when you get angry, Dominique. That was just a little warning of course – to show you we're serious. Do as we say and heave to. We just want to pay you a little visit."

Martin nodded.

"OK, just don't do that again or I'll ... 'ow did you know my name anyway?"

" I look forward to whatever you're going to do to me, *à bientôt, chérie.* "

Dominique snapped the microphone shut.

"Arrogant bastard, just let me get my 'ands on 'im."

"You may be able to do that sooner than you think, Dom. They mean business, so we have to play this one carefully. We'll get the mains'l down, and let them come alongside, but I want you to maintain course towards Kapsáli nonetheless."

"OK. But what are you going to do? Be careful, Martin."

"Let's just play this as it comes. I've been in this sort of situation before in the Caribbean."

They both went up on deck and started to lower the mainsail and secure it to the boom. Just off their windward side the Edelweiss watched their manoeuvre and waited to come alongside. Back in the cockpit, Martin eased the sheets to the jib and the mizzen and the Phalaris slowed even further to a steady two or three knots. On board the Edelweiss, Natalie began the approach from the stern, and eased the boat alongside, just forward of the damaged stanchions. Alain jumped nimbly onto the foredeck and helped Paul to follow. He landed heavily and cursed as he stumbled on the anchor post.

Dominique and Martin watched as the two men came towards them, moving along the safety holds on the cabin top as they coped with the roll of the yacht. They climbed down into the cockpit and greeted their reluctant hosts.

"Well, isn't it traditional to welcome us aboard, Mr Handley?"

"Cut the crap! Who are you and what do you want? This is piracy on the high seas in international waters."

"Piracy on the high seas, international waters! Did you hear that Alan? Our Brit friend is very posh. And what about you, *mad'oiselle?* What do you say?"

"Say what you 'ave to say and get off our boat, *salaud!*"

"Not sure what that means, but it sounded unfriendly. OK – let's cut straight to it. We want the helmet and you're going to give it to us. So go fetch."

"We don't have it any more …"

"Don't be stupid. We know you've still got it. Just fetch."

As he spoke Paul moved towards Dominique and with a practised movement caught her wrist, twisted her round and held a knife to her throat. Alain made as if to restrain him and then stepped back again.

"You'd better do it, my friend," he said to Martin. "He can be a touchy bastard at times and he means what he says."

"That's good advice, boy."

"Alright, alright. Just leave her alone. The helmet is in the radar housing on the main mast, but it would be crazy to try to get it down out here in this wind."

"Clever! We didn't think of that when we searched before. But you're going to get it down now and you're not going to drop it either. That would be even more stupid."

He tightened his grip on Dominique.

"Capisch?"

"I'll have to get the harness and someone will have to winch me up."

"Go with him, Alain. And no tricks, Handley, or your girlfriend will need a new face."

Martin went down into the cabin followed by Alain. Reaching into a locker he was beginning to pull out the harness when Alain grabbed his wrist and finished the task himself.

"Just making sure there was nothing nasty in there," he said with a smile.

Martin took the gear back out into the cockpit and began to strap it on.

"Get a move on, we don't have all day!" barked Paul.

It took good half hour to hoist Martin up to the radar housing and for him to manoeuvre the package safely into the bag strapped round his waist. The movement of the boat was much stronger twenty feet up and several times Martin lost his grip and was swung in an arc out into the void. Eventually, he pushed the package safely into the bag, closed the radar housing and began to abseil down. The scene below him was much as he had left it.

Paul had let Dominique go, but his knife was still in evidence. She was sitting huddled in the corner of the cockpit massaging her wrist and stretching her neck from side to side. Alain was staring up at him from the bottom of the mast. Just behind, the Edelweiss was following in their wake like a guard ship.

Martin's mind raced, seizing up the situation they were in and seeing no easy way out for the moment. He began his slow careful descent, trying hard to prevent himself being slammed against the mast and damaging the package. He reached the deck, unhitched his harness from the winch and worked his way back to the cockpit.

"Impressive! Just as well you didn't drop it!" Paul said.

"I told you it was stupid to try to bring it down out here – it would have served you right if I had dropped it, asshole."

"Temper, temper! I thought you Brits were supposed to be good losers."

"We don't have much practice at it."

Paul just grinned. He pushed Dominique ahead of him and they all went down into the cabin, where Alain placed the package on the chart table and began to remove the waterproof layers and the soft wool padding.

"This hasn't been opened! You haven't looked at it, have you?"

He looked up at Martin.

"You must be very trusting or just plain naïve, my friend."

He peeled back the final layer and they all stared in awe at the sight of the gleaming helmet. Even Paul seemed moved for a few seconds. Then he suddenly took out his knife and began to scratch at the gold. Alain grabbed his hand in an iron grip.

"What the hell do you think you're doing, Paul?"

Paul looked at him with a smile creeping round his eyes, despite himself.

"Look – it's new paint! We've all been well and truly screwed. It's a fake!" He fell back on the bunk half consumed with laughter, half angry. "So much for your friends, you mugs. You were just the patsies to keep us from following them. They've still got the real thing – or perhaps even the Italians have still got it. You silly bastards."

He reached over and threw the helmet across the cabin, where it hit bulkhead and crashed to the floor.

"So, what now?" asked Alain.

Paul was thinking hard. Either Handley or Krevine knew about the trick and had been acting as decoys or they had been taken for a ride. He didn't think their surprise had been faked, but it was possible. Why were they heading for Kýthira? Time to call their bluff.

"You, Handley. Where are you meeting Everidge and Robson?"

"We're not meeting them," lied Martin, still looking for a way out of their situation.

"You lie badly. Why? You owe them no favours. Team up with us. Call them and arrange to meet on the island. Then we'll sort out a nice reception party," Paul said.

"No way. You've hit us twice now. Just piss off and leave us alone."

"God, you Brits – you're so darned dumb. We're offering to work with you. Alright – if that's the way you want to play it, we'll leave you to it. Come on Alan, let's leave these saps."

Containing his surprise at how quickly Paul had given up, Alain followed Paul up the companionway into the cockpit and signalled to Natalie to come alongside. They stood watching as the Edelweiss approached.

In the cabin, Martin looked at Dominique who was still shaken by the experience of being threatened by a knife. He moved to her side, put his arm round her and held her tight for an instant. At the same time he whispered.

"Just stay where you are – I'll be back in a mo'. If there's trouble get the cabin door closed fast."

He reached behind her head and opened a locker, took out a flare gun, quickly fed a rocket cartridge in and climbed out into the cockpit. He stood quietly watching the two men concentrating on jumping across onto the Edelweiss from the foredeck. Alain leapt nimbly across and waited for Paul to join him.

Just as Paul was at his most vulnerable, Martin darted forwarded and aimed the flare straight into the cabin of the Edelweiss. Natalie lost control of the boat in her surprise and veered off sharply. Paul was left hanging desperately on to the side, his feet dangling in the waves as he was dragged along. The pressure of the water threatened to tear him away from the boat and Alain struggled to hang on to him. Natalie shut the engines down and rushed forward to help, but Alain brushed her away.

"Get the extinguisher – fast – or we'll go up in flames," he shouted.

He pulled Paul roughly on board and left him panting and lying along the deck. Through the cabin portholes Alain could see flames and rushed desperately to help Natalie. He knew they were seconds away from disaster.

On the Phalaris Martin shouted to Dominique to come on deck, fired the diesel engine and handed the helm to her.

"Get that headland between us and them and then head for Chóra, not Kapsáli. It's the capital and the harbour is easier to hide in. They won't be going anywhere for a while," he added, looking back with satisfaction at the scene behind.

He rushed forward to release the ties binding the mainsail to the boom and hauled the sail up from the cockpit controls. Within minutes the Phalaris was surging forward with the combined power of the sails and the engine. Behind them the Edelweiss was wallowing broadside on to the waves, a thick cloud of smoke billowing out of the cabin. Paul was in the cockpit, but there was no sign of the other two.

"That should see them off for a while, but it doesn't solve our problem. It's time we had it out with Charles and Ed – they have a lot of explaining to do. They set us up good and proper with that fake helmet."

"So, do we tell them to come to Chóra or do we risk going on to Avlémonas? I don't want to be 'ijacked again by that 'orrible man and threatened with 'is knife."

"No, it'd be safer to go on later to Avlémonas as arranged. Those bastards will have to make repairs before they can follow us again. There should be quite a lot of damage. They're lucky the fuel line didn't catch and the whole boat go up in flames."

"I hope you're right, Martin."

Dominique was beginning to shake as reaction set in and she looked so pale Martin thought she might faint.

"Do you want me to take over – or shall I fetch you a brandy, Dom?"

"*Un petit cognac* first. I'll soon be OK."

Martin went below and poured them both a generous shot of brandy and came out of the cabin holding two mugs. Dominique downed hers in one movement, while Martin sipped his more thoughtfully. He wasn't entirely sure his analysis was correct. He knew it would not take long before the Edelweiss would be back on the warpath and after serious revenge. He and Dom had been used by Charles and Ed as decoys – or was there more to it? Charles had seriously misled them over the helmet, but was it worse than that? Had he known all along they were in such danger? He certainly had some questions to answer.

He looked up and saw they were fast approaching the entrance to Chóra, its huge kástro dominating the headland. For the next hour their attention was taken up with entering the harbour and finding a spot away from prying eyes in a corner of the bay tucked in behind larger vessels.

*

"What's that over on the starboard bow?" Pierre picked up the binoculars. "It's a boat on fire. Head towards it, I'm curious."

Antonia spun the wheel and the Pericles approached the plume of smoke in the distance. Pierre continued to look through the binoculars fighting to hold them still to get a clearer picture despite the movement of the boat. As they came closer, he grew more convinced.

"Antonia, we're in luck today. I'm almost certain that's the Edelweiss. Let's pay them a little visit."

"Sure! I thought you were getting excited – this could be fun!"

As they drew closer it was easier to assess what had happened. The Edelweiss was drifting side on to the waves and had lost all power. Smoke was still billowing from the cabin, but the crew appeared to have the fire under control and were damping down with buckets of water. Two of them could be seen in the cockpit area. Antonia brought their boat to within hailing distance.

"Hi there! Do you need assistance?"

Pierre was standing in the cockpit using a megaphone. One of the crew looked across and cupped his hands to reply.

"Yes, thank you! Could you give us a tow?"

"Stand by. We're coming in."

Antonia manoeuvred the boat alongside and Pierre put the fenders over before lashing the two boats together. Antonia powered round, turning the Edelweiss head to wind and waves. As the movement became easier, Pierre crossed over onto the Edelweiss, helped by Sondheim.

"Thanks. That feels a lot better. I was getting really fed up with the roll. It's Paul, by the way."

Pierre put out his hand.

"Pierre. Glad to help. What happened here?"

"Oh! Just a fire in the galley, which got out of control. My fault I guess – I never was one much for cooking. We sure are pleased to see you guys. This is Natalie and this is Alan," he added, as Alain emerged from the cabin, his face streaked with sweat and the soot from the smoke.

"How is it in there, mate?"

"It's OK now – no thanks to your cooking, Paul. But I am not keen to start the engines until the fuel lines have been checked. We don't want to set the fuel off. We would appreciate a tow into Chóra."

"No problem, though it'll be uncomfortable in this swell for you."

"Not as bad as wallowing out here without power, I can tell you!"

"Right, let's get underway, but Kapsáli would be better. There are more boatyards there."

"Fine by us."

Ten minutes later the tow-line was fixed and with Pierre at the wheel of the Pericles and Paul steering the Edelweiss behind, the two boats began to make towards the harbour of Kapsáli and the nearest boatyard. It took a good three hours to reach the harbour and to tie up. Paul went off ashore to find a mechanic, leaving Natalie and Alain to continue clearing up inside. Antonia went over to give a hand and took advantage of the opportunity to explore every area of the boat, as she helped tidy up and move things around.

The cockpit was soon full of burned, stained and soggy bunk cushions, charts, books and clothes as they threw the ruined items out through the cabin door. Little runs of blackish water ran out everywhere in streaks from the pile, as they stuffed the mess into black bags and heaved them up onto the quay. A crowd of excited tourists gathered looking down at them as they worked. No-one offered to help, but there were plenty of comments in French, English and Greek and the cameras were out in force as the scene was recorded for story telling back home after the holiday.

"Anyone would think this was the highlight of their trip," Alain said bitterly. "I wouldn't mind so much if I thought it wasn't true!"

Later that afternoon a local engineer returned with Paul to look at the engines and Antonia left the Edelweiss to return to her own boat.

Back on board, she stripped off her soot stained clothes and stepped into the shower, describing to Pierre through the shower curtain what had happened on board.

"I searched the Edelweiss from top to bottom, Pierre. I'm sure the helmet is not there," she said, her voice half scrambled by the sound of the running water.

"Maybe they were telling the truth and it really was a galley fire. Maybe they didn't catch up with the Phalaris," Pierre said.

"They caught up with them alright – I heard Alain swearing under his breath several times about Brits and what he would do to them when he caught up with them again. I saw him pick up a spent flare cartridge amongst all the mess and try to hide it from me. The galley definitely was not the start of the fire. It began with the flare," she replied.

"OK. Then we need to know more about what happened. Handley and Krevine are not here in Kapsáli, I'm sure. I went to have a good look round the harbour while you were helping and there's no sign of them. As far as we know Everidge and Robson are still heading towards Avlémonas, so the meet is still on. Or, maybe Handley and Krevine still have the helmet and were able to fight off the Edelweiss," Pierre said.

"Well, this lot aren't going to tell us. I'm worried though that although it's been a good chance to search their boat, we may have blown our cover."

"Do you think they suspect us?"

"Not yet, at least I don't think so, but we can hardly keep popping up wherever they go now."

"True. I was thinking we might go straight on to Avlemonas tonight and wait for things to happen there. That way it will look as if they're following us, rather than the other way round."

"Not a bad idea, Commissaire."

Antonia stepped out of the shower, with her towel wrapped round her.

"Come on, I'm hungry after all that excitement," she said taking Pierre's hand and leading him into the front cabin.

He could smell the fresh scent of her soap as he followed. In the cabin she turned towards him, let the towel drop to the floor and began to loosen his belt.

Later, Pierre was in the galley cooking, when he heard the shout from the quayside. He put his head up through the hatch and saw Paul standing there looking down at him.

"Sorry to interrupt, mate. We'd like to thank you guys for towing us in – the damage is not too bad by the way. The engines are fine. We're going ashore soon to grab a bite to eat and want you to be our guests."

"That's very kind, but we have to move on as soon as we've eaten. This has been a detour for us as we were expected in Avlémonas this evening."

Paul Sondheim's eyes narrowed, and then the smile returned to his lips.

"Well, we may see you there. We'll be going in that direction ourselves later tomorrow with any luck. Thanks again – and have a good trip."

He moved away. Pierre watched him return, head bent in thought, to the Edelweiss. Perhaps Sondheim had not been convinced by the coincidence. Or perhaps he had spotted something on board which had made him suspicious. Either way, he and Antonia would have to go on to Avlémonas now, despite the late hour.

Chapter 10

Pierre returned to the cabin to find Antonia sitting at the chart table plotting the course to Avlémonas.

"I heard. What do you think?" she said without looking up.

Pierre put a hand on her shoulder and distractedly massaged the back of her neck as he replied:

"I think he's no fool and he's uneasy to say the least. The coincidence was suspicious to him, but he's not sure. After all, if we were returning to the mainland, going on to Avlemonas would be the next logical port to go to."

"Mm, that's nice; don't stop," she said, stretching her neck from side to side under the pressure of his fingers. "Where did you learn to do that?"

She turned towards him.

"Well, we've no choice now but to go there and to wait and see if the Phalaris turns up. Shall I get on to Kahn to see if he is still tracking the Artemis despite the loss of the bug?"

Pierre nodded. He checked the simmering ratatouille in the galley and went up on deck. They had about 20 nautical miles to do that evening to get to Avlémonas and he was keen to get away. He busied himself with the mooring lines, but was really looking to see what was happening on board the Edelweiss. The lights were on in the cabin and he could see the three of them deep in discussion. What we need, he thought, is a bug inside their cabin. Perhaps Antonia could arrange that.

Dusk as usual was falling quickly and lights were starting to come on along the harbour front and in the houses behind. The smell of cooking reaching him from the restaurants and souvlatzídiko stalls reminded him he hadn't eaten since lunch. Time to get back to the galley. No time to go ashore to get in more supplies, he thought ruefully. He freed all the mooring lines except the bow line and went below.

Antonia was tasting the ratatouille with a wooden spoon as he entered. She added a pinch of salt and announced it was nearly ready.

"Major Kahn reported in to say that the Artemis has been spotted and Everidge and Robson have definitely arrived in Avlémonas. So we presume the meeting is still on. Kahn said they did go on to Volos after we left them. The Greek police followed them to the church by the harbour, but no-one appeared to meet them. All the tombaroli, except Samborini as we know, were arrested. So, if they were expecting someone, it had to be Samborini himself."

"Or perhaps they were waiting for instructions from their collector?"

"That's possible, but in any event no-one turned up. The mystery at the moment for us is where the Phalaris is. We have no tracker on it. So, do we still go on to Avlémonas and wait or do we search for the Phalaris?"

"I think we should go on. In the dark we've no chance of finding them here or in the bays nearby and I'm sure they'll be all more keen to meet up with their so-called friends after what has happened today. They will want to have it out with them, for sure. All we have to do is to wait for them to arrive at the rendezvous."

"*A vos ordres, Capitaine,*" Antonia said, in that mocking tone he had grown to appreciate:

"Let's eat first – I'm hungry," he replied, putting plates on the table and reaching for the casserole. "Any chance of getting a bug inside the Edelweiss, do you think? We need to know where Sondheim and friends are all the time now and what tricks they are planning. We may have to remove them from the scene if we are to let Handley and Krevine deliver the helmet safely to London, assuming that's still the plan."

"Especially since we don't know for sure if they do have the helmet," Antonia added, helping herself to more *ratatouille*. "I'll make some calls."

Pierre mopped up the last of the juice from his plate with a piece of bread, drained his glass, got up from the table and went to start the engines. Leaving them in neutral, he released the bow line. With a final glance at the Edelweiss, which lay silently at the quayside giving nothing away, he took the wheel, put the engines in gear and headed out of the harbour. He could see the lights of Chóra harbour across the bay to the west. Soon he was out clear of the harbour roads and heading east. Pierre rounded the headland off Chalkos and set a course for Kastri. He could just make out the sea caves and the lights of Fyri Ammos.

"*Merde,* I'm still hungry," he said aloud, making his way below to see whether they had anything else on board to eat. This life at sea certainly gives you an appetite, he thought. Images of steak-frites were passing before his eyes. Not much chance of that though, he mused.

Antonia was opening the small fridge as he reached the galley area. She glanced at him and took delight in the amazement on his face as she asked:

"And how do you like your steak, *Capitaine*?"

"*C'est pas possible!* How did you know I was dreaming of such a thing?"

"We Greeks are good at bearing unexpected gifts – or hadn't you heard? I slipped out for a while when you were off looking for the Phalaris."

Pierre took over the cooking while Antonia told him what she had been able to arrange with the Greek Interpol section. As she talked a saláta kritikí took shape in the bowl on the table in front of her.

"No chips!" sighed Pierre, serving up the steaks and helping himself to the salad.

"There's no pleasing some people," she said, shaking her head with a smile.

While they ate he watched the radar screen. A couple of boats also heading north appeared, but they were well clear and moving more slowly. After an hour and a half Pierre altered course to round the last headland before the final leg to their destination. High above them the age-old church of Agios Geórgios looked down upon the sea as it had done for fourteen centuries, watching the boat-dots on the surface of the water. The church was already old when, two centuries before, it had looked on with satisfaction as the HMS Mentor plunged to the bottom of the sea below, loaded with some of the Elgin Marbles looted from the Parthenon, Greece taking back its own.

Feeling the evening cold, Pierre pulled on a sweater. Sitting close together in the cockpit, he and Antonia watched the lights on the shore-line, as the boat made passage towards Avlémonas. Out of the clear night sky, the stars were sending Morse code messages to planet Earth below. For a while the two of them were lost in their own thoughts far from the events of the day, but comfortable with the silence which had fallen between them.

The evening ferry from Diakófti to Crete suddenly appeared from round the last headland and passed them heading south in such a blaze of intrusive lights that it robbed them of their night vision, blotting out the stars. Its appearance tore them from their reveries and they turned their attention to navigating their way in to the port. A Coast Guard launch approached, but their Interpol ID quickly satisfied the officers on board and they saluted respectfully before veering off to intercept other late arrivals, having recommended a spot in the small harbour for Pierre and Antonia to moor up.

"Now the whole port will know we're here," sighed Antonia. "We can expect a visit from the local Chief of Police. So much for keeping our cover. I had better make some more calls to put a stop to unwanted publicity. The last thing we want is for Sondheim to see police or customs officials crawling all over our boat tomorrow morning saluting us and smiling broadly."

"You're right. It's bad enough the Coast Guard radioed ahead for a pilot boat to guide us in. Let's hope Everidge and Robson are too busy eating to notice when we enter the harbour."

As he spoke the small pilot launch drew alongside and they turned to follow it in to the berth reserved for them. Half an hour later they were on shore and heading towards the restaurants on the water front. They passed the pontoons and spotted the dark shape of the Artemis, with just the riding light showing. It was impossible to tell if the dealers were on board, keeping watch from inside in the dark, or whether they had gone ashore. Pierre felt the hairs rise on the back of his neck. Antonia, sensing the tension in him, whispered:

"Relax. Why should they recognise us even if they are on board, they're looking out for Handley and Krevine, not for us. My guess is they are much more likely to be eating and drinking somewhere on shore. Come on, you owe me a drink after those steaks – your face was a picture."

"You're right. Let's find a good French wine."

With a sigh of resignation, she took his arm and guided him towards the lights of the restaurants up ahead.

*

"So how exactly do you plan to tell Martin and Dominique you knew all along they were being followed?" asked Ed.

"I'll think of something, don't worry."

"Well, you'd better come up with something fast, 'cos after that attack on the beach they were none too pleased to put it mildly," replied Ed. "Did it ever occur to you that when they realised they'd been set up they might join forces with the other lot?"

"Well they didn't, so stop fussing."

"Don't you get shirty with me, Charles. You took a hell of a risk and you planned this without telling me either, so it's you who is going to have to square it with them, not me. What bothers me more, frankly, is that I'm sure we were being watched in Volos in the church."

"Now you're being paranoid. Those Greek churches are always creepy inside – there was no one there apart from us and a few old women praying. More's the pity, but I guess all the other finds had already been seized so Samborini would have had nothing else to give us, even supposing he had escaped and been able to come to the rendezvous."

"Let's hope you're right – but we can't be sure all the Italians were caught in Çanakkale. If any of them did escape and guessed it was us who tipped off the Turkish police, they will be out for revenge. They could also be after Samborini too for that matter, to get the helmet back. That would explain why Samborini didn't show."

"Calm down Ed, for goodness sake. The Turks are pretty hot on this sort of thing and will have rounded them all up," Charles said.

"If you say so," replied Ed, beginning to think of his stomach again as the mood lightened. "OK. That's enough of the 'what ifs', where shall we eat tonight? Martin and Dominique aren't due till the morning, so we can at least have a good supper before the fireworks start."

"That's more like you – keep thinking of your stomach. As it happens I do know of a good taverna in one of the back streets here."

*

In Chóra, harbour Martin and Dominique had eaten aboard and removed the last traces of their unwelcome visitors. The stanchions on deck were nearly straightened out and the wires taught again. The replica helmet was on display on a shelf and, impressive despite being a fake, brightened up the whole cabin. It also served to remind them that no-one at all was to be trusted and they were on their own. The rules of the game had changed.

Martin doubted Sondheim and the others would attack again, but he was sure they would certainly try to follow them, hoping they would lead them to Charles and Ed, which was in fact exactly what he had in mind to do. Perhaps the moment had come to teach Charles a lesson and for him to know what it felt like to be threatened by a man like Sondheim.

"Martin, if that man does reach Charlie and Edouard before us, we may lose everything. They may even – 'ow do you say – make a deal with them."

"You're probably right, Dom, so we must make sure they don't get there first. But we could also use them to frighten

Charles into playing fair with us. We still want our full share in this. Charles owes us the other half of the money and we're going to make damned sure we get it. Especially now we know he planted a fake on us and used us as decoys."

"Now you are starting to frighten me, Martin. I 'ave not seen you so angry before. But you're not in the Caraïbes now – why can't we just go back to Chaniá, or even to France and leave all this?"

"Mainly, because I don't want to let Charles get away with it..."

"That's silly, you know it …"

" … and partly because we know too much for Charles to leave us be. We can't back out now. He'll come looking for us if we don't show up."

Martin moved towards her and put his arm around her shoulders.

"We do have one trump card – the fact we know things about the Sondheim gang that Charles doesn't know. We may be able to use that to bargain with him and still get something out of all this."

He fell silent, still thinking out the possibilities. Somehow he had to both use Paul Sondheim against Charles, but also to stop Sondheim from following him and Dominique. A way of completely disabling the Edelweiss might come in handy.

"I think we should go round to Avlémonas tonight Dom – that way we'll have a head start and Sondheim won't be able to find us so easily. I doubt whether they'll be able to move before tomorrow anyway, depending on the repairs they have to do, and whether they had to call for help to get into port."

"OK. I'll get things ready."

"I need to go ashore first Dom, won't be long."

"Where are you going?"

"I'll tell you later."

He was on deck before she could warn him to be careful and she watched anxiously from the cabin door as he strode swiftly along the quay in the direction of Chóra town.

Chapter 11

The Phalaris was making good speed, well out from the coast, in a moderate breeze. They had managed to slip out of Chóra harbour in the falling darkness without attracting attention. There had been no signs of Sondheim or of any other boat following and they were as certain as they could be that their departure had gone unnoticed. There was a feeling of relaxation on board which had been missing since the attack. Martin was satisfied that by choosing Chóra rather than Kapsáli they had shaken off their pursuers for the moment. Aphrodite was smiling upon them, at least for the present, as they left her island.

The stars shone sharply against the black velvet backdrop of the night sky. The Milky Way was living up to its name, a hazy pale shadow draped across the window into the home of the gods. Martin was on the first watch, barely awake, but, as ever, under the vast expanse and mysterious silence of the night sky, he was prone to thoughts of the fragile insignificance of man. From time to time, the winking of the port and starboard lights of an aircraft heading for Athens or heading south towards Africa and beyond, introduced alien colours into the sky.

His eyes were so used to the darkness that he could see communication satellites cutting unnaturally straight lines through the apparent chaos of the universe. Every now and again shooting stars sliced fiery trails through the millions of pin points of light. The scars they created healed in split seconds leaving traces only on the watcher's retina. Alone out at sea, gazing into this vast void of pinpricks of light and the ghostly shadow of the Milky Way with nothing tangible to hold on to, Martin understood why the Ancients had imposed order on this chaos, seeing patterns and giving names to a zodiac of images. He understood their need to anchor the unfathomable to their own world.

Dominique had slipped quietly out of the cabin and was snuggling up beside him for warmth. For a while she said nothing as she too gazed at the sky and Martin remained silent, knowing that when she was ready she would tell him what was troubling her.

"What did you do ashore when you went off like that, *chéri*? You promised you would say it to me."

"I went to ask around amongst the fishermen whether there had been any boats in with fire damage, or whether there'd been an English speaking foreigner looking for help with repairs. One of them told me the whole story. His cousin works out of Kapsáli. He was potting for crabs in the shallower waters outside the harbour between there and Chóra and saw smoke rising from a motor yacht some way out at sea.

"Then, soon after, another boat went along side and took the burning boat in tow. They passed him as they came in to the harbour and he could see signs of a fire on board the damaged boat. The whole cabin looked blackened but not badly burned, at least as far as he could see from the outside. Most probably just smoke damage. The boats went into Kapsáli together and tied up at the quay. When the cousin returned to harbour with his crab and lobster pots, he said there was quite a crowd on the quayside watching the crew clearing up the mess."

"So, what happened then?"

Dominique sat up and pulled the hood on her waterproof up over her head to keep out the wind.

"One of them went ashore – the 'Englishman' he thought – and got help. The word is that the damage was mostly superficial, but the repairs will take a day at least. The crew put it about that it was an accident with a bottle of gas in the galley. The boat which towed them in was moored just in front of them, but left later on."

"So that horrible man Paul is stuck in the harbour for a while – I wish he had fallen into the sea and got eaten by a shark."

Martin pulled her even closer to him, bending forward to kiss her on the forehead.

"It was nasty, Dom, and there was no need to hold a knife to your throat, but it's over now and they won't attack us again, since we don't have anything they want. I'm sure they will try to follow us though to get to Charles and Ed – that's what I am counting on to have a hold over Charles when we see him."

Dominique suddenly sat up and pulled away from him.

"But that's not all you did. You still haven't said to me why you bought that new pack of fusées – flares?"

"Just a precaution. They're very useful for fending off sharks."

"Don't joke about things like that, Martin. I am not stupide."

"You're right, I'm sorry – but it is just a precaution, Dom, I promise you. Just in case they do threaten us again."

*

Back on board after their meal Antonia had spent some time communicating with the Customs officials and Interpol. Despite the lateness of the hour in Greece, because of the time difference, she had been able to speak to the duty officer and to contact Interpol HQ in Lyon.

"The local customs are going to look out for the arrival of the Phalaris and will keep us informed. In Kapsáli they've agreed to send an safety officer to inspect the damage to the Edelweiss and to start an investigation into what happened. They'll require it to have a new seaworthiness certificate before they allow the boat to depart. That should clip Sondheim's wings for a while, but not for long I think."

"Any luck on planting a bug on board?" asked Pierre.

"You do want it all at once don't you? Well, prepare to be impressed with your Greek partner. The spooks are going to send a man down to pose as a customs officer and he will plant a bug in the cabin as you command. We will be able to hear everything they say – assuming that is, Sondheim is not as clever as he thinks."

"*Impressionnant, Inspecteur.* What can we do to celebrate this success in international relationships and cooperation? Perhaps a bottle of champagne?"

Antonia just smiled her smile.

Pierre put some ice in a bucket and selected a bottle from the small '*cave*' he had assembled on board for just such an occasion. He went into the forward cabin and placed it by the wide bunk. Then he returned to the main cabin to close the boat down for the night. He checked the moorings and the fenders protecting the hull from the rough quayside. The boat was equipped with motion detectors and he set the switch, though the chances of unwelcome visitors were slim as there was a discreet armed guard on duty thanks to the status they had been accorded by the local police.

He went below again, shivering slightly from the chill of the evening. He slipped out of his clothes and warmed up under the hot water in the tiny shower cubicle. Wrapping a towel around him, he went into the cabin. A low glow from a single lamp revealed the bunk was occupied and, discarding the towel, he slid in beside the reclining figure who was turned away from him on her side. He ran his finger lightly along her back from the neck and down along the spine until he felt her tingle in response to his touch and leaned forward to nuzzle her ear.

"Le champagne avant ou après, madame?"

In reply, she turned towards him and gently guided his hand between her legs.

*

It was around six in the morning towards the end of his watch when Martin saw the launch approaching. The Phalaris was not far off the little harbour and still making good speed in the breeze. The launch circled round and drew in close from behind. On deck two Customs men stood either side of the cabin. peaked caps shielded their faces, conferring on them the badge of officialdom. The megaphone mounted on the cabin roof sprang into life and the metallic voice cut across the wind to reach him. Martin touched the side of his forehead as a salute in reply and, calling to Dominique, he let out the main sheet to slow the yacht and began to roll the jib from the cockpit control. Dominique came up from below, started the engine, and went up to gather in the mainsail while Martin held the yacht into wind. The Customs men watched as the Phalaris completed its preparations to receive the boarding party. The launch then drew alongside.

Dominique took the helm while Martin went forward to help the two men step across and the three of them joined her in the cockpit.

The officers saluted.

"*Kaliméra, Captain. Madame.*"

"*Kaliméra*. Welcome aboard gentlemen. What can we do for you?" Martin replied.

"Just a routine inspection, if we may, and a few simple questions, Captain."

"Of course. May we offer you a cup of coffee and something to eat?"

"Very kind, Captain," replied the senior of the two, looking at his colleague. Ena Nes, perhaps?"

"I'll see to it myself. My partner will answer any questions you have in the meantime."

"I'll happily remain with this charming lady, Captain, but my colleague will help you with the coffee."

"Of course," replied Martin, recognising the manoeuvre

Martin and the young lieutenant emerged a few minutes later with four cups of coffee and four glasses of iced water. A plate with baklavá completed the presentation. The younger officer learned forward and whispered something in the ear of his colleague, while Martin passed the tray.

"Madame has been most helpful, Captain. But I am not entirely clear why you're coming to Avlémonas."

"That's easy. We have some friends from England who have come down by boat from Volos and we're meeting them here for few days before they have to return home. Also, we do not know your beautiful island well and would like to do some walking ashore and explore. We heard the old church of Agios Geórgios is particularly worth a visit."

"You're right, Captain, it is very old and has watched over our heritage for many centuries now, as your Milord Elgin found out when he stole our sculptures from the Parthenon. I believe Saint Geórgios is also your – how do you say – patron saint?"

"Yes, he is. What Elgin did was wrong, but I think at the time he thought he was preserving your heritage rather than stealing it."

"I am pleased to hear you say that, Captain. Could you perhaps explain more about the helmet on the shelf in your cabin?"

"Ah! Indeed. It was a present from friends who bought it at the replica museum shop on Skópelos. They had it sprayed gold to match the finds from the tomb of King David which they had seen in the museum at Vergina. It is a magnificent souvenir, isn't it?"

"So my colleague tells me. May I perhaps see it for myself?"

"Of course. Please follow me."

The two of them went down into the cabin and the Customs officer stood for a moment looking at the helmet gleaming in the corner. The nose protection piece and the dark holes either side for the eyes stared back at them, as their own eyes became used to the duller light in the cabin. It would be easy to believe there was a head inside. The captain went towards the shelf and with a nod to Martin as if seeking his permission, picked it up and turned it over to look inside. He seemed satisfied and held the helmet out at arms length twisting and turning it to catch the light at different angles.

"You are right, Captain, it is a lovely copy. Thank you for your cooperation. Welcome to our island. I hope you find your friends and enjoy your stay."

They went back up to the cockpit and the young lieutenant signalled to their launch to come alongside. They both saluted before crossing back to their boat, which quickly left them behind in burst of spray and white wake, sparkling with the colours of the rainbow in the rising sun.

"*Tu étais magnifique, Martin!*" Dominique put her arms round him trembling with relief. "I was so afraid they would search the boat and find the fusées."

"Don't worry. There is nothing suspicious about having flares on board. In fact it's compulsory. But you're right, we'll have to be careful when we're in port. He wasn't fooled, Dom."

"Per'aps it was just a coincidence and they're controlling all the boats which come in to the port."

"Checking them. Possibly, but I don't believe in coincidences. We'll have to warn Charles and Ed that Greek Customs may be onto us and they'll be able to link us together now that we're meeting."

"Why should we warn them of anything after what they 'ave done to us? They lied to us and put us in danger. It is our turn to 'ide something from them."

*

At around seven Pierre went up on deck to savour the early morning freshness and to look over the boats assembled in the harbour. The local fisherman had been up and about for some time already and little blue fishing boats were setting off piled high with lobster and crab pots. With a sigh he went back into the cabin and switched on the computer. The bleeper informed him there was a new message and he opened the emails to see what could be so urgent at this hour of the morning.

Antonia stepped out of the shower and came into the cabin, her wet hair hanging down one side of her face as she tilted her head and rubbed it dry with a towel. She looked over his shoulder, dripping water onto him, to read the message.

Memo:

Greek Customs and Coast Guard Squadron, Kýthira, reporting to Commissaire P. Rousseau and Detective Inspector A. Antoniarchis, Interpol.

Yacht Phalaris *intercepted at approaches to Avlémonas at 0600 hours. Two crew on board: Handley, Martin [British passport] and Krevine, Dominique [French passport]. Reproduction helmet, painted gold, on open display in the cabin. Possible source: Museum shop on Skópelos. Latter not confirmed, but helmet definitely replica.*

No legal infringement. Inspection ended 0630 hours. Yacht Phalaris *proceeding into harbour to meet friends arriving from Volos. End of report*

"So now we know why Robson and Everidge stopped off at Skópelos on their way to Skiáthos and what they were doing in the museum shop. Plenty of questions still left unanswered though," Pierre said.

"True, but it also confirms what we suspected. Sondheim's lot forced them to show them where the helmet was hidden. Then they all discovered it was a replica. That's why Handley displayed it openly in the cabin afterwards. If he had known beforehand it was a fake they wouldn't have hidden it up the mast in the first place," replied Antonia, with a final flick of her hair into a towelled bundle on top of her head.

Pierre wiped the back of his neck dry with his hand as he began to read a second email, this time from Major Kahn, sent the previous evening. He read out aloud from the screen while Antonia went back to their cabin.

"Khan says there was a split in the ranks of the tombaroli. When questioned after they were arrested, they claimed Samborini had gone off with some of their share of the money. They said he had taken one of the items – a helmet – to another meeting place with the foreigners. Later he returned to the harbour to watch the rest of the haul from several tombs being loaded onto the fishing boat. But that Samborini didn't go aboard the fishing boat when it was loaded with the finds, but slipped away before the raid.

"Kahn has a complete inventory of the finds but…" he hesitated as he ran his eye down the list "…there is nothing there which interests us. The helmet alone will lead us to the collector, so we are back where we started."

"Not quite," Antonia called through from the cabin "but I know what you mean. OK, so we concentrate on the meeting between Handley and Marceau with Everidge and Robson, who must still have the real helmet, since it is not apparently on board the Phalaris. They could have off-loaded it in Volos, but Kahn's watchers would have seen that."

*

It was about eight o'clock in Kapsáli when Paul looked up from the cockpit and saw an official looking group, in uniform, heading along the quay towards the Edelweiss.

"Hey you guys, looks like we've got company. I'll do the talking, you just keep quiet."

Alain and Natalie glanced at each other, eyebrows raised, but did not reply.

"I still reckon our two rescuers were just a mite too friendly."

He was talking to himself as he hadn't noticed that Alain and Natalie had gone down into the cabin to continue the clearing up.

"The woman," he continued, "Toni something … was much too keen on helping out. Did you see how she poked her nose into everything? They were both just too nice to be real.

Not a bad boat either — had a load of hi-tech stuff on board. Must have set them back a lot."

The officials had reached the Edelweiss and the senior officer, looking down, saluted.

"*Kaliméra*, Captain. May we come on board?"

"Sure, General. What can I do for you?"

"Just Brigadier, I regret. Thank you."

He came down the ladder onto the deck followed by his men, who stood on the foredeck awaiting his instructions.

"Brigadier Papadopoulos at your service."

He showed Paul his ID card identifying him as from the Greek Customs and Excise.

"We were informed you had at accident at sea which has necessitated big repairs."

He continued firmly as Paul tried to interrupt: "According to Greek law I must check that these repairs have been carried out and issue you with a new seaworthiness certificate before I can permit you to leave port and to sail in Greek waters."

"And how long will that take, Brigadier?"

"No more than a couple of days, if everything is in order. I'll need to see your ship's papers."

"Oh for Chrissake, it was nothing — just a small fire in the galley. Take a look for yourself."

"My men will do just that. Thank you, Captain."

He looked up and nodded to his two officers, who immediately went below.

"Hey, couldn't we just come to some arrangement, so we can settle this quickly?"

Paul had dropped his voice.

"Be careful Captain Sondheim, I might misunderstand you. This is Greece, not South Africa. I know your country well and would not like to have to be unfriendly."

"OK, sure. Whatever you say. But just hurry it up, will you?"

The customs men reappeared and had a conversation in rapid Greek with their superior. The men then left the Edelweiss and climbed the ladder back up onto the quayside where they stood waiting.

"My apologies, Captain, for the rudeness of speaking in Greek, but my men do not speak English. They confirmed everything seems to be in order and that your colleagues are even now cleaning off the dirt caused by the smoke. Come to my office this afternoon around five o'clock with your papers and I'll see your case is dealt with as a matter of urgency. The certificate will be ready tomorrow morning."

"Sure thing, Brigadier Papidapolis. Thanks."

"Papadopoulos. Good bye, Captain Sondheim."

He saluted and rejoined his men.

As the customs men left the quayside and returned to their car, Alain and Natalie came up out of the cabin to find Paul angry, but deep in thought.

"So tell me what the shit that was all about? What exactly did they do down below?"

"Nothing very much – they just looked around and checked the galley. They didn't speak to us. Then they went into each cabin and opened a few lockers."

" 'nothing very much' – for Chrissake, how stupid are you, Frenchy? Of course they did something. We just don't know what. They're deliberately trying to slow us up. I bet it's down to those bastards who towed us in. I knew they weren't what they seemed."

"Don't shout at me, Paul. You weren't very clever trying to bribe Papadopoulos and insulting him by getting his name wrong. Now he knows for sure something's not right. We'll be lucky not to be arrested if you go on like this."

"OK, OK – so I messed up. So what do we do now?"

"We hope Papadopoulos gives us the papers tomorrow to continue and we're not too late when we arrive in Avlémonas."

"Hey, look, why don't you two catch a bus there today? Or rent a car if that's possible in this dump. I'll follow in the boat tomorrow."

"First sensible thing you've said today, Paul. OK, good idea. Come on Natalie, let's get going and leave Paul to calm down."

Sondheim watched the two of until they were out of sight and then reached for his cell phone. He dialled a number quickly and, looking around as he spoke, talked quietly for several minutes. With a final glance round the harbour, he snapped the phone shut and went below.

Chapter 12

Antonia was sitting at the chart table when the computer came to life again and signalled another message. She opened the file.

"Pierre," she called, "there's another message, this time from the Istanbul Museum. It's longish, so I'll print it off."

Pierre stuck his head out of the shower and looked across to where Antonia was sitting.

"How long? Long enough for you to join me in the shower, Inspecteur?"

"I've already showered, Commissaire, but I thank you for thinking of me. Long enough for me to put some coffee on and for you to put some clothes on."

"You spoil me," Pierre replied in mock resignation. He pulled the shower curtain aside and disappeared into the fore cabin, as curious as Antonia was to read the Museum's comments.

It was still early, but already the sun's rays were warming the cabin and he went quickly up on deck to rig up the awning over the cockpit. The Harbour Master would let them know where the Phalaris moored up and when Handley and Krevine made a move to go ashore.

He dressed quickly and he and Antonia sat down to read the message coming off the printer.

Report from the Head Curator, Arkeoloji Müzesi of Istanbul, to Commissaire P. Rousseau and Inspector A. Antoniarchis, Interpol.

Following receipt of several crates of illegally excavated artefacts from various sites around the ancient site of Troja, intercepted by Major S. Khan of the Turkish army, the Museum makes this preliminary report on the contents.

The artefacts appear to have come from a number of different tombs. It will take some time and further interrogations of the alleged thieves to identify which sites the individual items came from, if indeed it proves possible.

Our researches will be helped by the careful records kept by Major Kahn of the positions of each tomb opened by the Italian tombaroli. The most recent tomb to be opened may prove to be more important than the rest and the contents of this tomb, already separated from the other finds and identified, may be linked with the siege of Troja by the Greeks as described in the Iliad.

A funeral urn has been identified as coming from the right period and there are well preserved pieces of armour. A helmet appears to be missing, which confirms the initial statements made by the Italian tombaroli to Major Kahn.

Our experts are convinced of the importance of all the tombs that have been found and it has been decided to release funds to continue immediately the work that the tombaroli have started and to protect the tombs from further pillaging.

Progress reports will be sent to the Interpol team once these measures have been put in place and further researches have been undertaken.

(Signed) Head Curator, Arkeoloji Müzesi, Istanbul

End of Report

"Interesting attitude the Museum is taking. It's almost as if they're grateful for the help of the tombaroli. Maybe they are," Pierre said. "Nice compliment referring to Kahn too."

Antonia picked up her mobile on the second ring and listened intently.

"The port authorities are telling us that the Phalaris is preparing to enter the harbour," she relayed, "and will keep us informed as to where they moor up. With any luck they're in direct contact with Everidge and Robson, and will tie up alongside, saving us a lot of time searching, not that it will be difficult here."

Pierre was about to comment when she held up her hand to silence him.

"They also report that a cell phone call has been made by Sondheim to a phone in Volos. He spoke outside the cabin so the bug they planted in Kapsáli did not pick up the conversation clearly enough for them to be able to hear what was being said."

She spoke slowly as she translated:

"Sondheim will be unable to leave before tomorrow because they're delaying the issue of the new certificate of seaworthiness, but it seems the other two on board have caught a bus here from Kapsáli."

"The usual suspects are gathering! We've a long day ahead of us. Did you say something about coffee? I've completed my part of the deal. I'm fully dressed."

"So you are, Commissaire. I hardly recognised you."

*

The Phalaris nosed gently into port under motor, sails down and furled. Dominique took the helm, while Martin stood on the foredeck guiding her past the yachts and fishing boats to where the Artemis was tied up. He was speaking on his phone to Charles as he made hand signals to Dominique so she knew where to turn. He shut the phone when he spotted their boat and with a nod acknowledged Charles' greeting.

Dominique edged the Phalaris alongside and Martin threw a line across to Charles who pulled the Phalaris along the last few feet, all the while chatting and asking them how the crossing was. Martin avoided eye contact and concentrated on keeping the boats just far enough apart to avoid scraping the sides. Still not responding to Charles, he checked the height of the fenders between the two boats, while Ed and Dominique saw to the line aft and the springers.

Martin and Dominique then stepped across and followed Charles and Ed into their cabin. Neither of them smiled a greeting.

"So what the hell is going on, Charles?" Martin said.

"What do you mean 'what the hell is going on?'

"You know bloody well what I mean. You send us out like lambs to the slaughter with hardly any warning. We are attacked twice, drugged, boarded at sea, Dom has a knife held to her throat and is in fear of her life and you have the balls to ask 'what do we mean'! All that for what? I'll tell you for what – for a bloody fake you painted gold and planted on us."

"Oh! Stop whingeing for god's sake, Martin. You've been around, you know the score. Of course we didn't warn you – it would've been worse if you'd known. You wouldn't have acted in the same way if you had – at least Sondheim realised you'd been misled too and so didn't carry out his threats. Now we've flushed them out into the open and know who they are."

"So how the hell will that help?"

"Well firstly, I've heard of Paul Sondheim – this is not the first time he has butted in to a job like this. I might be able to pull strings and have them seen off and even arrested," Charles replied.

"You know you won't do that – it would draw attention to yourselves. In fact it's too late, since the customs and the police have already made the connection between the four of us already. They are probably watching us right now."

"How do you figure that?" asked Ed.

"We were boarded by Customs early this morning on our way in. They're suspicious already. The Customs guy knew exactly what he was looking for – discovering the fake helmet on display in the open didn't fool him at all. They weren't born yesterday. And that's not all – I'm sure I spotted the other two from the Edelweiss on the quay when we arrived here. They must have come by car or something."

"You didn't tell it to me, Martin."

"I didn't want to worry you, Dom; you've been through enough already."

"Maybe he's right Charles," broke in Ed. "Now they know about our meeting they'll watch us even more closely. In fact they've probably already made inquiries back in London and know exactly who we are. I told you there was someone else in the church in Volos when Samborini didn't show. That's how they know we're here."

"Listen to 'im, Charlie. Edouard is talking sense."

Charles sat back thoughtfully. A silence fell. He was pleased to have got the real helmet as far as they had without it falling into the wrong hands, but the circumstances had changed. Using Martin and Dominique as a decoy had taken the pressure off himself and Ed. One more short step out of Kýthira and the Phalaris would be clear of Greek waters and have a better chance of getting through to England. The Italian authorities had enough problems of their own to bother with requests from Greek or Turkish police to intercept boats in international waters. They were too busy trying to stop their own sites being plundered. The main danger came from the Sondheim gang. Since Tremblay and Marceau were already here it was obvious they knew all about this meeting. They would have guessed that he and Ed were the ones with the real helmet.

"Since we are all in *la merde* – how do you say, 'ze sheet' – we should work together instead of fighting each other."

"The shit. Dom's right Charles – we've got to come up with a solution to save all our arses. There's no going back now. So where do we go from here?"

Charles remained silent for several minutes longer as he weighed up the options, aware the others were all watching him. He knew the danger was coming from several directions. He realised it must have been the tombaroli who squealed to the police about himself and Ed after their arrest with the finds. Anything to get back at Samborini for double-crossing them at Çanakkale. Customs also knew about Martin and Dom, but he wondered whether the tombaroli knew about them too?

"OK, you're right. Here's the idea. Let's assume the main danger remains the Sondheim lot. I don't think Customs will bother us once we leave Greece. They may be suspicious about you two, but they found nothing on the Phalaris so they can't do anything. As far as Ed and I are concerned I think the best thing would be for us to abandon the Artemis here and to slip away on the ferry to Gýtheio on the mainland with the real helmet. From there we can get to Pátra and take the ferry across to Bari. No, hang on, better still – this time we'll take the replica and give you the real helmet."

Charles paused. The others were tempted to break in, but realised he was thinking aloud and held back.

"From Bari we'll make our way to Catania on Sicily, probably by ferry from Reggio. How long would it take you to sail there, Martin?"

"About a week, maybe less."

"That's fine. We'll meet you there in the Porto Vecchio."

"What's your plan, Charles? I don't get it," Ed said.

"Divide and confuse. As you said, Greek Customs and possibly Interpol now are watching us. If it was just Customs, they would have arrested us by now. The tombaroli must have sung like birds to save their own skins when the Turks caught them."

"So what does the Interpol want?" asked Dominique.

"Tell her, Ed."

"Charles means Interpol are more interested in finding out who's behind all this, who commissioned the original search, than in getting the helmet before it leaves Greece. They don't want any of us, or the tombaroli for that matter. So they won't intervene until the last moment. They'll just follow until we lead them to the private collectors, ours and Sondheim's."

"And I suppose the Greeks would like to recover the helmet, but can see the point of arresting the collectors, so they'll wait until we deliver the goods," continued Martin for him. "So why don't you just take the damned thing straight to London and let them follow you?"

"Because I want the rest of the money off the man who owes us for doing this and because we have to shake off Sondheim as well as Interpol if we are to make the delivery. I think I know a way of fooling Sondheim. If we play this right, it'll be the collector *he* is working for who'll get caught and not ours."

"Charles is right. I've got some info on Sondheim which will interest you."

Ed passed round a sheet from the printer. There was a pause as each of them scanned the information.

"Where on earth did you get this, Ed? Sondheim sounds a nastier character than I thought. In fact, we're lucky to have got away as lightly as we have."

Martin was beginning to feel angry again as he remembered the attacks and the knife threat on Dominique.

"I just hacked into the Interpol computer, same way as I always do when I want to know what paintings are missing and might reach the market," replied Ed with a grin. "They had a file on Sondheim – nothing proven, but he's been suspected before of being involved in some dodgy deals."

"Edouard ! You are a dark sheep."

"Horse, but thanks anyway!"

"Let's keep it serious," interrupted Charles. "If Ed and I use the ferry and keep our heads down, we'll be able to leave the country with the fake helmet. Even if we are stopped there is no law against taking out replicas. Sondheim won't know whether we have the real thing or whether you do Martin, so they'll have to split up."

"So who will have the real helmet?"

"This time you will have it – I promise," he added seeing the expression on their faces, including Ed's. "Ed and I will get out of Greece and meet you in Catania. We'll take the real helmet off you and fly on with it to London from there. You'll be out of the whole business and free to do what you like."

Martin looked doubtful.

"What if customs search us again as we leave? And won't Sondheim have another go at us as soon as we're in open water? He'll know something went down here."

"Well, it's a risk, but my guess is the police and customs are more likely to follow Ed and me, especially when they see we've abandoned our boat. All you have to do is to get outside Greek waters. Until then you do the double bluff and put the real helmet on the shelf in exactly the same position as the fake one is now. I could see it through the cabin porthole as you came alongside," he added.

"Clever – but it may just work," Martin said.

"When you leave here the Edelweiss will have to follow, but they will have to split up too as at least one of them will have to follow us."

"They'll need two on board the boat, so most likely it will be Sondheim who follows us. He wouldn't trust the other two," Ed said. "Not a bad plan, Charles. I'll go with that. We should be able to shake him off easily enough. You two happy?"

"What do you think, Dom?"

"As long as Sondheim is following you, not us, it is OK – I don't want to meet that 'orrid man again. You're welcome to 'im."

"Agreed then. We'll swap the helmets tonight."

"OK," Martin said. "But we have to wait until Sondheim gets here with the Edelweiss. They already knew we were meeting you here, when they threatened us during the hi-jack. He must have sent Alain and Natalie on ahead by bus. I don't think the damage to their boat was great – unless I was lucky enough to seriously foul up their engines – and so he won't be delayed much. We'll need them to see us together first and then to realise we have split up for this to work."

"Good point, Martin. OK, so we stay on board and visible, so that Tremblay and Marceau can report to Sondheim," Ed said.

He put his arm round Dominique and gave her a hug.

"How about some of that French cooking you promised me, Dominique? I'll give you a hand."

*

Just before darkness fell the following day, Paul brought the Edelweiss into the harbour and picked up Alain and Natalie from the small quay.

"Hi! You OK? I got away earlier than I thought. Papawhatsisname didn't fuss in the end and let me leave.. Did you make the meeting? Could you hear anything?"

"We arrived too late to do much last night. We found the Brits easily enough, but Handley and the girl didn't get here till early this morning. Handley went straight to moor alongside the Artemis and all four stayed together on their boats last night. Customs are on to them though and have set up a surveillance op. We also think our so-called rescuers are watching too. They've had several visits from the Customs and police. They are tied up in the next bay not far away."

"What the hell sort of visits do you mean?"

"*Amicables* – friendly. They are obviously police themselves, which means our rescue was not just good luck. They must have been following us and knew who we were all along," Natalie said.

"But how did you get away so quickly from Kapsáli, Paul? Did you try to bribe the Brigadier again?"

"Don't worry, Alain, the General and me are the best of friends – he just wanted me out of his hair, I guess."

"That I can understand – so he warned Customs here exactly when you'd arrive and posted a guard over there to watch us meet up. We were also followed on the bus and have been watched ever since."

Paul ignored him and continued:

"… so the Toni woman and her Frenchman are police bastards, are they? I thought they were just too innocent to be true. Well, I called our collector in Volos and he said to keep a tight watch on everyone's butt and that's what I intend to do."

"You did what, you brainless idiot? They can monitor calls like that," Alain said. "And they'll know we've got a contact in Greece for certain now."

"Well, I'm going to put a stop to some of this and pay our rescuers a visit while they're tucked up in bed."

"Don't be stupid, Paul. It's time to lie low, not to draw more attention to ourselves," Natalie said.

"Come on – just a little bang, nothing serious."

"For Christ's sake, Paul, will you just listen to yourself? We're not even sure where the Brit dealers are now – they don't seem to be on board their boat and they're not with the other two on the yacht either. In fact, we don't know the hell where any of them are."

"Shit! Well, don't just stand there you idiots – go and find out where they've got to. Do I have to do everything myself? There are not many places they can go in this dump, so maybe they've done a runner with the helmet."

*

"Did you get all that, Brigadier?"
"Loud and clear, Commissaire."

Chapter 13

At around four o'clock in the morning a dark figure crept out of the cabin on the Edelweiss in full diving gear carrying a compressed air bottle. After struggling into the harness and settling the bottle comfortably on his back Sondheim adjusted his mask, sat on the stern, and slipped quietly into the black waters. With a final check everything was working as it should and a glance at his watch, he swum gently away across the harbour towards the next bay where the Pericles was moored. His flippers created little white flecks of wake. On board the Edelweiss, Alain and Natalie, lying on their bunks in their sleeping bags, were talking quietly together in the dark.

"The silly bastard. He really is going to do it. There's no way we're going to get away with this. All hell will break loose. "

He looked out through the porthole in their cabin. Suddenly he tensed and moved away. "Oh shit! We must be being monitored somehow. I'm sure those are watchers on the quay. Keep back from the porthole, but look over there, that car, to the right of the bollard. That's it."

"There's definitely someone inside, Alain. Two I think. I can see the green of their night sight binoculars."

Natalie moved across to Alain's bunk and sat on the edge.

"Do you think we're being bugged? Remember when the customs men came aboard in Kapsáli? Maybe they planted a bug. They didn't have much time and we were in the cabin with them, so it shouldn't be hard to find, if they did."

They both began running their fingers along under the edges of the lockers and the central table of the main cabin. Natalie went down on all fours to check under the bunks. It took them half an hour to find it – a small black microphone sticking to the front of the cooker in the galley, looking as if it was one of the controls. Alain unclipped it gently and leaned over to the next boat. He placed it carefully on the back of the cabin door.

"Clever! So obvious, we didn't notice it. They must know everything we've said since leaving Kapsáli," he said.

"So they'll know exactly what Paul is about to do – he's walking straight into a trap."

Traces of a smile were beginning to play about Natalie's eyes.

"Time for a quick exit?" Alain said, catching her mood.

"You mean, leave Paul? Shouldn't we warn him?"

"You don't mean that! It's either go now or wait for the police to come for us too. We might just get clear of Greek waters if we make a run for it, but it has to be now. I doubt they'll bother to follow us, as there's nothing they can charge us with apart from being accessories. Paul will have to take his chances – we did try to warn him off."

"OK, let's do it. It'll be a relief. I never liked the bastard anyway. Arrogant chauvinist."

Alain looked at her, read the expression on her face and without a word went up on deck to slip the moorings, while she started the engines. The noise burst loudly into the gentle stillness of the early morning, but soon the diesels warmed up and the noise settled back into a gentle purr. She eased the Edelweiss as slowly as possible out into the channel and turned for the entrance to the harbour. As made their way towards the open water, Alain could see movement in the watching car. The binoculars swivelled in their direction, but no one got out or came running along the quay.

"They're going to leave us alone, Nat. We might just get away with this."

She put her hand on his shoulder as they both peered forward into the shadows and weaved their way through the boats outside riding at anchor, seeking out the main channel. Soon the gleam of the beacons on either side of the harbour entrance began to fade behind them. Natalie eased back the throttle to speed out through the narrows to the freedom of the open sea.

When Sondheim could see the Pericles ahead of him, he sank slowly beneath the dark waters with hardly a ripple as his flippers arched over like a whale's tail fin and slid beneath the surface. He swam slowly towards the hull, lighting the way with his torch. At the stern of the boat, he steadied himself against the eddies by holding onto one of the propellers and reached into the pouch around his waist. He took out a small limpet mine and was about to set the timer when he saw the flash of an underwater camera and felt a tap on his shoulder. He whirled round to find himself looking straight into the mask of another diver.

Despite being temporarily blinded by the torch shining in his eyes, he made a move to take out his knife from his belt, but a restraining hand gripped his arm from behind and a ring of torches came on all around him. The diver nearest to him signalled he was to surface and with a shrug of the shoulders he kicked his flippers and headed upwards.

He pulled up his mask as he broke the surface and was again blinded by searchlights all around. He could just make out the barrels of the police guns trained on him. A hand reached down and pulled him closer to the ladder at the stern and he heard an order to climb aboard.

Sitting in the cockpit he pulled off the face mask and the dry suit hood and acknowledged the policemen surrounding him.

"*Kaliméra*, Captain Sondheim. We meet again under changed circumstances. You're under arrest of course."

"Hi, General. Well, well, our brave rescuers," he said, looking at Pierre and Antonia. "So pleased to see you again."

"You've not lost your sense of humour I see, Captain. I admire that, but I'm afraid this time it will not – how do you say? – get you off the hook."

The Brigadier's body language changed as he turned to his men and gave his orders.

"Take Captain Sondheim away and lock him up. Get him a change of clothes and arrest the other two."

One of his men stepped forward and whispered in the Brigadier's ear.

"Oh dear, how silly of us to let them slip away. Your friends have left port, like the rats deserting the ship which is sinking, Captain. You have no friends now, no clothes, no boat, nothing. "

"Typical – running for cover at the first sign of trouble."

"You would no doubt have done the same under the circumstances, Captain Sondheim. Do not worry however, we will pick them up later."

The Brigadier's men removed Paul's flippers and bundled him off the boat into the waiting police van on the quay. Pierre and Antonia watched him go with some misgivings.

"Excellent operation, Brigadier. The only problem is that a man like him will not talk and I doubt we'll ever discover the identity of the collector he is working for if you keep him here," Pierre said.

"Maybe we can get more information from the other two when you catch up with them," Antonia said.

"I'm sorry to have to say to you, Detective Inspector Antoniarchis, I doubt that will happen. They'll soon be leaving Greek waters and we would be wasting our time trying to get the Maltese or Italian authorities to extradite them back to us. They have not committed a crime in Greece, so we would have no grounds on which to make such a request."

"I quite understand, Brigadier," Antonia replied with a smile.

*

Out at sea the Edelweiss was making fast passage away from the Greek mainland. Dawn had arrived in a burst of sunlight, and morale on board was high as Alain and Natalie found themselves alone on the boat for the first time in weeks. The presence of Paul Sondheim had coloured their whole existence for so long they had almost forgotten what it was like to be able to think for themselves. The sense of freedom and release they felt gave them a lift as if they were on holiday and they smiled and laughed together, opening the throttle to let the boat bound across the waves and throw up the spray on either side. The growing warmth of the new day made itself felt and they shed their heavy waterproofs.

Alain went below to prepare coffee and search for something for breakfast. They had left Avlémonas so precipitously they had not been able to stock up on bread, so on the spur of the moment Alain decided to make a traditional Canadian breakfast – something he realised Paul would have scoffed at had he been with them, but for him it would be a powerful reminder of home in Quebec and he knew Natalie would love it.

The cabin was soon full of the smells of frying bacon and steaming waffles. With a final added touch of maple syrup, he came up from the galley with two mugs of coffee and the loaded plates to the delight of Natalie, who quickly set the autopilot and took her seat at the table on the top deck. The silence between them as they ate was the silence of contentment at being able to forget the outside world for a moment. Alain looked up after a few mouthfuls, his elbow resting on the table, fork holding the next mouthful of waffle dripping with syrup.

"So what do we do now?"

"How do you mean? We disappear for a while. Perhaps spend some time in Malta – we've enough fuel to get us there if we don't go too fast. We could sell the boat and head back to La Roquette perhaps or even start up a diving school on Malta."

"Be serious, Natalie. We're too deep into this to be able to just walk away. Our collector - the Man - as Paul calls him – won't just let us drop out; we know too much. We'll have to tell him what's happened and find out what he wants us to do now."

"*Merde*! But you're right. Just for a few moments I was loving the thought of being free of all this. I'm pissed off with this cloak and dagger stuff – and I shocked at the way Paul held his knife to that poor girl's throat; she looked terrified. I'm glad he got caught, he crossed too many boundaries for me."

"Oh! Don't assume they'll hang onto him for long. The Greeks will do a deal and get him out of the country as soon as they decently can. He's just an embarrassment and not the man they want."

"Don't spoil it, Alain, I was beginning to enjoy today. Anyway how do we contact the collector?"

"Paul left his cell phone on board – I'll bet the number is on it somewhere."

"Good idea! He called a number in Volos, I think."

Alain went below and searched Sondheim's cabin for his cell phone. It was still on, and he searched the address book. Near the end he found what he was looking for. A mobile phone number with no name attached.

"Could be this one. No name."

He pressed the number and could hear the ring. Immediately a voice responded:

"I told you not to call except in an emergency!"

"This is an emergency. Paul has been arrested."

"Who is this?"

"Alain – Paul has been arrested by Customs in Avlémonas and is probably being interrogated by Interpol right now. Natalie and I are outside Greek waters so we're safe for the moment. What do you want us to do?"

"Can you still watch and track the yacht transporting the helmet?"

"Probably, if it comes this way as we expect it to."

"Do it."

The phone went dead and Alain looked at Natalie.

"He says we're to go on tracking the Phalaris."

"Shit!"

"He didn't wait for me to say what happened when we searched their boat. Maybe Paul already told him?"

Alain put his arm round her.

"At least we don't have to attack them. He said just to follow. We don't even know if they'll have the real helmet. It's like the three cup shuffle. They won't want to be caught again, this time with the real thing, but we can't be sure. They may be bluffing. They may well expect us to try to get revenge for the fire too, so they'll be ready for us this time and I doubt we'd be able to board as easily as before."

"So, what's the plan?"

"We wait off shore and watch out for their sail. The tan colour should be easy to spot and shadowing them will be no trouble."

Natalie took her coffee out into the cockpit from under the awning, stripped down to her bikini and stretched out on the bench seat to enjoy the sun before it became too hot to bear.

"You know, Alain, this is first time I feel comfortable like this for weeks. I always hated the way Paul looked at me. Remember when we were on the beach and drugged the other two before searching their boat? The whole time I was distracting Handley, I felt as if Paul was watching me too through his binoculars from the back of the beach, stripping my clothes off me."

"Maybe he was, but he won't be doing it any more, so relax!"

She closed her eyes against the sun and murmured:

"The Phalaris won't be anywhere near us for ages yet. Come and join me."

Alain, now down to his swimming trunks too, came across and sat down beside her. Her hand moved to his thigh and he leant over to kiss her.

*

Antonia yawned loudly as the Greek officers went ashore, leading their prize away. The Brigadier followed soon after, leaving them on their own. It was still early and they had had a long night of watching and waiting. Pierre too was feeling the lack of sleep, but couldn't rest until he had worked out their next move.

"We'll still have to keep watch on Handley and Krevine," he said. "I'll get Papadopoulos to post some men and keep us informed. We know Everidge and Robson are still here, but they must have worked out a plan. They won't know yet that Sondheim has been arrested and the other two have fled. But they soon will."

"They must have suspected the Edelweiss would follow them as soon as the repairs were finished. But since it came and went after dark, they may not even know it got here."

Pierre reached for his phone and spoke with Brigadier Papadopoulos.

"Sondheim's not saying anything as we thought. He's being charged with attempted sabotage, so there's a good chance in the end he'll do a deal. For the moment he's being left to cool off."

As he finished speaking his phone rang. It was Major Kahn. Pierre listened for a few moments and looked across at Antonia as he was speaking, raising his eyebrows. She looked back at him questioningly, but he gestured to her to say nothing and continued to listen intently. After a few minutes he closed the phone.

"So, what did he say?"

"The Turkish authorities have decided to let the tombaroli go without charge. They're being deported. They saved their skins by fully cooperating with the police. The Museum is so impressed with the finds they made I think they would employ them as official archaeologists if they could!"

"What about Samborini?"

"He's disappeared completely. No one knows where he is – I suppose he's back in Italy now. I wouldn't like to be in his shoes though. The others will hunt him down if they can, I'm certain."

"What does Kahn think of all this?"

"He's going to be promoted for arresting the tombaroli and for saving so many relics of the Turkish heritage. We have a friend for life there."

"I'm really pleased for him. I had a soft spot for the Major."

"Not too soft I hope!"

Chapter 14

The four of them walked along the quay towards the harbour-side restaurants. They quickly found a taverna popular with the local fishermen, where they could have a leisurely breakfast. They drew up chairs, but almost immediately Ed got up again and, without a word, left the others with a nod towards Charles. The waiter approached and Charles ordered for himself and for Ed. Martin and Dominique chose more slowly from the menu and ordered coffee. Charles looked carefully about him, then relaxed and settled back in his chair to enjoy the atmosphere and observe the morning's activity in the harbour.

"Ed'll be back soon – he's gone to find out what the latest gossip is amongst the fishermen."

"I didn't know he could speak the language that well."

"Ed has hidden talents, that's why we make such a good team."

Charles shifted round in his seat and was looking about him again, eyes darting back and forth.

"So I'm beginning to appreciate," Martin said, puzzled by Charles' unease.

He too began to scan the crowd, sensing that Charles felt they were not out of danger. He could see no sign of Sondheim and the others, but caught sight of Ed almost running back towards them. He made his way quickly through the tables, nearly crashing into a waiter. He finally eased himself back into this chair.

"Come on then, spit it out Ed. You look like a cat that got the cream."

"You'll never guess – Sondheim's been arrested! A couple of hours ago, early in the morning."

"Whatever for? Tell it to us, Edouard. Come on, don't tease," Dominique said.

"Well, he was caught trying to blow the prop shaft off the Interpol launch. They were waiting for him apparently and he was caught red-handed."

"That at least answers two questions for us. Interpol is definitely on their case as well as ours, and Sondheim did manage to bring the boat here after the repairs. We didn't see him arrive, so it must have been late last night or very early this morning," Charles said.

"We didn't seriously think we'd shaken them off by going into Chóra instead of Kapsáli," Martin said. "There's always someone watching and we hardly avoided drawing attention to ourselves when we set fire to their boat."

"So, what 'appens now? We 'ave the Interpol and the *douane* – how do you say – customer, still tracking us."

"Customs," Ed corrected with a laugh. "But I haven't finished yet, Dom. The fishermen also said the Edelweiss left again very early this morning just before Sondheim was caught. So the other two chickens have fled the coop and left Sondheim in deep shit."

"Interesting. OK, but we stick to the plan. Ed and I will slip away leaving the boat here. We can leave in daylight now since Sondheim can't follow us. You two leave when you like and we'll see you in Catania. It's still possible Tremblay and Marceau are waiting out at sea for you and will follow, so be careful."

"We'll need some stores first and to refuel – it's a long trip across."

"No problem, Martin. That might be an advantage. Interpol will stay to watch your preparations and then track you. That'll take the attention off us. By the time they realise we're not still here, we should be well on our way."

"When we've finished our meal here – there's no hurry, the ferry doesn't leave from Diakófti for another two hours – Ed and I'll go back to the boat and swap over the helmets as we agreed. By the time you get back we'll be gone. I'll set a timer for this evening so that our cabin lights come on and off."

"OK. We'll get our supplies this morning and refuel this afternoon. We'll stay on board the Phalaris this evening and make it clear we're settling down for the night. We'll leave at about seven tomorrow morning, before it gets too warm," Martin said, looking across at Dominique for her approval.

"That's fine. We'll be on the mainland by then on our way to Pátra."

They finished eating and ordered more coffee and a bottle of wine, relieved now that the plan was firmed up and knowing Sondheim was out of the picture. Anyone watching would have had the impression they were settling in for the morning without a care in the world.

Papadopoulos' team posted in the next taverna along, watched the second coffees arrive and the wine being opened. Strictly against orders, they too ordered a bottle. When they next looked across, Charles and Ed had left and Martin and Dominique were setting off to go into the town for their stores. Reluctantly, the men abandoned the rest of their wine and set off in pursuit.

*

Vincenzo Samborini returned to San Gimignano after dark and made his way through the dusty narrow streets to his house in the via Piandornella. The houses on either side leaned across to each other and whispered as he went by. Hidden eyes followed his progress as he climbed the hill, but there was no one outside on the doorsteps to greet him after his long absence. There was no one inside the house either. That was how he liked it.

The house had lain empty for nearly three months and he had to push the front door hard to go through into the only room on the ground floor. As the door scraped across the dirt floor he could hear the rustling of mice scuttling out of sight into the dark corners of the room. The smell of droppings was overpowering. The stale air trapped inside, rushed past him as he opened the door wider, escaping at last into the cooler air of the evening and the freedom of the street.

He paused for a moment on the threshold, listening for other sounds or signs of the presence of danger. Hearing nothing, he entered and strode confidently across the room, despite the gloom, to where a rough wooden table stood. The lamp was where he had last left it and he reached for the matches to light the wick. The eyes of the mice were reflected in the sudden flare of the match flame for a split second before instantly going out as they fled down the holes they had burrowed into the walls, emphasizing the density of the blackness all around. Samborini lifted the glass mantle and lit the lamp. The room filled with yellow light and strangely shaped shadows cast by the jumble of objects accumulated over generations played on the walls.

The ground floors of the older houses in the town had always served as the barns and stables for the animals. In some cases this had continued until only a few years before, such was the tenacity of the country way of life.

Samborini picked his way sure-footedly across the earth floor holding the lamp to where the light revealed a wooden staircase leading up to a modern door. He climbed the stairs and with his free hand fumbled in his pocket for the key. The lock was well oiled and key turned easily and almost silently releasing the catch. He turned the knob and opened the door, which led directly into the main room.

The lamp revealed surprising luxury: modern rustic style furniture and comfortable armchairs. The walls were covered in shelves on which stood a mass of small statues, earthenware pots, bits of plates, glass bottles and small ornaments of all sorts. On the floor there were groups of amphora stacked together against the wall. There were two full-size statues in surprisingly good condition. The corners of the room were dark and Samborini's eyesight was still flared out by the harshness of the gas lamp's flame. He set the lamp down on the small table to the side of the door and reached for the electric light switch.

"*Buonasera, Vincenzo.*"

Samborini's hand froze in mid-air half way towards the switch.

"I wouldn't do that. We have things to talk about, you and I. Come. Sit down. Hands on the table where I can see them," said the voice in the local accent, which he recognised only too well.

Using the next few seconds to regain his composure, Samborini moved slowly across towards the table and sat at one end as he was bidden. His eyes were adapting to the gloom and he could see into the recesses of the room. He made out a dark haired thick-set man, settled back in the carver at the other end of the table – his right hand man in the gang, Giovanni Lucca.

"*Salute, Giovanni.* What can I do for you?" he said.

"I want my share, Vincenzo," came the reply.

*

It was three in the morning when the radar sounded the warning and Alain dragged himself out of the warm bunk, pulled on a sweater over his pyjamas and went out into the wheelhouse. The radar screen showed a blip about a mile off the starboard bow. Alain looked out through the cabin porthole, but there was nothing to be seen. Wide awake now he rushed out into the cockpit. Shivering, he peered into the blackness, but there were no stars and no moonlight to guide him. The morning sea mist was dense and impenetrable. It swirled around him and he pulled his sweater down over the gap at his waist to keep out the intense cold. He could hear the sound of foghorns in the distance, though how far away he could not judge. He well knew that in fog sounds were deceptive and deadened and even their direction was difficult to determine.

Staring into the dark with no references to estimate direction or speed was always eerie and disorientating. How on earth had they managed in the olden days? he thought to himself, as he returned to the warmth of the wheelhouse and the reassurance of the modern electronics on board. The blip on the radar screen was growing bigger and the Edelweiss was heading straight for it. Not seriously worried, he switched the steering to manual, turned the wheel a few degrees to starboard to avoid the collision course and increased the speed to 10 knots.

The blip still grew larger and then to his consternation split in two.

"Shit, there are two of the buggers out there!" he said out aloud.

He shouted to Natalie to come up on deck and frantically swung the wheel again hard to port to come off the collision course with the second vessel. He could clearly hear the throbbing of engines now and make out the lights of a container ship towering above them, already frighteningly close.

"Natalie!" he shouted again.

As she came quickly out of the cabin below, scared by the tone of his voice, they were both flung sideways as the Edelweiss took a glancing blow on the bow and was flipped almost on its side. The next thing they knew they were scraping along the hull of the huge cargo ship and bits of the port side of the Edelweiss were being ripped off by the roughness of the metal plates on the side of the vessel, which hung over them like a curtain, blotting out the sky. The sounds of the Edelweiss rapidly being ground to pieces and the roar of the ship's engines were deafening.

"Christ! Get the life-jackets! I'll do the raft."

Alain scrambled out into the cockpit and released the catches on the life raft perched on the afterdeck. It dropped away into the sea and began to self inflate. The Edelweiss was taking on water fast and he knew they had only seconds left to get into the raft and to cut it loose before they would be at the stern of the cargo ship and caught in the drag of the huge propellers. He screamed again to Natalie who was struggling towards him through the waist-deep water in the cockpit carrying the life-jackets.

"No time to put those on. Just hang on to them and jump – now!"

He grabbed her arm and pulled her with him as he leaped across towards the raft. His heavy sweater weighed him down when he hit the water, but he managed to seize one of the safety ropes looped around the outside of the raft and pulled them both towards the entrance. As he started to haul himself inside, the raft was whirled round by the speed of the vessel and catapulted him into the side of the ship. He lost consciousness and was sucked beneath the hull by the turbulence and thresh of the propellers. The Edelweiss was low in the water by now, the cabin top only just above the waves, trapped air keeping it just afloat.

Natalie hung grimly onto the loop-line, grabbed her knife and hacked desperately at the painter attaching the raft to the Edelweiss. A few seconds more and the raft too would be pulled down towards the vessel's huge propellers, dragging her with it. The line gave and the raft floated free of the Edelweiss. Already it was tossing about crazily in the violence of the wash and, tiring fast, she could no longer keep her hold on the loop-line. Her fingers slipping, she made a final frantic lunge to hook her safety harness onto the inflatable and then was pulled under as the raft toppled over.

*

Martin came out on deck in the early dawn to be greeted by a thick mist hanging over the harbour. Perfect cover he thought as he shivered and went back inside to pull on more clothing.

"*Bouge-toi, Dom.* Time to go. Put plenty on, it's bloody cold out there."

"*Merde!*" she said sleepily, turning over in the bunk. "What time is it? I don't want to get up – I'm nice and warm here. Come back."

"About six. Time to go. Just put some coffee on and stay below – I'll do the rest."

He went back up on deck, released the bow line and let the Phalaris drift soundlessly away from the quay. The engine started up noisily joining the background hum of the fishing boats leaving at the same time. He put it in gear and steered gingerly out into the main channel. Peering into the mist he could dimly make out the entrance to the harbour, the lights on either side shining in halos of diffused light through the damp air. He had decided to head north and to pass between Kýthera and the smaller island of Elafonisi. He then planned to swing south-west out into the open sea and to set a course for Catania on the east coast of Sicily, avoiding the main shipping lanes crowded with vessels heading east for Piraeus.

Once clear of the harbour, he went forward to release the ties on the mainsail. Back in the cockpit he raised the sails to assist the engine rather than to take over, since the sea mist had deadened the wind. Soon, as the air warmed, the morning breeze would spring up and he would be able to save fuel and rely on the sail alone.

Thank goodness for GPS and the radar, he thought as they made their way up the channel. He knew that without it they would have been stuck in port until the mist cleared, with no chance of slipping out. At least they had left unobserved thanks to the conditions. The genuine helmet now stood on the shelf where the fake had been. The ruse might work if they were inspected again, but he still preferred not to be spotted if possible and to run the risk of the bluff being called. They had not seen Charles and Edward since breakfast the previous day, but, as promised, the cabin lights on the Artemis had come on when darkness fell and then gone off later.

He just hoped the two of them had caught the ferry unobserved and were now on the mainland. Dominique appeared with two mugs, coffee for him and hot chocolate for her. They huddled together for warmth staring out ahead for signs of ships or trawlers. They sounded their low-tech foghorn every five minutes or so and from time to time heard an answering call from somewhere far off. Like pigeons cooing to each other Dominique said. More like screech owls Martin had replied.

The mist began to lift and by nine o'clock the sun was strong enough to see off the last wisps. The breeze sprang up sufficiently to allow them to let the sails take over. The instant quiet as the motor was shut down added to their sense of escape after the recent events. Martin trailed a couple of fishing lines in the hope of catching something for breakfast and soon had brought in a couple of sea bass – a rare treat. He gutted and filleted them outside in the cockpit, attracting a flock of gulls as if from nowhere. He threw the guts and the heads overboard and the birds argued and dived and fought each other in a raucous ballet above the waves in the wake of the yacht. Soon Dominique could smell the fish frying below – Martin's speciality and her favourite. Martin emerged carrying two warm baguettes dripping with butter and stuffed with fresh sea bass.

The Phalaris was making 6 or 7 knots with the sea breeze behind them and they were able to set a new course straight for Catania. Martin continued to keep a lookout while Dominique dozed on the foredeck, learning back against the cabin top beside the mast, basking in the warmth and enjoying the breeze on her face. Towards the end of the morning, far out to their left under the port bow Martin noticed a red and orange blob which appeared and disappeared in the troughs. He turned towards it easing the sail.

The change of direction roused Dominique who soon spotted what it was that had attracted his attention. She stood up and, shading her eyes, stared out across the waves. Martin had reached for his binoculars and they both exclaimed at the same time that it looked like a life raft.

As the Phalaris bore down on the raft, they both kept their eyes glued to it looking for signs of activity. Nothing stirred aboard, though the continual bobbing up and down made it difficult to be sure from a distance. Soon they were close enough to see that the entrance flap was open and that the raft was low in the water. They swept past and Martin slackened the sails and rounded up into wind to make the approach.

Dominique stood ready with the boathook and deftly caught one of the loops around the outside. Martin dropped the sails and started the engine to keep the ketch head to wind while Dominique secured the raft alongside calling out to anyone inside. There was no reply.

She jumped across to the entrance and wriggled her way in on her stomach. Inside the raft there was a foot of water and bits of equipment floating all around. The water was red with blood and a woman lay in the corner, her arm looped through a hand hold as if she had deliberately tied herself to the side to prevent herself from slipping unconscious down into the water and drowning inside the raft. She had managed to get her legs into a survival suit, but above the waist was wearing only a thick sweater. Dominique splashed her way across, half crawling, half stumbling. She quickly examined the reclining figure

"There's a woman in here," she shouted back to Martin," but she's very cold and injured. She 'as a gash on her fore'ead and she's lost a lot of blood. I can feel a pulse though."

"Can you get her to the entrance?"

"Yes, but then you'll 'ave to 'elp me."

Dominique put her hands under the woman's arms and began to drag her across to the entrance. The raft was rocking violently in the swell and the water inside was creating waves as she fought her way through the debris sloshing about. Martin came onto the raft and they swapped places. He heaved the woman up onto the edge of the raft and they eased her across onto the stern platform of the yacht. He quickly jumped back on board and the two of them gently pulled the woman into the cockpit.

"She's still breathing, but probably hypothermic. Better get her onto a bunk and wrap her up in blankets to raise her body temperature."

They pulled off the survival suit and her wet clothes and wrapped her in layers of blankets. When Dominique had carefully cleaned the wound on her head wiping away the blood before bandaging it up, she exclaimed:

"*Merde, c'est Natalie Marceau!* I wonder what happened to their boat."

"Something made them abandon their boat and she was lucky by the looks of it to make it to the raft. There's no sign of Tremblay. And we know Sondheim was not on board."

"What were they doing out here?"

"You remember Ed said the Edelweiss had been seen leaving? Well, perhaps Charles was right and they were just out here waiting for us."

"Or perhaps they were just trying to get away, when they knew Sondheim had been arrested."

"Mm, that's possible."

"Should we call for 'elp or wait till she wakes up?"

"I'd rather wait. I'm sure she'll come round when she's warmer and that gash on the head is not as bad as it looked when she was covered in blood. I'd like to get some information out of her before we decide what to do."

"I'll stay with 'er if you can manage."

Martin went up on deck and scanned the sea around. He hoisted himself up to the first spreader on the main mast to get a better look, but there was no sign of anyone else in the water. Over to the south there was something floating and he decided to go closer. The raft was so waterlogged that though he would have liked to have taken it in tow, it would have been too dangerous, so he cut it loose, thinking they might be able to salvage it later. He turned towards the objects he had seen and soon the boat was surrounded by bits of wood and clothing. A torn life-jacket bobbed forlornly alongside, but there was no sign of Alain. He turned away again and headed back to where he could see the life raft.

Coming alongside this time he secured the raft and went aboard. It took time to pump out the water and he was both soaked and tired when it was done. He returned to the Phalaris, closed the entrance to the raft and tied it to the stern.

Dominique called out that Natalie hadn't come round yet, but that her body temperature was rising. Martin hoisted the sails, reset the course for Catania, engaged the autopilot and went below.

"I think we could risk massaging her to get her circulation going now she is warming up."

About half an hour later Natalie opened her eyes and looked around her in fright. She did not seem to recognise either of them at first but when Dominique spoke to her in French she relaxed a little.

"*Ne t'inquiète pas. Tout va bien maintenant. Tu es avec des amis. Tiens, essaie de boire un peu.*"

Dominique raised Natalie's head and held a cup of warm soup to her lips. She managed to drink a little before slipping off again into a deep sleep.

"She'll be OK now, I think so. We must let 'er rest," she said.

Martin went back to change out of his wet clothes and finished off the hot soup before joining Dominique at the helm. They discussed what to do now they had a passenger from the enemy camp. What line would she take when she woke properly? Should they take her to Sicily and let her go or would that be too dangerous? They could hardly keep her captive on board. They would have to lock her in the after cabin at night in case she tried to take over the boat while only one of them was on watch.

Dominique was looking out over the stern as they talked, half watching the life raft bobbing in their wake.

"Martin, I think we should cut the raft loose, it's slowing us up. And it makes us more visible if anyone is following us."

"It's possible too that a collision has been reported and they'll send out search aircraft. It seems a shame to dump it though."

"Why not collapse it and stow it on board?"

"Easier said than done, but it's a good idea. Let's do it."

*

In the harbour at Avlémonas, Antonia was waking. It was still early. She looked at her watch – just after seven. She fell back against the pillows. Later when she pulled back the curtain to look out of the porthole, the morning mist had cleared. Turning on her side she saw that Pierre was no longer there and he did not answer when she called out. She crawled across the bunk and squeezed into the small but efficient shower. Quickly drying herself off and pulling on a warm sweatshirt against the early cold she went up on deck and looked out along the quay. In the distance she spotted Pierre returning to the boat carrying bread and a small bag. Very French she thought: can't exist without fresh bread in the morning. No bad thing nonetheless, she reflected, realising she was ravenously hungry.

Pierre came on board and placed the bread and rolls on the table, looked around him and asked:

"*Et le café, madame?*"

"You Frenchman! Not ready yet, *monsieur*. And I never make coffee before I've had a decent hug from my partner."

"In France, we do not have partners, we have lovers or wives or preferably both."

"Chauvinist! OK, OK, I'll put the coffee on, but you tell me what you've been doing as well as collecting the bread."

"The Brigadier has told me they have tracked the Phalaris to," he took out a piece of paper, " 36'52" N by 22'45" E. It seems they diverted south for a while and then resumed their course. It looks as if they're heading for Sicily, so that means possibly Catania or a smaller harbour nearby."

"What about the two in the Edelweiss?"

"That's the interesting bit. They tracked them to 35'11" N by 22'42" E and then lost them."

He went over to the chart table, spread out the chart and traced the positions of the two boats with his finger. Antonia stood by him watching and calculating as he marked the two spots with crosses. They both stared at the chart and tried to interpret the movement of the boats. It appeared the Phalaris had turned briefly south in the direction of the last sighting of the Edelweiss and then resumed its course after a short while.

"So what do you think?" asked Antonia.

"I've no idea. We'll have to go out to see for ourselves – but only after I've had my coffee," he replied.

"Coming up."

After a final check with Papadopoulos on the latest position of the Phalaris, which, he reported, was maintaining its course towards Sicily, they released the mooring lines and headed out to sea. The mist had gone and the visibility was good. Heading south back round the bottom of the island of Kýthera they headed off in search of the Edelweiss. It took about three hours to reach the last known coordinates. There was no sign of the boat, but Antonia spotted some driftwood and bits of equipment. They headed towards the floating debris and scooped it aboard. A torn life-jacket and some bits of clothing gave some cue as to what might have happened. A few scraps of wooden decking floated around them. Nothing they saw could be definitely connected to the Edelweiss, but the coincidence was too great for there to be much doubt in their minds.

Antonia put a call on the ship's radio through to the Brigadier.

"Kaliméra, Brigadier."

"Kaliméra, Inspector."

"We've found debris in the area of the last contact with the Edelweiss, but no sign of survivors or of a life raft. We'll follow the Phalaris, but will keep well back until we're sure where she is heading."

"Efaristó, Inspector. We will keep you informed of their latest position every three hours. Over and out."

The heat of the day was beginning to make itself felt, but remained bearable because of the light breeze and the wind they created by their own speed. Pierre calculated a course which would bisect the probable track of the Phalaris. Their speed of about 20 knots would bring them within sight of the yacht in a few hours, then he proposed to reduce speed and to follow them in case any rendezvous at sea had been arranged.

He soon heard the sound of aircraft engines in the distance. A Greek Navy helicopter was circling over the area of the last sighting of the Edelweiss. A man of influence the Brigadier, he thought to himself. He was still puzzled at the lack of a life raft. He distinctly remembered seeing one attached to the protruding afterdeck when they had taken the Edelweiss in tow. Perhaps this time there really had been an explosion which had sunk the boat. He wondered if Papadopoulos would tell Sondheim his associates had probably drowned.

In the middle of the afternoon they spotted a tan sail about three or four miles ahead. Pierre throttled back to about 6 knots and they kept just out of sight below the horizon, watching on the radar.

Chapter 15

Paul Sondheim sat on the quayside in Bari working out his next move. After he had done the deal with the Greek authorities his feet had literally hardly touched the ground, so keen were they to get rid of him. He had been bundled onto a plane bound for the little airport of Bari. They wanted him quickly out of Greece.

On arrival no one had given him more than a cursory glance as he went through the passport check, armed with a new passport, his old one still being on the Edelweiss. He had no more than a small overnight bag with him, thanks to Natalie and Alain deserting him. I'll get those bastards one day, he thought to himself, as he settled back in a taxi taking him the short ride into the town. There he headed for a trattoria on the waterfront.

On the way he picked up a copy of La Republiccà and sat down to order a beer. He flicked through the paper, but was distracted as the ferry arriving from Pátra docked right in front of where he was sitting. Half watching the foot passengers coming down the gangway and half reading the paper, he stiffened as he read the headline about the murder of a tombarolo. The name was not familiar to him, but the coincidence made him think. He looked up from the paper and, with hardly seeing eyes glanced across to the ferry. Two backpackers caught his attention. They were older than the usual run of young people struggling with their rucksacks and there was something familiar in the way they walked.

"Hell! that's those two Brits," he exclaimed aloud.

He jumped up knocking over the table, threw a couple of notes onto the chair, abandoned the paper and ran quickly towards the foot passenger exit.

*

The two scruffy-looking travellers who alighted from the ferry in Bari harbour were wearing the unremarkable backpackers' uniform of jeans and T-shirts. The crossing from Greece normally took about 24 hours, but a storm had slowed the ship up and the deck passengers in particular had had a rough time with next to no shelter. The two men, with two or three days' growth of beard, looked tired and relieved to be ashore. Most of the passengers were waved through customs without formalities and the two of them were no exception, although they sensed the customs officials scrutinised them more piercingly than most of the other foot-passengers. Out on the quayside in the Porto Nuovo, they consulted their guide book and crossed almost immediately into the Città Vecchia.

"So far so good, Ed. OK let's find a small hotel here and rest up, I'm knackered. That was some crossing."

Charles shrugged his pack up a little higher to ease his sore shoulders and started out along a narrow street leading into the centre of the old town.

"I'd kill for a wash and change of clothes and something good to eat. The food on the ferry was disgusting and the smell of everyone puking up put me off anyway. I just hope all this hide and seek is worth it," Ed said. "I'm not cut out for carrying backpacks like this."

"You shouldn't have put so much in it – I told you you didn't need all that stuff you bought."

"It isn't what I bought that's heavy, it's the damned … "

Ed stopped for a moment to buy a copy of La Republiccà from a street vendor, while Charles looked again at his town map and started heading confidently down another side street near the Castello. Half-way down he turned in through a narrow doorway and entered a small courtyard. The pensione was modest, but clean and comfortable and they took two rooms. They agreed to meet in a couple of hours to go for a meal when it was dark.

Later, Ed had to bang on Charles' door to wake him up.

"Come on Charles, I'm starving."

"Always thinking of your stomach as usual. Alright, alright, I'm ready. Let's go."

Back in the street they headed towards the Piazza Garibaldi and soon found a trattoria. They had both abandoned their backpacker image and looked more like the thirty-something tourists they were. The evening was warm and the streets noisy. Ed was carrying the newspaper which he had not looked at yet, having spent the last two hours either in the shower or crashed out on his bed in the hotel. They chose a table at the back of the terrace from where they had a good view of the passers-by.

"I'm going for the local speciality tonight," Ed said. "The *capretto ripieno al forno.*"

"Ever the bloody linguist. What's that when it's at home?"

"Roast kid."

"Goat! No thank you, I'll stick to *spaghetti alla Norma.*"

Ed ordered for them both and added a bottle of the local ciro red. He opened the paper and spread it out on the table, while Charles continued to watch the passers-by.

"Shit! Look at this Charles. Samborini has been found dead – throat slit. Revenge killing the police think."

"Bloody hell! What does it say?"

Speaking slowly as he translated, Ed read out the account.

"Vincenzo Samborini, long suspected by the police of being a top tombarolo, but never caught nor charged, was found dead by neighbours at his home in San Gimignano yesterday. He had not been seen in his home town for over two months but had apparently returned a few days ago. Local people suspected something was wrong when, after having been empty for so long, a light in his house remained on all night and all the next day. When they forced their way in, they discovered his body in the main room on the first floor. He was toppled over, lying on his side on the floor, still tied to a chair. With his throat slit. Police report that he had been tortured before he died and there are rumours of a rag being stuffed into this mouth."

"Bloody hell, Ed. That sounds like the Mafia," Charles said, putting his glass down.

"Hang on, I haven't finished yet. There's more."

"Vincenzo Samborini was a native of San Gimignano and knew the hills around the town intimately. He allegedly made his living by breaking into old Etruscan tombs and selling on the finds to agents who specialised in the illegal exporting of artefacts and works of art to museums and art galleries all over the world. It is said that he had personal contacts with wealthy collectors who commissioned him and his gang to find specific objects. Police think he had just returned from just such a commission, but this time in Turkey. They speculate that the gang fell out and that this was a revenge killing … etc., etc. …"

"OK, enough," Charles said. "I don't like the sound of this at all. We should get out of Italy pronto."

"You're right. I don't fancy staying either. Poor bastard. Our fault too," Ed said. "If the other tombaroli were after him because of the double-cross, then sure as hell they're after us too. So much for your great idea!"

They ate their meal in silence, each lost in his own thoughts. Being followed by the customs or by Interpol just went with the territory, but angry tombaroli were a different matter altogether.

"I guess the one who came to us with Samborini to hand over the helmet told the others about the extra payment and Samborini paid the price for not sharing it."

"Maybe, but now the others know how valuable it is, they'll want to get their hands on the helmet too. Especially since they lost the rest of the finds."

"Maybe Catania is not such a good meeting place after all. It might not be too late to get Martin and Dom to go to Malta instead," Ed said.

"OK, do it, but don't tell them why – better ring them now rather than wait till we get back to the hotel. How's the goat?" asked Charles.

"Better than a sacrificial lamb," he replied reaching for his phone.

"Very funny."

*

Later that evening Charles and Ed made their way back to the pensione. The padrona seemed nervous when they went in and asked for their keys.

"*Grazie, buonasera, signora,*" Ed said giving her a smile and a nod, but she had already disappeared into a back room and his thanks were addressed to a still swaying curtain behind the desk.

"Odd," he said to Charles. "I wonder what's bugging her."

Charles shrugged his shoulders and was already climbing the stairs. He was still tired after the journey on the ferry and the wine with the meal had made him feel sleepy again. His key wouldn't go easily into the lock on his door and he struggled with it for a moment.

"Here, let me help you with that," Ed said. "You are knackered, aren't you? Time for some real kip and then let's get out of here pronto."

Ed turned the key and pushed open the door. The sight that greeted them was like out of a gangster movie. The room had been ransacked. The drawers of the chest had been pulled out, the bed tipped over and wardrobe door pulled off its hinges. Charles' backpack lay in the middle of the floor, the contents emptied onto the carpet. In the only armchair still in one piece, lay the helmet. Behind the chair stood a man idly tapping the blade of a knife into the palm of his hand.

"*Buonasera*, Engleesh."

"Shit, who the hell are you?" Charles said.

"For me to know it, and for you to divine it, *signore*."

He pointed to the helmet.

"What is zees piece of shita, as you say?"

"Oh, bugger. You and your plans," Ed said, turning to Charles. "Now we're really fucked."

"Zees is not ze 'elmet we want. It 'ees worth nothing." The man reached over and threw it contemptuously onto the floor. "Now you are going to tell us where ze real 'elmet is."

"You sure as hell are, mate ..."

Ed whirled round, but was too late to avoid the blow to the back of his neck from Sondheim who was standing behind the door. As he fell, he saw Charles stagger when the knife was plunged into his thigh. But Ed had lost consciousness before the sound of Charles' scream reached him.

*

All through the next day Pierre and Antonia tracked the Phalaris, taking care to stay back just below the horizon. The weather was kind – a steady breeze for the yacht and calm seas. For the two Interpol agents it was a time to catch up on report writing.

There was a constant stream of messages coming in on the emails and over the ship to shore radio. Papadopoulos let them know he was keeping Sondheim in custody for as long as he could, but that his superiors saw no point in charging him. Pierre and Antonia were happy with that as they preferred to let him run and to follow him when he was released. Sondheim was still unaware the Edelweiss had been sunk.

They received reports from the harbour authorities in Piraeus that a Greek cargo vessel had reported a collision in the fog and had some minor paint scraping along the water-line. Since nothing had shown up on their radar in the fog they supposed their vessel had hit a submerged container, but the incident could explain what had happened to the Edelweiss.

Major Kahn kept them up to date with the analysis of the finds that had been seized from the tombaroli. It seemed that they had proved to be invaluable and a whole new impetus had been given to the Archaeological Museum authorities. Turkish Government funds had been made available and several teams of researchers were out following up all the leads and opening up the tombs for proper scientific survey.

On the second day, just after they had breakfast on board, the phone went. It was Major Kahn. Pierre picked up the phone continuing with one hand to work at the galley.

"Hello, my friends, how do you do?"

"We are fine, Major, but what about you? We hear you are quite the hero."

"No more Major, I am Colonel now. Everyone think I am expert in archaeology and I want to thank you."

"*Félicitations, mon Colonel!* That is wonderful news. We will drink to your promotion, it is well merited."

"You will visit us again soon, no? I wish you good luck with the case. We are very happy here. We will drink to you also."

Pierre passed on the news to Antonia. He had caught a couple of sea bream earlier and was busy preparing them Greek style. Antonia looked up from time to time from the report she was writing to see the fish disappear into the little oven wrapped in foil, sprinkled with olive oil and red wine and surrounded by chopped aubergine.

"Pity we don't have any *romarin* to season them with," he muttered to himself as he worked. The lettuce was looking rather jaded, but he managed to put together a passable salad and chased Antonia off the cabin table so he could set it all out. He opened a bottle of cold white Entre-Deux-Mers which he extracted as if by magic from the small fridge.

Dusk was falling and he set the radar and the auto-pilot before they raised their glasses to drink a toast to the new Colonel. The fish was exceptionally good and they said little as they ate. Not to be outdone by her French colleague, Antonia reached across into a cupboard behind her and brought out a small package. Inside were very sticky slices of baklavá which they ate straight from the paper accompanied by much laughter and licking of fingers.

After the meal, Pierre returned to the wheelhouse to check their course and Antonia followed with the coffee. She saw the expression on his face.

"What's up?"

"Bad news. Everidge and Robson have been found in Bari. Their bodies were in a small pensione in the old quarter.

There was blood everywhere and it's clear they died slowly. A reproduction copy of the helmet was lying on the floor. The padrona of the hotel was murdered too – presumably because she would have been able to identify the killer or killers."

"That's terrible. There's curse on this helmet," Antonia said, her hands shaking as she set the cups down.

"We're going to lose the link to the collectors at this rate. It must be the rest of the tombaroli gang who are doing this," Pierre said. "Samborini must have given Everidge and Robson away to save his own skin, and now the whole gang are after the real helmet in earnest."

"Sure. And they're serious opposition, Pierre. We could become targets ourselves."

"So, if the helmet Everidge and Robson had with them in the hotel was the fake, the real thing must be on board the Phalaris this time. The question is – did Everidge or Robson tell the tombaroli that? It's like the famous three card trick. If they did, Handley and Krevine are in big trouble."

"Maybe they don't know which one they've got. I wouldn't put it past … "

The ship to shore phone interrupted her.

«Parakaló? Nai, nai. Kaliméra Brigadier...» She listened for a moment. «Entáxei, entáxei. Efaristó." She turned to Pierre.

"It's looking bad. Papadopoulos sounded embarrassed, but he said he had been instructed to do a deal with Sondheim and deport him fast. They put him on a plane from Kalamáta to Bari earlier today."

"You're joking!"

"Wait! In return, Sondheim gave them his contact number to reach the collector he's working for in London, so all is not lost. And that's not all, the Phalaris has changed course and seems to be heading for Malta. I wonder if they've heard the news about Everidge and Robson. But that should be impossible. The Italian police have imposed a news blackout."

"OK, whatever the reason, we follow. I'll get onto headquarters in Lyon and ask them to get the Maltese coastguard to meet the Phalaris and to escort it into Valletta. It's time we had a talk with Handley and Krevine."

"What do you have in mind?"

"I don't know. We can discuss that together, but you agree it's time we spoke with them?"

Antonia nodded and took over the helm to set the new course, while Pierre went below to make the call.

Later that evening in the warmth of their bunk, they lay together propped up against the pillows, bare legs touching down to their toes, quietly mulling over the events so far. Another bottle of wine stood on the shelf by the bed and each of them cradled a glass against the movement of the boat as they discussed their next moves. Antonia put her glass back on the shelf, wriggled down slightly and put her head on Pierre's shoulder. As her fingers slowly began to walk their way teasingly down his chest, exploring, the phone shrilled in Pierre's ear. With a sigh, he reached up to take it off the hook and listened intently. Antonia's hand paused. Pierre turned towards her.

"That was the Italian police. Samborini has been found – murdered – throat slit. The body count is growing."

*

Natalie woke slowly early that evening. She felt the sudden movement of the boat and heard the noises on deck as the yacht changed tack and the sails were reset for the new course south to Malta. The sound of voices reached her as she came to and tried to make out where she was. All she could see in the tiny forward cabin was a dim light round the edge of the door. She tried to sit up, but the dizziness which immediately overcame her forced her to lie back again. She tried to remember what had happened and how she came to be in a bunk on board an unknown boat. Panic rising she realised she was naked under the blankets. The last thing she could recall was struggling to climb into the life raft and retching sea water. She slipped back into half-consciousness, her brain still whirring and reliving the nightmare.

The noise of the engines is deafening. For what seems like an eternity she is held under and tumbled over and over by the powerful turbulence of huge threshing propellers. Several times she manages to surface and gulps desperately for air for a brief second before being sucked down again. Finally the raft saves her life by acting like a buoy pulling her back to the surface on the end of her safety line and away from the grip of the vessel's suction. She bobs in its wake as the ship retreats like a ghost into the shroud of the night fog. Her initial sense of immense relief as the vessel disappears into the blackness is replaced by panic and loneliness. All hopes of rescue are dashed and she is alone and deserted in the dark waters. There is no sign of Alain and no reply when she frantically shouts his name.

At last the raft rights itself and she struggles to haul herself inside, vomiting up water and most of the contents of her stomach. The inside of the raft is full of water, but she somehow succeeds in dragging herself to the far end and in attaching her harness to the loops on the inside to stop herself sliding down into the water. She grows colder and colder and slips into unconsciousness.

Reliving the nightmare caused her to cry out. The door of the cabin opened. In the half light she saw a figure coming towards her and, pressing herself back into the bulkhead, Natalie froze with terror.

"*Calme-toi, Natalie! Shh! Ça va, ça va. Personne ne va te faire mal.* It's alright. I'm not going to 'arm you. You're safe now.

You're on our boat and we're looking after you. You've slept fo1 twenty-four hours, but you 'ave no serious injuries and you'll soon feel better."

"But how did I get here? *Où est Alain*?" She looked around the cabin desperately.

"You were the only one in the life raft. You were unconscious. There was no sign of Alain – I'm so sorry, we did search for 'im, but we saw nothing. What happened?"

"A cargo ship ran us down. I think Alain was sucked under by the propellers – he was trying to save me. I don't know."

She looked at Dominique, silent tears pouring down her cheeks, her whole body shaking. Dominique sat beside her on the bunk, put her arms round her and rocked her like a baby.

"That's enough. You're safe now. You must rest, but first you must eat a little. I'll be back in a minute."

She stood up and pushed Natalie gently back down onto the pillow.

"Why are you being so kind? You know who I am and what we did to you."

Dominique turned in the doorway.

"Don't talk about that now and don't worry. We know more than you think. I'll be back in a minute."

First she went out into the cockpit to tell Martin what had happened:

"I think she must know Sondheim's been caught – she didn't ask about him – just Alain."

"We must go carefully though until we know for sure whose side she's on," replied Martin. They had only recently received the cryptic message from Ed about the change of plan and he was worried something had gone seriously wrong on shore. Why were they being told to go to Malta now instead of Sicily?

"Don't worry — I'll be careful."

She disappeared again into the galley to prepare some more soup to take to Natalie. When she entered the forward cabin taking a mug of soup with her, Natalie was calmer and sitting up. Dominique handed her the mug and sat down again on the bunk facing her.

"So tell me more, Natalie. What is all this about and why are you working with a bastard like Sondheim?"

Natalie took a sip from the mug and said:

"Paul made us an offer we couldn't refuse. It sounded so easy. All we had to do was to use our boat as a base from which to follow your friends — the dealers. If the Italians did find the helmet, then we would try to steal it from them. Paul said there was another private collector who would pay good money for it. We never spoke to him, Paul did all that. He made all the contacts, firstly in London and with someone in Volos. It all seemed like a game. We knew it was illegal, but no real harm was being done, no-one was getting hurt and it was a way of earning some much needed cash."

She paused and took another sip from the mug. The colour was returning to her face and she was looking stronger.

"Paul didn't seem to know about you two at first, so that was an added complication when you turned up. Alain and I didn't want to search your boat or to harm you, but Paul said we were too involved to back out and you wouldn't really get hurt. So we went along with the first attack on the beach.

"Then later on when Paul insisted we board your yacht at sea, he went too far. I was so shocked when he put that knife to your throat, really I was Dominique — you must believe me."

Dominique took her hand.

"It's alright — that's all behind us now."

"Alain was worried too about how far Paul would go, especially after you set our boat on fire. Things were getting out of control and we both knew what a temper he has. He was frighteningly angry.

"Later we were rescued and towed in to Kapsáli by those two who turned out to be police from Interpol. When Paul realised they already knew all about us. He nearly threw a fit. He wanted to blow up the Interpol boat. We tried to stop him, but of course he took no notice, so when he left the boat to swim out to put the limpet mine on the Interpol boat, we decided that was enough and slipped out of the port."

"You don't know that Sondheim was caught and arrested before he could set the mine?"

"We found a bug in the cabin after he had gone, so we knew all our movements had been monitored and they were laying a trap for him. That was one of the reasons why we left, before they got to us too." She paused. "We put the bug on a boat next to us before we went so they couldn't track us. We just wanted to leave the bastard to get what was coming to him. If we got caught we knew we would lose everything we had built up together in France."

Remembering again what she just escaped from and how Alain had died, she fell back on the bunk, tears welling up in her eyes.

"*Mais, calme-toi.* You don't have to worry about Sondheim any more."

Dominique stroked her hair and brushed it back off her tear-stained face. "But I am very sorry about Alain for you."

After a few moments, Natalie asked:

"So, where are you taking me now?"

"We were going to Catania, but there has been a change of plan and we have changed course to go to Valletta."

"Funny, Alain and I dreamt of going there and starting a new life together."

Chapter 16

Natalie stayed out on deck and left her to her own thoughts, leaving the questions for later. She seemed genuinely distressed about Alain and was still exhausted. The Phalaris was well on her way to Malta. Dominique had set a course of 190°, and calculated an arrival time of early afternoon the next day. They would have to keep a close watch all night if they were to avoid what had happened to Natalie and Alain. The dangers would be greatest as they approached Valletta harbour and crossed the shipping lanes. It was growing dark, but the moon was up and so at least the visibility was good. However, they still kept their eyes on the radar and scanned the horizon for shipping.

"So, whose side is she on, do you think?" asked Martin.

"Difficult to be certain at the moment, but she's not on Sondheim's side that's for sure. I'll talk to 'er again when she's 'ad time to recover more."

"We need to know. If she's not with us, it'll be dangerous. I just don't know yet if we can trust her."

"Edouard sounded very worried when 'e talked to me on the phone. 'e said Samborini was dead and that 'e would phone again."

"But he hasn't, Dom."

"Maybe something bad has 'appened. Shall I call him back?"

"OK. Tell him about the Edelweiss and that we have Natalie on board."

The number rang several times with no answer and Dominique waited impatiently for Ed to speak. Then a voice came over the air – it was not Ed's and she almost dropped the phone.

"Who is this? It is not you, Edouard?"

"No, it isn't your Edwaah. It's your uncle Paul. You remember me?"

"You bastard – what do you want? And why have you got Edouard's phone? What have you done to 'im?"

"Great accent I remember when you're worked up."

His tone changed.

"Now listen up, and listen good. Your Edwaah died a nasty death – no, it wasn't me, but I was there. He and Everidge blurted everything out in the end, but it didn't save them. The Italians still finished them off. Not a pretty sight. I wouldn't be alive myself if they didn't need me.

He fell silent for a moment.

"They want the real helmet and you've got it."

He heard her gasp and laughed.

"Oh! Come on, you're kidding me. Don't tell me you don't know which one you've got – again! You sure as hell are suckers."

Dominique was so shocked at the news about Charles and Ed that she didn't bother to correct him

"But this time your luck is in," he went on. "Because you can give the helmet to me, seeing as there's no one else to give it to except the tombaroli guys and they would slit your throat to get it if they could."

Dominique gripped the side of the cockpit and sat down heavily. For a moment she couldn't speak for the nausea rising in her throat. Martin looked across and mouthed a 'what's up?' but she shook her head.

"Why should we give it you, when we can take it straight to our collector?" she said, regaining some of her composure.

"Because you'll never get that far. If you work with me, I'll take the thing off you and you'll be clear of the whole business," he replied.

" 'ow much will you pay?"

"That's better. Sense at last. Tell me where you are and we'll work out a deal."

"No, you tell me a price first. I'll be in touch," she replied, ending the call.

Dominique shut the phone and recounted the details to Martin. He remained silent for a while as he thought about what had happened to Charles and Ed. He knew now they were in real danger from the tombaroli. Ed must have known he and Charles were targets when he rung and diverted them to Malta for their own safety.

"Trouble is, Dom, I don't trust Sondheim as far as I can spit. Once we hand over the helmet, what's to stop him telling the tombaroli where we are? We're only safe while we have the helmet – it's our insurance now – and while neither he nor the tombaroli know where we are."

"The Italians have eyes everywhere. It won't take them long to find us," Dominique said, shivering.

"I know – somehow we'll have to convince them we haven't got the helmet any more."

The rest of the night passed slowly. They took it in turns to be on watch, but neither slept well during their down time and the arrival of dawn was a relief to both of them. Natalie had slept through and not made a sound.

At first light they sat in the cockpit cradling mugs of hot chocolate in their hands, still trying to think out what to do about Sondheim and his offer. Without Charles and Ed they felt isolated, unable to contact their collector and uncertain about the best course to take. It was not so much about the helmet now, more about staying alive.

During the night Martin had stared again at the helmet gazing down at him from the shelf. He found himself mesmerised by its non-seeing eyes despite himself and by its power and age. Unable to stand it any longer he got up in the middle of his off-watch time and packed it away. The more he thought of the history behind the helmet the more he thought handing it over for money was wrong. Maybe they could do a deal with the authorities, so it would reach a proper museum for everyone to see.

There was a noise below and Natalie came up from the cabin. She looked more rested and smiled as she sat down beside them.

"I'll get you some 'ot chocolate," Dominique said, getting up to go to the galley.

"It's OK – I can make it myself, you stay there, you've been up all night."

Natalie was about to return to the cabin when her smile faded as she looked out over Martin's shoulder.

"What's that?" she asked, pointing to an approaching boat coming up behind them. Dominique and Martin turned to look where she was pointing.

"Oh, shit! It looks like a customs launch. Not again. How the hell did they know?" Martin said.

"They mustn't find out who I am or what happened to Alain and me," Natalie said. "You won't tell them, will you? Just say you met me in Greece and I hitched a lift to get to France."

"Calm down, Natalie, it's not you they're after, it's us."

The launch from the Maltese Customs drew alongside and instructed them to heave to. One of the officers transferred to the yacht and ordered Martin to alter course to St. Paul's Bay in the north of the island, well away from Valletta.

*

Pierre picked up the phone.

"They're taking them to St. Paul's Bay. We're to meet them there. The Maltese report there are three on board, not two as expected – two women and a man. They've put an officer on board and he has spotted an extra life raft stowed on the deck."

"Sounds like they found the girl in the life raft after the Edelweiss went down. That could be useful. OK, give me a course for St. Paul's Bay. We should be there in a couple of hours if we step on the gas," Antonia said.

"That didn't sound very nautical!" teased Pierre. "Turn left a bit."

"I bet Napoleon didn't have this trouble with his crew. Just give me a proper heading, sailor."

"Napoleon was no sailor, that was Nelson."

He consulted the chart.

"Steer 224° S, Admiral."

*

It was mid-afternoon and the atmosphere on board was tense. In the distance the Qawra Tower appeared at the southern entrance to the bay and the Maltese officer took over the helm to pilot them in. St. Paul's Bay no longer looked like the old fishing port it had once been. Modern blocks, flats and hotels, lined the waterfront and looked down on them as the launch led the Phalaris into the harbour and Martin and Dominique prepared to pick up the mooring assigned to them.

Two senior officers came aboard soon after and began to question them about the life raft and Natalie's presence on board. Unable to deny the silent witness of the life raft, Natalie gave them a full description of what had happened and of Alain's disappearance. Martin confirmed her account and continued by describing her rescue and their search for further wreckage and survivors.

"Why did you not report all this to the Greek authorities and ask for a sea search for the missing man?" asked the Maltese officer.

"I think we can answer that," Pierre said, as he and Antonia came aboard from the dinghy they had used to row over from where they had dropped anchor.

The Maltese saluted the two Interpol officers and reported what they had learned so far.

"Thank you, officers. We can take over now. We are grateful for your help and will send you a full report later," Antonia said.

Realising they had been dismissed, the customs officers merely saluted and left the yacht.

Without a word the five of them went down below and squeezed round the table in the main cabin of the Phalaris.

"Time for cards on the table, I think," Pierre said by way of preamble. "You already know who we are. You have only us left to deal with now, so we must make a plan, not least to protect you."

None of the others spoke. Raising an eyebrow, Pierre looked in turn at Martin, Dominique and Natalie. They remained silent.

"You haven't asked me why you should need to be protected so, tell me, what do you know already?"

"We know Samborini is dead ..."

"How?"

"Ed Robson told us – they saw it in the paper. We also know that Ed and Charles are dead too."

"And how do you know that?" broke in Antonia. "It hasn't been in the papers or on the radio – so how do you know?"

"Sondheim told us on the phone. He was there."

"What! You've spoken to him? How does he know? Did he kill Everidge and Robson?"

"No, he said the tombaroli did it and that he couldn't stop them."

"I bet he couldn't. But how did you know Sondheim was free and how did you get in touch with him?"

"We didn't mean to," Dominique said. "I dialled Edouard's number and Sondheim answered. He had picked up Edouard's phone after he and Charlie had been murdered."

"That could be useful," murmured Pierre, looking at Antonia. "A point of contact."

"You bastards! Is that all you can think about? 'e was a lovely man Edouard, and Charlie too, and now they're dead. All because of that bastard Sondheim."

"You're right, I'm sorry. That's why we must make a plan and why you need us – to protect yourselves – and to avenge their murders," Pierre added.

He looked again at each in turn and saw his last remark had hit home. Martin was thinking fast. A plan was beginning to form in his mind. He knew their best chance now was to work with Interpol.

"We must lure Sondheim into a trap and take him out of the play altogether if we can," Antonia said, reading Martin's thoughts and taking the words out of his mouth.

"Did you tell Sondheim Natalie was on board?" asked Pierre.

"No, there wasn't time and I was too *émue* – how do you say?"

"Shocked, but not so shocked you weren't ready to deal, Dom," Martin said.

"Tell us more," said Antonia.

"Well, we do have the real 'elmet with us this time. Charlie told us they were taking the fake one with them when they left Avlémonas and that we would have the real one. But he lied to us before and I wasn't sure which one we really 'ad. But he was too clever for 'is own good and this time he told us the truth." She looked across at Martin. "Perhaps if they 'ad had the real one, the tombaroli would not 'ave murdered them."

"I'm sure they still would have. So what exactly did Sondheim offer?" asked Antonia.

"'e said 'e would pay us for the 'elmet and that we should meet. 'e said the tombaroli were after us and they would slit our throats if they caught us, even if we handed over the real 'elmet."

She shivered and looked across at Martin. "I am sorry, *chéri*, but I am frightened – I have had enough of this and I want to get rid of the *sacré* 'elmet."

Martin squeezed her hand. There was a pause, as the others remained silent. Antonia broke in.

"I'm sure Sondheim's right about the tombaroli. That's why we need to set up this meeting with him and to arrest him for good this time. He doesn't know Alain is dead and that Natalie is with you. I think we can use that. We can make sure he thinks you're both alive," she said, looking at Natalie.

"Your best chance is to talk to Sondheim as if you and Alain were still following the Phalaris and had not deserted him in Avlémonas. That way he'll think he has support when he fixes a meeting with Martin and Dominique to take the helmet off them. Agreed?"

Natalie took a deep breath and nodded.

"OK. Here's what you do," Pierre said.

Chapter 17

The next morning Martin and Dominique went ashore in St. Paul's Bay to stock up on provisions for the crossing to Corsica. Natalie stayed on board, while they rowed across from the mooring to the town quay. Neither said very much. They had talked well into the night after Pierre and Antonia left and were exhausted when they finally fell into their bunks. The Pericles was still there in the harbour, but there was no sign of movement from the Interpol team.

It had been agreed the meeting with Sondheim would be set up in an old church high in the hills above the port of Calvi on the north coast of Corsica. The plan was for Dominique to keep in contact with Sondheim via Ed's phone and to arrange to meet him there to hand over the helmet in exchange for the cash he was offering. Natalie would stay on board the Phalaris and the Pericles would keep within range as a precaution just in case Sondheim tried to find them and hi-jack them at sea again during the crossing. Martin reckoned the trip to Calvi would take about five days under sail.

Walking into town he and Dominique could reflect properly on the events of the past few days for the first time since they had rescued Natalie. Only now did what had happened to Ed and Charles sink in. The little information Sondheim had given them played on their minds and imaginations.

"I just can't bear to think of what those tombaroli did to them. Sondheim was there, but he did nothing to stop them."

"I guess he couldn't on his own. But then again he had no real reason to. He wanted to know where the real helmet was just as much as the tombaroli did."

"How did he find out where Charlie and Edouard were staying, I wonder?"

"And even odder, how did he make contact with the tombaroli?"

"He must have made a deal with them too – or they would have killed him also, I think."

They finished buying the supplies and walked slowly back to the harbour discussing the chances that the plan hatched with Interpol would work. When they reached the Phalaris, their arms aching from the bags they were carrying, Natalie reported that the Pericles had left its mooring.

It took them the best part of an hour to stow away the supplies safely, to top up the water and diesel tanks and to prepare the boat for sea. By noon they were ready. Dominique took the Phalaris out of the bay accompanied by a customs launch to pilot them through. They suspected however that the Maltese were just making sure they left their jurisdiction. The Maltese Customs had not been pleased by the Interpol intervention and had not appreciated being outranked on their own patch. The pilot launch stayed with them until they were well clear of the St. Paul's Islands, from where with a final dip of its ensign, it headed back to base.

Soon the Phalaris was crossing Mellieha Bay. Dominique used the Madonna Statue on the tip of the headland as a reference point. Next they passed Ahrax Point and the White Tower and, leaving Comino and Gozo well to port, they headed out into the open sea and a stiff breeze. For the rest of the day they were in the lee of Sicily, but knew that once clear and heading north the wind would be fresher. The night passed without incident despite the presence of tankers in the shipping lanes of the Malta Channel heading for Valletta or Piraeus and by mid-morning the next day they had left the Italian island of Pantelleria well to the south of them and were heading north past Cap Granitola, on the tip of Sicily.

Natalie was gradually recovering from the shock and fatigue of the collision and rescue and began to reveal more about how she and Alain had become involved with Sondheim. In the cool of the evenings, as the three of them sat in the warm cabin and the yacht continued under her self-steering gear, she worked out her grief at the loss of Alain by talking about how they met.

"When I left school in Geneva I didn't know what to do with my life. I had spent all my time up until then as a spoilt little rich girl and my parents wanted to marry me off to the son of a business partner. For a while it seemed almost a good idea to me too. He was a nice enough man, but had the same background as me and really was just a rich playboy. All we did was ski and sail and travel. Some people would say it was an ideal life, but I began to get interested in art galleries, while he began to get interested in other girls, so we drifted apart. Finally, I persuaded my parents to let me go to university in Bern and I lost touch with him."

"How did you like being a student?" asked Dominique.

"It was fantastic. I met so many new people from outside my own background and started to think for myself. I read every book there is on art and art history and spent hours in galleries all over Europe. I even spent six months in London and six months in Paris."

She flicked her hair out of her face and lay back on the bunk seat.

"Then I did my final year and passed with a decent degree. A gallery in Nice took me on – a friend of my father's owned it – and I spent two years arranging sales and buying pictures and ancient sculptures for rich clients."

"So you didn't escape your old social circle then?"

"No. Quite the opposite; I found myself being sucked back into it. The art world is a small one and you get nowhere without contacts. But what got to me in the end was the fact that the clients were buying the pictures as investments, only to sell them later at a profit. Most of them weren't interested in the beauty of the pictures or the sculptures, just in the profit. Some of the pictures were even put straight into bank vaults. They never hung them in their houses at all and nobody got to see them."

"But you stuck with the job?"

Martin was lying on the bunk seat on the other side with his head in Dominique's lap.

"Yes. Wouldn't you? It paid well and I could travel all over the world at other people's expense. I did a bit of buying and selling for myself and bought a small house up in the hills behind Nice in a village called La Roquette sur Var. It's a dream up there."

"But where did you meet Alain?" asked Dominique.

"He was working on one of the yachts in the harbour in Monaco owned by one of our clients. He was a breath of fresh air to me. What the English call a rough diamond."

"He was French Canadian wasn't he?"

"Yes. From Quebec. He had had some close brushes with the American authorities. They thought he was drug dealer, but really he smuggled immigrants into the States mostly from Cuba. When things got too difficult he came to Europe and worked as a skipper for rich playboys who had bought their yachts, but didn't know one end of the boat from the other."

"I know the sort," Martin said. "I did a spell of that myself in the Caribbean."

Natalie continued telling them about herself – letting it all out in a rush like water behind a dam which had suddenly burst. It was her way of grieving for Alain and the loss of the dream of a life together. Martin and Dominique were content to listen and to let her words wash over them – it was a kind of therapy for them too. They knew she was coming over to their side and that they could trust her now.

Later, at Martin's prompting, she took a deep breath and plucked up enough courage to phone Sondheim. She followed the plan they had worked out and told him she and Alain had lost the Phalaris at first, but now they were shadowing the yacht again. She said it was heading north, probably heading for France. The electrics on the Edelweiss had packed in and they had not been able to contact him before. He seemed satisfied, but offered no details of what he had been doing or where he was, beyond the fact the Greek authorities had deported him to Italy without charge.

Martin listened intently for any sign that Natalie was still on Sondheim's side, but had fewer doubts now that she had told them so much about herself. He still needed to know how Sondheim had come into the picture however, and how she and Alain had teamed up with him in the first place.

"You did well; so far so good," Martin said, when she closed the phone. "He didn't tell you what he told Dom about the tombaroli or about Charles and Ed then?"

"Not a thing, the bastard. Not even that he was going to make a deal with you two. He just wants us – Alain and I – to keep him informed of where you are. He spoke as if he was choosing his words very carefully. Do you think the tombaroli could have been listening in?"

"That's a thought. Anyway, we'll keep him dangling a bit longer and then Dom can ring him again on Ed's number to finalise the deal and tell him where to meet us."

*

Antonia was sitting in the cabin staring transfixed at the treasure on the table in front of her. The helmet gleamed back afresh from over three thousand years ago as if it wished to reveal its story to her. Despite the damage to one side it was an impressive sight. Antonia examined it with an expert eye – instantly the academic researcher again which she had once been, no longer the police officer. She called through to Pierre to come down to see it.

Pierre entered the cabin and sat beside her. He too was mesmerised by the power the helmet transmitted from an age long gone.

"Is it the real one?" he asked.

"It's a genuine helmet of the period alright. I would have to know a lot more to be able to say if it were likely to be Achilles' helmet – more details of where it was found, what else there was in the tomb and so on – but yes it's genuine. The tombaroli knew their stuff – but it didn't do Everidge and Robson much good. It's a cut-throat world when money is involved – literally it seems.

"It's fortunate for us that they decided to give the real helmet to Handley and Krevine this time. If they hadn't, the tombaroli would have it now."

She turned the helmet round so Pierre could see the damaged side.

"Look at this."

Her finger traced the indent.

"At first I thought this must be later damage, but look how the gold is not cracked and how it covers the splits. The gold was applied after the damage had been caused, not before.'

"Whoever did the gold plating wanted to preserve the damage, not repair it?"

"Exactly. This helmet was used in a fight and then preserved. We must get this to Athens as soon as possible."

"I thought we were going to give it back to the Turks."

Antonia shrugged her shoulders and frowned.

"Why should we? Kahn's already got his promotion without it. Istanbul doesn't know for certain it exists. Anyway, Achilles was a Greek; this is as much a part of our heritage as theirs."

"I'm not sure the Turks would see it quite the same way," he said with a wry smile, "but it's up to you – I'm not going to get involved in this one. We do need to get a replica made as soon as possible though. In fact," he added thoughtfully, "don't we need two if you're sending the original back?"

"That's already in hand. The Maltese police photographer has faxed over a series of photos and measurements to the museum. The replicas will be delivered to Pantelleria tonight by plane. There's a small airport on the island."

"You have moved fast – and I thought you had just gone shopping! I'm impressed!"

"You'll be even more so when I tell you the Italian police found Everidge's cell phone in the hotel and there's a number in Scotland on it – Edinburgh to be precise – which they think belongs to the collector they were working for. The phone will be on the plane from Athens too and we can give it to Handley and Krevine so that they can contact him, or maybe it's a her."

"*Incroyable, mais vrai,* as we say; you're right I am even more impressed. So we stop off on Pantelleria," Pierre said, checking the navigation display. "I only hope they have good restaurants there – even if they are Italian."

Antonia just looked to the heavens.

*

"Tell us again how Sondheim come into the picture? Was he a friend of Alain's?" asked Martin.

The wind had held up all that day and they were not far off the southern tip of Sardinia. They had settled down to a routine on board and Natalie had taken her turn on watch through the nights with one of them. Martin was nearly sure he could trust her, but had one more line of questioning he knew he had to follow to be absolutely certain in his own mind. Although he knew already she hated Sondheim as much as they did.

They were all three in the cabin of the Phalaris, relaxed after the evening meal. Natalie put down her glass and thought back to her first encounter with Paul Sondheim.

"Well, we were in Hyères in a restaurant one evening and suddenly Alain jumped up from the table and ran over calling to a man who was walking past. The man stopped and the two them shook hands like old friends, all smiles. Alain brought him back to our table and introduced him as a friend from his days in Florida. I didn't take to him at first, but he had an amusing way of telling fascinating stories about how he was involved in smuggling all sorts of things and it sounded exciting, romantic even."

Martin leaned over and topped up her glass and then his own and Dominique's.

"He began to talk about artefacts being brought out of Italy and Greece and being sold to private collectors all over the world. This was something I knew about and I was fascinated with what he was telling us. The gallery I worked for had once even been suspected by the police of being involved in such deals in Switzerland. I didn't believe it at the time, but looking back, knowing what I know now, I'm not so sure."

"Go on about Sondheim," Martin said, as she paused.

"Sorry, yes. He told us that contacts in London had heard two London dealers had been asking questions about the possible whereabouts of Achilles' tomb. It sounded all too fantastic, after all a lot people still think the Iliad is just a good story. But apparently they asked the opinions of so many well-known archaeologists that it became common knowledge that someone must have commissioned a contract to find the helmet Achilles wore at the siege of Troy. Someone who was convinced the story was true."

"Charles told us it's almost certain there's some basis of historical evidence for the siege," Martin said. "Apparently, a German archaeologist called Schliemann carried out some digs on the site which showed a city existed there at the right time and that it was an important and strategic trading power."

Natalie nodded in agreement and continued:

"Paul said he knew of a French collector who would pay well to have the helmet for himself, so he kept watch on Charles and Ed in London."

She took another sip of wine and lay back again, remembering the details of the conversation.

"Eventually, Paul said he'd followed them to Italy where they had recruited a team of Italian tomb robbers. When he realised the tombaroli were going to Turkey, that was enough confirmation for him."

"He made a deal with the French collector and formed a plan to follow Charles and Edward and to steal the helmet off them if they found it."

"And that's where you came in?" Dominique said.

"Yes, we were to smuggle the helmet away by sea – just like you. Doing it by plane is too difficult these days with all the security, as you know."

"So, you agreed, and the rest we know!" Martin said.

"Yes – it sounded like an adventure and not too dangerous or even much outside the law. It's so difficult to prove that goods have been stolen or exported illegally, we thought the most we risked was that the helmet would be confiscated. But then later when it all became violent, it was too late to back out."

She looked at them both.

"I really am so sorry about the attack on you at sea. When Paul pulled that knife on you Dominique, I was very scared. Luckily, Alain calmed him down. It was at that point we both realised it was no longer a game and the stakes were too high."

Neither Martin nor Dominique responded to her apology, so she hesitatingly continued.

"Then when Paul became so angry at being fooled by the Interpol team who towed us in to Kapsáli after the fire, he threatened to blow up their boat. We thought we'd persuaded him not to be so stupid, but when he set off early in the morning like that with the explosives we realised there was no stopping him. He had simply lost all sense of judgement and was putting us all in danger. So we seized the chance and left the harbour as you know."

Silence fell between them as they pictured what might have happened if he had been successful.

"Our story with Charles and Ed is much the same, without the violence of course," Martin said. "Now that's all changed too – we want the bastards who killed Charles and Ed to be caught."

"And that includes Sondheim," Dominique said, on the verge of tears as she pictured the attack again. Natalie put her hand on Dominique's.

"You must believe me when I say I am on your side. I've lost Alain too – I wish we had never got into this."

"OK, we do this together then. But no tricks!" Martin said, looking her in the eye. Natalie held his look and replied:

"You needn't worry, Martin – I want the bastard as much as you do."

*

They were soon approaching Pantelleria Island. The black volcanic Montagna Grande looked down on them in the diminishing light of the evening and wisps of cloud around the summit reflected the dying sun in ever-deepening orangey pink streaks across the skyline. They could see the dark lines of the terraces covering the slopes of the mountain. Here and there Moorish-looking houses dotted the landscape. They tied up at the quayside and were met by the local police who took them off to the little airport and out onto the tarmac of the runway. There was an anxious wait for almost an hour, but finally they heard the engines as the small plane from Greece approached, landed and taxied over to them.

Antonia got out of the car and walked across to the plane which stood with its engines still running. Antonia carefully passed a large package to the pilot and received two parcels in return. The plane took off again immediately and she stood watching until it was just a tiny dot in the sunset sky. Silently she walked back to the police car.

She and Pierre ate that evening down by the harbour and set off again around midnight to make up the distance between themselves and the Phalaris. The rendezvous was to be in the shelter of the Golfo di Orosei off the coast of Sardinia.

Later the next day the two boats sighted one another three miles out from the tiny harbour of Cala Gonone. Antonia went aboard the Phalaris with one of the new replica helmets and Everidge's mobile phone. Martin was to use it to contact their Scottish collector in Edinburgh and to inform him of what had happened to Charles and Ed, now that the blackout in the Italian papers reporting their murder had been lifted.

The plan was for Natalie to report to Sondheim that she and Alain were still tracking the Phalaris.

After a suitable gap Dominique would phone Sondheim using Ed's mobile as before to negotiate a pay-off and to arrange the meeting on Corsica in two days time to make the exchange.

Once Pierre and Antonia were sure everyone was clear about their roles, the Phalaris returned to the open sea and Pierre and Antonia headed into the little harbour of Cala Gonone. They had decided to spend the night there and then to move as fast as possible up to Calvi.

To avoid being spotted by Sondheim or the tombaroli, they would pass through the difficult Strait of Bonifacio and approach Calvi from the south round the west side of the island. The Phalaris would continue up the east coast, past Elba and then round Cap Corse to approach Calvi from the north. Pierre and Antonia would have about twenty-four hours before the Phalaris arrived in which to set the trap.

Chapter 18

Two days later the Phalaris entered the thriving harbour and coastal resort of Calvi. Martin headed straight for the marina and tied up at a quay reserved for visiting yachts. Although it was early in the season, the main beach in the sweep of the bay was well populated by tourists, the sea dotted with swimmers, and the beach mottled with the multicoloured parasols of the sunbathers. The fierce heat of the day had kept the wiser locals in the shade of the cafés and bars.

All three of them felt nervous at what lay ahead and were conscious their arrival was being observed from the shore by many unseen eyes. Some of those eyes were there to protect them, but others would be hostile and calculating. Natalie kept well out of sight in the cabin, in case Sondheim himself was already watching them. He would surely be there somewhere.

Sounds of jazz from one of the many festivals which the town hosted each year came across to them on the breeze as Martin and Dominique stood on the deck surveying the scene. The cafés and restaurants of the *quai Landry* were full of the bustle of tourists. Pairs of smartly dressed légionnaires from the base, with their distinctive white képis, strutted their stuff along the wide waterfront, pretending not to notice the admiring glances of the visitors.

Martin and Dominique left the Phalaris and chose a restaurant on the front from where they could easily keep an eye on it. That afternoon would be a busy one and they wanted no hitches to their carefully prepared plan. They ate mechanically, hardly tasting their food, their minds elsewhere. After the meal Martin went to collect the car they had arranged to hire and Dominique went back on board.

When he returned and parked the car near the yacht, Martin had to push his way through a crowd of local men who were leaning on the railings idly watching Dominique as she sun-bathed on the deck, well aware of her audience. When Martin went aboard, Dominique followed him down below to the vocal disappointment of the observers on the quay.

"We thought with those silly men eyeing me, no one would ambush us," Dominique said, laughing.

"I think you enjoyed the attention! OK, back to reality. The plan is that we take the car to the Chapelle de Notre-Dame-de-la-Serra, here to the south."

He pointed to the map laid out on the cabin table.

"Sondheim will meet us inside and we will do the swap."

"How can we be sure 'e'll bring the money?"

"We can't, but there will be plenty of tourists there so he won't want to attract any unnecessary attention. There would be no point in him trying to double-cross us now he is about to get what he's convinced is the real helmet. For him it'll be cheap at the price, compared with what he hopes to get from his collector. Relatively we're not asking for much."

"Let's hope this new replica Antoniarchis had made is good enough for him this time to think he has the real thing. He was fast enough to spot the fake last time."

"That was just a shop replica, this one is made by specialists and he won't unwrap it in the chapel with all the people about."

"When we boarded your yacht in Crete," Natalie said, "he was all fired up and very suspicious. We just didn't know whether you had the real thing or whether you were just a decoy to distract us. Anyway, this time he'll see what he wants to see."

"I really hope you're right, Natalie," replied Dominique.

Later that evening Martin and Dominique left the yacht and carrying the package over to the car in a beach bag. They turned out the lights and locked the cabin door as they went. Natalie stayed inside, only a little reassured by the gun which Martin had produced and showed her how to use. He had carried arms when he worked in the Caribbean and had kept it since those days in case he ever went back.

The road up to the chapel wound its way through the maquis and some newly planted olive groves. The view in the evening light across the perfect curve of the Golfe de Calvi was spectacular and there were plenty of visitors there to enjoy it. Many had done it the hard way, taking the rugged path on foot up from the town, but there were several cars parked by the chapel too.

They entered and approached the altar. After a moment standing before it, they sat down in a pew and knelt as if to pray. There were several tourists inside walking up and down the aisles, admiring the statues and the roof of the nave. Some were resting in the pews enjoying the cool of the inside of the building. Most of the tourists were dressed in the usual bright colours of holidaymakers, which contrasted with the darker clothes of the local people who lived and worked on the land and with the old women dressed in black, observing the Catholic custom of wearing a lace shawl to cover their heads.

A priest, himself in a long black cassock, approached them in the front pew and signalled to Martin to go into one of the confessionals. The priest followed him and entered the other half. Through the grill, a voice whispered:

"Open it and show me. No tricks this time."

Martin carefully unwrapped the helmet and held it up to the grill, turning it this way and that to show the damaged side and to make the gold shine in the feeble light of the booth.

"OK, wrap it up again and leave it on the seat."

"Not before I see your side of the bargain."

The priest held up a bundle of notes.

"Split it up and pass the notes under the grill."

The priest didn't move.

"If you don't, Sondheim, I'll walk out with the package."

"You're learning, at last. OK. Stay cool."

Martin spread the notes about his pockets as Paul passed them through the confessional grill and left the booth to rejoin Dominique who was still kneeling in the front pew. Martin took up the same position beside her.

"Your prayers are answered. Get ready to drop flat on the floor."

At that moment the doors of the chapel opened and a squad of gendarmes burst in. The tourists screamed and took cover wherever they could. The Italian tombaroli, who had been mingling with the local people inside the chapel, drew guns and crouched low behind the pews. Realising they had fallen into a trap several of them tried to take tourists as hostages, but backed down when they saw they were out-gunned and out-numbered.

Within minutes the Italians had been disarmed, handcuffed and bundled out of the chapel. The police vans outside drove off, sirens wailing, with an escort of motorcycle outriders. The tourists began to pick themselves up and to comfort their frightened, crying children. Martin and Dominique dusted themselves off and made their way up the aisle to the main door. Out of the corner of his eye Martin saw the curtain of the confessional move and Paul, still dressed as a priest, walk calmly, but quickly, towards the side door carrying the package, just as Pierre and Antonia entered the chapel.

"Quick, Sondheim's getting away," shouted Martin. They sprinted towards the side door, only to see it slam and to hear the sound of a key turning in the lock. By the time they had turned round, pushed their way back through the tourists to reach the outside of the chapel, a car was accelerating away down the track in a cloud of dust.

Pierre did not seem particularly perturbed at Sondheim's escape and made no move to pursue him. Antonia had taken no part in the chase, staying to comfort the tourists and the children.

"You never intended him to be caught here did you? That was all part of your plan too, I suppose," Martin said.

Pierre said nothing.

"You bastard! We trusted you. Now we're the targets again. Sondheim'll be after us as soon as he realises he's been fooled."

Hearing his raised voice, Antonia approached, took Martin's arm and said:

"Heh! Cool down! The replica's made by experts and he doesn't know enough to be able to tell whether it's genuine or not. Anyway, from what you said he was already convinced you had the real thing, so he won't doubt he has the genuine helmet and will just think he was clever enough to escape the trap we set."

"He knows Everidge and Robson are dead and the helmet they had with them was a replica, so where else could the real helmet be but with you two? Your replica was just a museum shop reproduction, though a good one. This time the replica is professionally made," continued Pierre. "We want him to take it to London, so we can follow and trace the French collector who's paying him."

"I hope you're right. 'e is not a fool and I am afraid of 'im," Dominique said, who had joined them outside the chapel.

"And how exactly do you propose to track him? You've lost him once already," asked Martin, still angry.

Pierre reached into his jacket and brought out a small GPS monitor. The screen showed a map and a moving red dot. He held it up.

"There is a chip inside the helmet."

"My god! I'm glad we're on the same side now. How did those Italian tombaroli get here, by the way? We didn't spot them when we came in. I suppose you arranged that too?"

"Someone tipped them off that Sondheim was up to something, so they followed him," Pierre said, his expression betraying nothing.

"As simple as that! OK, but what about Natalie now?" Martin asked.

"As we agreed, I think it would be better if she continued on with you and stayed down in the south once you have reached the French mainland. We want you two to continue on to England with the real helmet and to make contact with the collector Everidge and Robson were working for."

"I suppose that's now bugged too?"

Pierre merely smiled as Antonia handed over the package.

"That's why we needed to borrow it for a while. You're in no danger, since we shall know exactly where Sondheim is all the time," Antonia said.

"And where we are too," Dominique said.

"But of course," Antonia said. "For your own protection."

*

When Martin and Dominique arrived back at the Phalaris Natalie was asleep in the cabin.

"I'm sorry. I couldn't keep awake any longer; it was so dark and peaceful. So tell me what happened – did they catch Paul? Did you get the money?"

Dominique recounted what had taken place in the chapel and how they had been out-manoeuvred by the Interpol officers.

"But we did get the money, so perhaps it's not as bad as all that," Martin said, placing the package with the helmet on the table. "Come to think of it neither Rousseau nor Antoniarchis asked for it back. Perhaps it's our reward for helping them."

"That's all very well, but Sondheim is still out there and will be after Alain and me, thinking we're still together."

"I doubt it, Natalie," Dominique said. "He thinks 'e has got what 'e wanted and will 'ave realised the *flics* don't really want to arrest him. They can charge the tombaroli with murder without mentioning him. I think 'e will do what Rousseau said and run straight at London."

"To. He'll feel safer there, away from any other tombaroli who might be on the loose, and it's his best chance of getting some money out of this," Martin said.

"Are you sure he won't suspect the helmet he has with him is a fake?" Natalie asked, still unsure.

"Antoniarchis didn't think so. She said the replica is very good and would fool all but an expert. He'll take it to London and bargain for the best price he can get from his French collector. They will be tracking him all the way."

"So what now?" Natalie asked.

"We'll sail to the mainland tonight and drop you off. Then we go on to England via the Canal du Midi. We'll contact Charles' and Ed's collector, confirming we have the real thing and he can ignore anything else that has suddenly reached the market."

"You think 'e'll believe us?" Dominique said.

"Now you have told him about what happened to Charles and Ed, he'll know we mean what we say. I'm sure it'll work."

Despite what they had said aloud to each other, all three had nagging doubts about exactly what Sondheim or any remaining tombaroli might do next and decided to leave immediately for mainland France, feeling safer at sea than in the harbour. They set about preparing to cast off and were soon moving out of the bay. They rounded the headland and quickly passed the lighthouse on the Punta de la Revellata.

Martin set the course at 290° for Hyères, checked the navigation lights and engaged the self-steering. They had about thirteen hours of sailing time ahead of them and would need to keep a sharp lookout during the crossing, particularly near the end. He hoped to reach the islands off Hyères just after dawn and the harbour by nine or so.

That night, as they took turns on watch, Martin and Dominique continued to listen to Natalie, who revealed more about herself and her relationship with Alain. With the stars and the moon to light their way, the Phalaris flew across the twinkling carpet of the sea and the memory of what lay behind them faded. They even began to feel they had over-imagined the dangers which lay ahead. When they finally tied up in the harbour at Hyères and it was time for Natalie to leave, there was sadness on both sides at the thought of parting and of losing the camaraderie of those who had shared dangerous moments and come through.

Natalie was planning to return to her house in La Roquette and Martin and Dominique planned to leave for the

Canal du Midi immediately after they had restocked their
supplies.

*

After two days waiting and watching in the harbour in Calvi,
Pierre and Antonia were aware their private world on board the
motor yacht was about to be abruptly broken into and normal
life would be resuming. They had spent so many hours together
on the Turkish hills and on the chase around the Mediterranean
that the world beyond had seemed far away despite the
electronic contact they had regularly made with their offices
throughout.

Even the assistance of local officers on Kýthira, Malta
and Corsica had seemed like just temporary intrusions into their
privacy at times, a necessary part of maintaining the dramatic
backdrop of their adventure.

The mere thought that very soon they would both be
thrust back into the normal bleak environment of offices and
paperwork, of superiors questioning, supervising and interfering
after so much independence, induced a feeling of lethargy and
resentment in both of them. They wanted to cling on to the
almost fictional world they had inhabited for so many weeks.
The intensity of the professional and personal relationship
which had grown up between them had become the real world
and life beyond, an alien land. With very little time to adjust,
they would soon be subject again to the rules of others.

It was clear from the microchip in the helmet that
Sondheim had already left Paris and was heading for London.
First he had made a detour to a small village behind Nice,
apparently just to pick up a car, but somehow he had become
involved in a hit and run incident. Then he had moved quickly
north, changing cars every few hours. In Lyon, he had taken the

TGV to Paris. The French police had kept Pierre and Antonia well informed about his movements and their last message showed he had boarded the Euro star for London. It was the final confirmation they needed.

The next day they would have to catch a plane to London themselves. Colleagues from Scotland Yard would already be tracking Sondheim and their reports would soon be arriving by email.

On their way back to the boat after their final meal together on shore, Antonia asked:

"You know that report about Sondheim stopping off at a small village apparently to pick up a car and being involved in a hit and run?"

"*Oui.*"

"Well, the name seems familiar – La Roquette."

"Could be."

Pierre's mind was elsewhere.

"Are you sure we were right to still send Handley and Marceau on to England with what amounts to a decoy? It seems a bit risky to me with Sondheim still on the loose. What if he does see through the replica he has?"

"Don't worry, thanks to the bugs in both we'll know where they are all the way. Sondheim is already in London and no longer a threat to them. He just wants to get his money quickly from his own collector. He's too greedy to suspect anything."

"Let's hope you're right."

Pierre put his arm round Antonia's shoulders and they continued along the waterfront enjoying the warm breeze off the sea.

That night they lay together in the snug forward cabin quietly at first, each of them privately wondering whether their relationship would survive the shock of the abrupt change of environment. Was this just a sudden romance, a short fling? Both reflected on when they had first met at the briefing in Athens before they left for Turkey.

All Antonia had seen then was a pleasant youngish looking French Commissaire, still in uniform despite the heat, somewhat hot, bothered and disorientated. She remembered that at lunch in the headquarters, he had been full of suspicion over whether the food and the wine in Greece would match up to what he was used to in France. He had a greeted her in a friendly enough way, but with that slight northern reserve.

She had found herself observing him uneasily, wondering how well they would be able to work together. She knew that if the assignment lasted as long as she thought it might, they would be thrown together for long periods. Did he have a partner back in France? A family perhaps? How would she react to him, after having so recently ended a relationship herself, one she had not yet completely got over?

For his part Pierre had seen an attractive dark haired Greek woman who didn't seem to fit the usual image of the police officer. Well tanned and fit looking, she had made him feel older than he was. She had not been wearing uniform and Pierre had been uncertain how to read her status and how to react to her relaxed charm and informality.

Later, he realised the fact she had had a career as a university academic before joining the police meant she would never be as institutionalised as those who spend their whole working lives in the service. This made her stand apart from her colleagues and her behaviour more difficult to anticipate. It gave her a maverick quality that attracted and intrigued him, but the strength of the mutual attraction that had drawn them together had caught him by surprise.

Antonia too had been uncertain whether she was ready for a new relationship. The pain of the last one had been with her still. They maintained a professional relationship for several weeks out on the hills above Troy, but in the end perhaps it was the sense of humour they shared that had broken the barriers and eased the path for both of them.

Pierre looked across at Antonia and reached up to turn out the light above the bunk. He started to say something, but Antonia put her fingers to his lips and whispered:

"Not now. I know. Let's just see what happens."

He took her face between his hands and kissed her as he felt her whole body press against him and her hand in the hollow of his back pulling him even closer towards her.

*

Natalie had hired a car and set off for her home, which until recently she had shared with Alain, in the little hilltop village of La Roquette-sur-Var behind Nice. Despite some regrets, she felt relieved at leaving Martin and Dominique since she needed time to herself to work out where her life was going without Alain. Could she settle back to her previous routine as a dealer, she wondered. Her old firm would certainly take her back after her extended leave and her life could resume where it had left off. But was that what she really wanted? Despite the loss of Alain, the dangers and excitement of the recent events had sharpened her appetite for adventure. Then she remembered that Sondheim had escaped the trap in Calvi and looked in the rear mirror to check the road behind.

Leaving the A57 and joining the A8 motorway occupied her thoughts for a while, but when she looked in the rear mirror again she thought she recognised a car she had seen earlier, about three vehicles behind. An hour later she turned off into a service area for a break and a coffee. The car behind did not follow her and she breathed more easily as she locked the doors and went into the restaurant.

When she returned to the car the Mistral had sprung up and the gusts were gathering strength. She would be glad to get back to the shelter and safety of her home, knowing the wind could last for days. Another hour and she turned off the motorway and headed north for the short stretch up the N202.

In the wing mirror she glimpsed a car like the one that had been behind her on the motorway. Impossible, she thought to herself; I'm just edgy and tired. There are hundreds of cars that colour. A few moments later it overtook her on the dual carriageway stretch and disappeared at speed into the distance. Her grip on the wheel relaxed, but the Mistral was making driving difficult and the trees were bowing before its strength, leaves and twigs breaking off and swirling across the road. Her car was being buffeted by the gusts and she had to concentrate hard as the sky darkened and cars turned their lights on.

What normally delighted her when driving back up the steep hill to La Roquette was seeing the tiny centuries-old village perched high up at the end of the narrow single-track road which entwined the rocky hillside. But that evening the village was silhouetted against a dark and threatening sky, a far cry from the endless blue skies of Greece to which she had become so accustomed.

Once, the Italian border had extended this far and La Roquette had been one of a string of fortified villages marking the frontier between the two countries. Now most of the houses belonged to rich incomers. She had been lucky to find her house through contacts of her father's. It was right on the edge of the rocky summit and the previous owners had even managed to fit a swimming pool into the small garden. The pool hung half over the edge of the cliff supported by pillars fixed into the rock. At night when the underwater pool lights brought out the blue of the water and patio lights were a soft glow under the stars, the effect was magic.

Below and beyond, the view extended right down to the lights of Cannes winking in the distance. On the warm evenings of summer she and Alain used to spend most of the night outside, sometimes falling asleep under the stars and only waking when the cool of the early morning sent them indoors to the warm comfort of their bed.

Natalie drove into the tiny square. She parked the hire car opposite her house. The wind was so strong she had to struggle to make her way across to reach her front door through the swirl of flying leaves. She was about to turn on the light in the hallway when her heart missed a beat. There were voices coming from inside. A familiar voice called out:

"Come on in, Natalie, you've got some explaining to do."

"And hello to you too, Paul," she said, forcing herself to remain calm, and entering the living room. Then she launched herself across the room to where Alain was rising from his chair. He winced as she threw her arms round him crying out his name.

"Alain! How is it possible … ?"

"So this is the same Natalie who said she and Alain were still in the Edelweiss shadowing the Brit and the French girl, but who had actually sold out to the police! Well, your little scheme has fallen apart now and you're going to pay for it."

"Paul, I didn't have any choice," she replied, realising he didn't know who exactly had rescued her and not correcting his misunderstanding.

"When the police found me in the life-raft, I was half dead. I thought Alain had drowned. What else could I do, but cooperate? I thought you had been arrested in Avlémonas and it was all over."

She clung even tighter to Alain and looked up at him.

"But Alain, what happened, how . . . ?"

"I managed to cling on to the life-jacket when I was sucked under and that saved my life. When I hit the surface again I was only half-conscious, but the automatic bleeper must have started up. Luckily it wasn't damaged by the hull of the ship. I was picked up by another cargo vessel about an hour later and taken on to Piraeus. I was unconscious most of the time, so I didn't know if they searched for you."

Paul got up and poured himself a cognac while Alain continued. He stood watching them.

"I was kept in hospital for three days, drifting in and out of a coma and badly bruised, but otherwise lucky to be alive. Nobody knew who I was of course. When I was finally able to leave I didn't know what to do so I came back here. I thought you were dead. There was no news of anyone else being picked up. Then Paul turned up and told me what had happened in Calvi and that you were still alive, but were working with the police."

"Did he also tell you he was there when Everidge and Robson were tortured and murdered?" asked Natalie, clinging to him.

"OK, that's enough you two! I'm out of here. I've got the real helmet this time, thanks to your botched scheme in Calvi and that's what it's all been about."

"What about us? You owe us our money, you bastard. You can't just walk out."

Natalie threw herself at him beating his chest and clawing at his face. Paul seized her hands and threw her backwards onto the floor.

"Sure I can. You shat on me when you ran out on me in Avlémonas and now I'm shitting on you. No way I'm giving you money – I've lost too much already as it is, thanks to you. Ask Handley and Marceau for the money I gave them."

Picking up a bag off the floor beside his chair, he walked out of the room and down the corridor. The front door was still open and banging against the wall in the wind. He grabbed the keys of Natalie's hire car from the side table and fought his way across the square to the where she had parked it, shielding his face against the flying debris.

Alain followed him out and ran over to cut him off. As he stood in front of the car to block its way, Paul drove straight at him and he was thrown over the bonnet as the car struck. The tail lights of the car glowed red as it careered round the corner and Natalie rushed screaming across the square. Alain was lying sprawled on the ground, his head at an angle.

When she reached him, blood was already trickling from the corner of his mouth. She cradled him in her arms, rocking back and forth, her hair a wild flag in the wind covering both their faces and soaked in his blood. Lights came on all around, and dark faces were silhouetted in the doors and windows as her wail of pain echoed round the square.

Chapter 19

Paul Sondheim stepped off the Eurostar in St Pancras Station and headed for the taxi rank. Standing in the slow moving queue, he thought back over his journey north from La Roquette, which, strangely, had passed without incident. He had abandoned Natalie's hire car a few kilometres up the road and stolen a series of different cars every couple of hours or so. He knew he had been lucky not to be stopped at a road block after the incident with Alain. Damned fool, he said to himself. Why did he have to do that? If he'd just stayed in the house instead of rushing out to be a hero, he could have been reunited with Natalie and be none the worse for his experience. But no, he just had to interfere and get himself killed.

When he had finally reached Lyon by car, he had taken the TGV to Paris. The security at the Gare du Nord before he boarded the Eurostar had given him some anxious moments, but of course when he said the helmet was just a present for a friend, a museum shop replica they had believed him. What else could it have been, after all? Finally in London, he felt badly in need of a shower and some rest before going to meet the collector. He would need his wits about him if he were to finish the job and to collect his money from that old fool.

A taxi drew alongside.

"Rubens Hotel," he said as opened the back door and slipped inside carrying the package.

He sat back on the bench seat and let the motion of the taxi lull him almost to sleep. He glanced out of the window from time to time and took in the crowded streets and grubby buildings of the capital. The drizzle had settled in for the evening and the streets were glistening in the lights, streaks of neon colours making patterns on the roadway. He learned forward and tapped the window behind the driver:

"Stop near to a Marks & Spencer will you and wait for me?"

"Right you are, governor," the driver said, doing a sharp U-turn, which threw Sondheim back into his seat. The taxi drew up as near to the shop as it could and Sondheim rushed out through the rain, nearly forgetting to take the package with him. He returned fifteen minutes later with a bag full of clothes and the driver took him on to the hotel.

He must have dozed off, since the driver's tap on the window woke him with a start. He checked in at the reception desk under his real name, showing the new passport he had been given in Greece. Once in his room he ran a hot bath and fell asleep in the warmth and steam of the tub. The tepid water woke him an hour later and he took a shower to warm himself up again. Back in the bedroom he called room service and ordered a meal. He changed into the clothes he had bought and, using his mobile this time, tapped in a number and listened quietly to the accented voice at the other end giving him instructions. He closed the phone and heard the knock on the door of his room.

"Room service!"

Keeping his hand on the knife in his jacket pocket, he opened the door and the waiter wheeled in a trolley with his order.

"Good evening, Sir. Shall I put it on the table for you?"

The waiter glanced round the room as he picked up the bottle on the trolley and began to pull the cork.

"No, leave that, I'll do it."

The waiter put the bottle down and went across to draw the curtains.

"Leave those too – that's all, thank you."

Sondheim picked a five-pound note up off the bedside table.

"Thank you very much, Sir. Good night. Enjoy your meal."

Sondheim closed the door behind him, checked the lock and, breathing more calmly, sat down to finish opening the wine. He switched on the television and tuned in to BBC World News, watching the images flash by, hardly taking in the commentary. His attention was caught for a moment by an item about a recent break-in to a museum in Amsterdam and the loss of a painting, apparently stolen to order. And so it goes on, he thought to himself.

The meal gave him fresh energy and when he left the hotel an hour later, a bag over his shoulder, he felt a surge of adrenalin and a lightness in his step. It's nearly over he said to himself. This is the last leg. The taxi took him to an address in Notting Hill and stopped outside an imposing Victorian terrace house. He climbed white painted steps to the front door, which opened as he raised his arm to knock.

Sondheim stepped inside the hallway and his eyes widened. Nothing on the outside of the house had prepared him for the sumptuousness of the inside. The English butler took his coat and led him to a study.

"Please wait here, Sir. Monsieur le comte is expecting you."

Sondheim glanced around him and took in the high ceiling and the old world furnishings of the study. The presence of a top of the range laptop computer indicated that it served as an office and the owner was not behind in his use of modern technology, despite the surroundings. Nothing he could see would give anyone the impression the man was a collector of expensive works of art however.

A few moments later, the door was thrown open and Le Comte Alexandre de Villeneuve, all smiles, came in to greet him. He was in his sixties, fit looking, greying only slightly and every inch the French aristocrat.

"Mr Sondheim! It is good to see you returned. You've done well. I see you have the package with you. Then you have done very well indeed."

Behind him a short dapper figure followed, wearing half glasses and carrying a small case. Without a word he went to the desk, placed the case carefully on it and released the two catches so that the lid sprang open. He turned expectantly towards Sondheim and his host.

"This gentleman is Dr. Braithwaite. He is a specialist in Greek and Roman arms. Be so kind as to give him the helmet, Mr Sondheim."

"Just call me Paul," the South African replied, handing over the package as requested, who took it from him without a word.

"No wait! This won't do at all," de Villeneuve said. "Let's go down to the gallery. It would be a much more appropriate atmosphere in which to see such a wonderful object."

Picking up the package himself he led the other two men out of the study and crossed the hall to a door at the far end. He took out a bunch of keys and turned the lock. The door opened to reveal a staircase leading down to the Victorian basement.

He led them down to another door at the bottom of the stairs and turned to a security keypad set into the wall to tap in a code.

"You can't be too careful these days, there are so many thieves about!" he said, with a smile.

Sondheim noted that this door was reinforced. The Count took out another key and the door opened to the hiss of hydraulic hinges. They stepped inside and de Villeneuve opened a lighting panel. As he switched on the lights, one by one paintings, statues and glass display cases were softly illuminated. The treasures revealed took Sondheim's breath away and he stood stock still, taking in the half-familiar objects, recognising styles but not quite being able to place the paintings themselves.

"Some of these have not been seen for years on the open market," de Villeneuve said proudly, noting Sondheim's reaction with pleasure.

"Now, let us open the package and see the helmet. I've waited a long time for this moment and have prepared a special place for it as you can see."

He handed over the package to Dr Braithwaite who carried it over to a table at the side. The Count stood at his shoulder as he began carefully to unwrap the helmet. They both gasped as the gold leaf glinted in the lights when the helmet was released from its protective packaging. Braithwaite placed it gently in the middle of the table and stood back to take it in properly. He looked at de Villeneuve, who nodded. The expert sat at the table, opened his case, took out a magnifying glass and began to examine the helmet in detail.

At that moment the door of the gallery opened and a group of police officers surged in, followed by Pierre and Antonia.

"I'm sorry, Monsieur le comte, but I ... " the butler struggled to say.

"Count Alexander de Villeneuve?" asked one of the men who had entered.

"Indeed, monsieur! But to whom do I have the honour of speaking?"

"Fine Art Squad, Sir. Detective Chief Inspector Williams."

He held up his ID for the count to read.

"Yes, yes, I can see. But what can I do for you, Detective Chief Inspector?"

"Alexander de Villeneuve, I am arresting you on suspicion of being in possession of stolen goods. You do not have to say anything, but anything you do say...."

"Shall I put the cuffs on him, gov?"

"I don't think that'll be necessary, Sergeant."

"*Mais c'est scandaleux.* It is an outrage. Do you have you any idea who I am, Detective Chief Inspector? I am a French diplomat. I have diplomatic immunity."

"Your ambassador has withdrawn your status, sir, and you're wanted by the Police Judiciaire in Paris. We have been authorised to arrest you and to take you into custody. I'd like you to accompany us to the station if you would, sir."

There was a movement at the back of the room as Dr Braithwaite tried to slip behind the officers and get to the stairs. His way was blocked by two smiling Interpol officers, who were standing in the doorway, watching the scene.

"Ah! Dr Braithwaite, I presume," DCI Williams said "We would like you to accompany us too, sir. To help us with our inquiries."

The detective sergeant and a DC began to shepherd de Villeneuve and Dr Braithwaite towards the stairs, whilst the other officers started to explore the gallery in more detail.

DCI Williams looked at Sondheim who was rooted to the spot completely at a loss as to what to do.

"You're free to go, sir," he said.

"You're letting me walk – just like that?"

"Well, as far as we know, sir, you've committed no offence in this country – unless there's something you want to tell me. Importing museum replicas is not against the law here …"

"That bitch! I'll ..."

He fell silent.

" ... and we're prepared to overlook the fact you may have known about Mr Villeneuve's gallery beforehand."

"So, Sondheim, you are just a fool of an amateur after all. You led them straight here like a silly goose," de Villeneuve said, looking back at him. "But I was a fool too, to put my trust in you."

"That's enough of that, sir. Come along now. Let's go quietly."

Pierre and Antonia caught each other's eye, just managing to hide their real feelings, and started to look round the gallery admiring the collection. Sondheim scowled, turned sharply on his heels, looked hard at Pierre and Antonia, and disappeared up the stairway.

"Keep an eye on him," Williams said to a DC, and nodded towards the departing figure. "And don't lose him. We're far from finished with him yet."

*

Back at their hotel in Piccadilly Pierre and Antonia went into the lounge bar and ordered a bottle of wine to celebrate the success of the first part of the sting. They settled into a discreet corner where they could talk without being overheard.

"So, one collector down and one to go. Martin and Dominique are heading for the Canal du Midi, but it will be at least two weeks before they're ready to cross the Channel from Brittany," Pierre said, pouring them out both some wine.

"Sondheim's face was a picture when it dawned on him he had been tricked. He was fuming when he went up the stairs. The most humiliating part for him in a way was not being arrested. They sent him off like a silly little schoolboy."

"The trouble is he's much more dangerous than a schoolboy – he may want revenge," replied Pierre.

"You think we'd better warn Natalie Marceau in case he goes back to France? She's suffered enough already. Losing Alain was tough."

Pierre's mobile sounded and he listened without commenting. He looked at Antonia as he concentrated, keeping her in suspense, but at the same time indicating the call was serious. After a few minutes he closed the phone.

"No, I don't think he'll go back. Remember that hit and run incident mentioned in the report of his movements? Well, it seems he deliberately ran down and killed Alain Tremblay in La Roquette. There will be a warrant out for his arrest and extradition from here too."

"But I thought Tremblay was drowned when their boat was sunk," Antonia said .

"So did Marceau, but apparently he was picked up by another ship and kept in hospital in Piraeus."

"Why were we not informed?"

"He was in a coma for a while and nobody knew who he was," Pierre replied.

"Who told you all this – Handley?"

"No, that was Marceau on the phone. She went back to La Roquette and found Tremblay and Sondheim already there. Sondheim took the helmet and her hire car and when Alain tried to stop him, Sondheim simply ran him over."

"He certainly is a nasty piece of work. Poor girl. She really has suffered – losing him once only to find him again and then to see him die a second time – that's rough."

Antonia paused, imagining what Marceau must have gone through.

"At least, that means Sondheim will stay here in England and wait for Handley and Krevine to bring over their helmet. But we'd better warn the British police to keep a tight track on him. He'll be even more determined now to get hold of it and to sell it on."

"I'll let the DCI know," Pierre said .

"What a day – time for bed."

"Yours or mine?"

Antonia smiled:

"Do you ever stop?"

"We French lovers have a reputation to live up to."

He signalled to the barman and asked him to have the ice bucket with the wine taken up to his room.

"Sorry, sir. I don't think we have anyone at this time of the evening to …"

"It's only eight o'clock! Oh! Never mind. I'll do it myself."

Pierre picked up the bottle, wrapped it in the cloth, gathered up their glasses and they headed for the lift.

"I suppose oysters are out of the question?" he asked the barman as they passed the bar on their way out.

"Oysters, sir?"

"Never mind," he said for the second time with a sigh. "L'Angleterre. Quel pays barbare!"

"You've never needed oysters before," Antonia said, slipping her arm through his.

Chapter 20

The journey through the Canal du Midi, down the Gironde estuary and out into the Atlantic had been uneventful. They had kept in touch with Natalie and were stunned by what she told them about the way Sondheim had run Alain down so cold-bloodedly. Their first reaction when she phoned them in near hysteria had been to leave the Phalaris at Sète before entering the canal and to go to La Roquette. But it would have been too dangerous to leave the boat as they didn't know what Sondheim would do next or where he would go. When they heard later from Natalie what had happened in London, and that Sondheim had not been arrested, they were even more relieved they had decided to keep going.

From La Rochelle on the Atlantic west coast they decided to make the trip round Finisterre in one leg and to head for the little port of Paimpol on the north coast of Brittany. Natalie promised to join them there and to cross over to England with them.

*

The passage round the Île d'Ouessant, off Finisterre, was not easy. The seas were as rough as their reputation, with Atlantic equinoctial depressions sweeping in, bringing long rolling waves, broken up by short chaotic breakers closer in shore. They had taken the outside passage, where, once they rounded the island and entered the English Channel proper, the westerlies favoured them and pushed them along the North Brittany coast at an exhilarating pace. The movement on board travelling in the same direction as the waves was much more comfortable, so they had delighted in the last leg of the journey. Dominique's spirits rose in tune with the feeling of being back in her native part of France and Martin too felt he was returning home.

They passed the busy ferry port of Roscoff, swung out slightly north to avoid the treacherous currents around Trégastel, keeping well clear until they sighted the Phare du Paon – the Peacock Lighthouse – on the Île de Bréhat. The approaches to the old fishing port of Paimpol are treacherous and complicated, but the beauty of the bay and the backdrop, combined with modern navigation aids, helped them thread their way through the strangely sculpted rocks and islets.

They passed the small island in the approaches to the port which is reserved as a bird sanctuary and watched the gannets diving all around them. Flying high, suddenly they would close their wings tight along their bodies and, beaks outstretched, in a flash of yellow, white and black, streak vertically down like crazy fighter pilots, hitting the water at the perfect angle and, with the neat splash of the expert diver, disappear only to emerge a few seconds later with a fish in their beaks. Such were their numbers that the sea boiled below them as they dived and resurfaced in their hundreds. One could only imagine the panic of the shoals of fish darting in every direction beneath the waves in a vain attempt to escape their pursuers.

In the 19th century the port of Paimpol had sent half the French fleet of sailing trawlers out to the Newfoundland and Icelandic fishing grounds and seen them return towards the end of summer, after six months at sea, laden with their catch. Now modern methods of fishing have turned the Atlantic cod banks into a desert, but Martin and Dominique too felt they were returning from their own expedition with a prize cargo on board.

Shedding the bonds of it's historic past, Paimpol has adapted to the new generation of seafarers by building a big new marina for the sailors of the leisure market. Martin and Dominique found a berth in the section for visiting yachts and checked in with the customs. After three days at sea they were ready for a good meal on shore. They would have two or three days to wait before Natalie joined them – time to reflect on the final stage of their journey and to prepare the Phalaris for the crossing to England.

Natalie arrived on their second day and found them on board making repairs. Dominique let herself down from the mast to greet her. As they hugged each other, Dominique said:

"Natalie, *ma chère*. What can I say? We're terribly sorry, it must 'ave been awful."

"It's all over now. Because I'd thought he had died in the shipwreck I'd begun to mourn him already. The surprise when I saw him alive for a few moments was like a dream – completely unreal. But at least I had one final hug and that was a way of saying goodbye too."

For a moment neither of them said anything and Dominique went on:

"We 'ave news of Sondheim in London."

"What happened there? I haven't heard."

Martin joined them from the cabin and, smiling, gave Natalie a hug.

"I thought I heard voices – I was down fixing the engine."

"Well," Dominique continued as the three of them sat in the cockpit, "they were able to track him right to London thanks to the bug in the replica. He checked into a hotel and delivered the 'elmet to his collector, someone called Alexandre de Villeneuve, a French diplomat."

"That old fool!" Natalie said.

"You know 'im?"

"Yes. We used to send him paintings from time to time. He is an old friend of my father's. I always thought he was one of the better ones who bought things because he appreciated them. I would never have suspected him of anything illegal."

"Well, beneath 'is house the police found a whole gallery of missing and stolen works of art," Dominique said .

"He did come over to Bern once a few years ago. More money than sense, but he bought some good paintings – all legal. We packed them up for him and he arranged the shipping himself. Probably to avoid duty at customs."

"Apparently, the police arrested 'im down in the gallery itself, but they let Sondheim go. Antoniarchis said his face was a picture when 'e realised 'e 'ad bought a fake off us and been fooled again."

"The trouble is," Martin said , "he'll be furious at being humiliated and all the more determined to get hold of the real helmet. We aren't free of him yet, by any means."

Seeing the look of fear on Natalie's face, Dominique quickly changed the subject.

"OK, Natalie – let's get you settled in. Is that your bag on the quay?"

Natalie looked at Martin: "First tell me again exactly what happened to Sondheim in London when they arrested de Villeneuve. Why didn't they arrest him? I don't understand. "

"Well, Antoniarchis said he was released because he hadn't committed a crime in England and there was no warrant out for him yet for the hit and run which killed Alain."

He paused and looked at Natalie, but she said nothing.

"They told him importing replicas was not illegal and let him go. They put a tail on him though."

"Yes, but what now? The French police told me there is a European warrant out for him which applies both here and in England – he murdered Alain, the bastard," Natalie said .

"He had a couple of days to cover his tracks before the warrant was issued and the British police lost him. They are still trying to find him, but there's no sign yet."

Martin looked at her carefully. Natalie was on the verge of tears, but he could see the underlying anger in her face. He knew she was holding something back. Getting up, he said:

"Come on. You're tired. Let's get your things into the cabin – same one as before."

He picked up her bag and put his arm round her to steady her.

"Later you can tell us why you really want to do the final leg with us to England."

*

"Still no news of where Sondheim is hiding out, but Handley and Krevine are ready to make the crossing from Paimpol," Pierre said .

"It's time to go to Dartmouth, I think. Have they let their collector know?" asked Antonia.

"Krevine says she's contacted him. He said to continue to Dartmouth as planned, but hasn't said how he'll contact them. He's not giving anything away."

"Has Scotland Yard been able to trace where the call came from?"

"Not yet, he always cuts off quickly and is using a pay-as-you go phone anyway."

The two of them had been allocated a small office in New Scotland Yard and had spent a busy two weeks since the arrival of the European warrant doing their report on the events leading up to the present. Pierre had been to Bari to see for himself where Everidge and Robson had died and to talk to the scenes of crime officers about what they had found. The room was a mess and there was a lot of blood about. Most of it had come from a severed artery in Everidge's leg. He had died quite quickly and would have fallen unconscious within minutes through loss of blood.

Robson had not been so lucky, but had finally died by strangulation. The members of the tombaroli gang who were arrested in Calvi told the carabinieri that Sondheim was present and he had forced Robson to tell him where the real helmet was. He had made a deal with the tombaroli to give them half of whatever he eventually sold the helmet for.

"That might explain why he needed to disappear and has done so very effectively," Pierre said. "He hasn't got the real thing and he's had to give up the replica. Samborini is dead and three tombaroli were arrested in Calvi. That leaves one more on the loose, if our information is correct."

"Perhaps he's the very one who was with Samborini when they did the deal in Yükyeri Iskelesi harbour on the boat," Antonia said .

"He might also be the one who murdered Samborini in San Gimignano. Sondheim will be next on his list."

Antonia had been back to Greece to trace Everidge and Robson's movements from when they left Kýthira and crossed to Bari. It seemed the Italian police had been aware of their arrival in Bari on the ferry and had them followed to the small pensione where later they had been murdered. They had reported the arrival to Interpol, but had no reason to continue to follow them or to post a watch on the hotel.

The owner had been murdered too. Her husband said an Italian and another man had entered the hotel together that evening and asked to borrow the Englishmen's key saying were friends and were going to wait for them to return. He claimed he had not seen either of them, only heard their voices through the curtain to the reception desk.

Antonia was also able to speak by phone to the captain of the vessel that had picked up Tremblay and talk to the doctors who had treated him. There was nothing of any use to learn from them.

Pierre had gone on to Corsica to talk to the *juge d'instruction* who had examined the case against the three tombaroli who had been caught in the trap in the chapel. He had granted their extradition back to Italy on suspicion of complicity in the murder of Everidge and Robson.

"This helmet, Commissaire, has already cost four persons their lives – let's hope there will be no more before this is all finished," the investigating judge had said.

"That depends on what happens in England, Monsieur le juge," Pierre replied. "I think we have not seen the last of Sondheim."

*

The crossing from Paimpol to Dartmouth had passed without incident and the lights on either side of the entrance to the river Dart barely showed against the dark stands of trees on the headlands as the Phalaris approached. The yacht hardly seemed to make headway in the half-light, slowly fighting against the fresh water current coming down the estuary seeking the open sea. Only the sharpening focus of the outlines of the rocks convinced them they were moving forward at all. The old ruined forts observing their progress from either side of the estuary had, ironically, been built in the fourteenth and fifteen centuries to protect the town against raiders from the ports of Brittany.

As the yacht quietly approached land, Dominique and Martin could sense the tension rising in each other. Neither said a word; physically they made themselves smaller as if this would help render them and their boat less visible to unseen watching eyes on shore. Dominique opened the hatch and went down into the cabin, where Natalie was looking at the GPS. The shaded light of the chart table flickered on for a moment and Natalie put her finger on a spot on the chart. Dominique went back up the companion way and spoke softly to Martin at the helm, conscious of the way sound carries so easily across water.

Martin passed the wheel to her and kneeling on the cockpit seat, one hand on the gunwale to steady himself, pressed his night-vision binoculars to his eyes to scan the shore on both sides of the estuary. At first he could only make out the lighter line of breaking waves on the rocks and the small beaches beyond. Then his attention was caught by a dark shadow low on the water, alternately shrinking and growing as it rode the swell.

"Over there," he said, pointing just forward and to the starboard side of the bow. "There's someone approaching."

A small motorboat was setting out from one of the little hidden coves amongst the rocks at the entrance to the estuary.

"It could be nothing. Just someone doing a spot of night fishing."

Dominique bent lower to see under the boom and looked out to where he had indicated. As she searched the darkness, a faint light flashed once, then a second time.

"No, that's the signal," Dominique said. "It's our contact."

Martin shone his torch on the sail with three answering flashes. The small motorboat increased its speed and headed towards the Phalaris. It passed by them slowly quite close, the man at the helm studying the yacht carefully, making no sign of acknowledgement when they waved to him. Then it dropped back a little way behind and began to approach from the stern, closing in on the port side.

"Get ready. He's coming alongside," Martin said.

As it drew closer the man at the helm threw back the hood of his waterproof and called across:

"This time I'll bet you do have the real thing. So hand it over. And I want the money back I paid you for that fake you palmed off on me in Calvi."

"Sondheim, is that you, you bastard?"

"Not friendly, Handley. Don't piss me about or I sure as hell will kill you this time."

"Like you killed Charles and Ed, and Alain?"

"Watch out Martin, he's got a gun. Just give it to him," Dominique said. "It's just not worth it."

"Good advice, pretty lady. So what's it to be Handley – death or glory?"

Silently Martin held up the package with the helmet. Dominique almost cried out with relief and turned away again to concentrate on keeping the yacht on course against the swirl of the current, which was becoming stronger as the river narrowed before the bend opposite Kingswear. At the same moment a squall hit the yacht and she veered away sharply under the sudden stronger pressure of the wind. The motorboat dropped back and started a new approach as Dominique regained control and put the yacht back on course.

Martin was standing behind her facing the stern, observing the motorboat's second approach and wondering how in hell Sondheim could have known where they were.

Sondheim was standing at the helm and not altogether balanced as he manoeuvred the boat closer. Suddenly, from behind Martin a shot rang out and he saw Sondheim stagger back. As Martin turned, there was a second shot, which left his ears ringing. This time Sondheim was spun round by the force of the bullet hitting him and his own gun went off as he fell forward onto the floor of the boat. Almost immediately he was engulfed in flames. His bullet had punctured the on-board petrol tank of the powerful outboards and within seconds the boat was a ball of fire.

The tank exploded and the whole motorboat was lit up. Flames shot twenty feet into the air and the bow of the boat reared up out of the water and then dropped back as the boat slid stern first, as if in slow motion, back beneath the dark waters, the flames choked out as it disappeared. Then it was gone. Bits of the cabin rained down like firework rockets burning up. The waves closed over the spot and a deeper darkness returned to the scene.

The shock wave had hit them almost instantly, the Phalaris heeled hard over and Martin and Dominique were thrown into a heap on the cockpit floor

"What the 'ell is 'appening?" gasped Dominique as she struggled to her feet and wrestled with the wheel to regain control. She reset the course and peered forward urgently into the darkness to check there was no danger ahead and to search for the on-shore navigation lights to keep them in the safety of the marked channel.

Martin picked himself up and looked out to where the motorboat had been a few seconds before, but by the time his eyes, temporarily blinded by the flash, regained their night vision, there was nothing to be seen, the existence of the motorboat now only a memory. He turned to see Natalie sitting on the bench seat shaking uncontrollably. He put his arm round her shoulder and gently prised the gun from her fingers. He wiped it and tossed it overboard. Still holding her tightly he said quietly:

"It's all over now, Natalie. Sondheim's dead. There'll be no trace. You've done what you came to do."

Natalie remained clinging to him and said nothing. The sound of his phone broke into the silence. Shaking himself, Martin put it to his ear.

"I saw that. It was neatly done," a voice said quietly. "You still have the helmet? Good. We will speak later."

The line went dead.

"Bloody hell, our collector's a cool customer. He's right here! He saw the whole thing, Dom," Martin said as he continued to keep his arm firmly round Natalie who was still shaking.

"But how the 'ell did he know it was Sondheim in the motor boat? I'll be glad when this is all over, Martin."

"So will I. I've no idea how he could've known."

Martin's voice betrayed the shock he still felt at the sight of the destruction of the motorboat. He had no reason to feel sorry for Sondheim, but the sheer calm of the caller and the assumption they murdered him, had caught him by surprise and for an instant he was drained of all energy, his mind blank.

Just as quickly he recovered and his mind started racing. If the explosion had been seen by the collector, then it would also have been seen by others from the shore and the lifeboat would soon be alerted by the Coast Guard. He knew they must turn back and look for survivors; not to do so would put them under immediate suspicion.

"Dom. Take her about. No-one could have survived that, but we will have to be seen to be looking. The lifeboat will be here soon and they'll want to talk to us as soon as we reach the mooring. Quick, there isn't much time; we don't anyone to think we're leaving the scene. If we raise their suspicions we'll be searched all the more thoroughly and they'll find the helmet.'

Martin called the Coast Guard and reported the explosion, while Dominique went about. He informed them there had been an explosion on small motor boat out night fishing and that they were turning back to search for survivors. The Coast Guard acknowledged and confirmed the lifeboat was already on its way down river.

"If our collector is watching, others are surely watching too, Martin," Dominique said, after she had completed the manoeuvre. "I'm scared."

Natalie put her arm round her.

"I am sorry – this is all my fault," Natalie said, through her tears.

"No Natalie, you 'ad to do it – for Alain's sake and you also protected us," replied Dominique. "I think if you 'ad not shot 'im, 'e would 'ave shot us to get the 'elmet."

"He'd been so humiliated at being fooled a second time, I think he was determined to get the helmet whatever the cost. We had a narrow escape thanks to you. But I still don't understand how our collector knew it was him on board," Martin said. "Assuming it was him on the phone – I can't be sure of anything now."

The Phalaris soon reached the spot where the motor boat had gone down and they circled the debris which was floating up from below. They could see odd bits of wood from the cabin and a lifebelt, badly charred. No body. Martin shone the torch all around. He let off a flare to light a wider area, but even in the ghostly reddish glare given off he could see nothing substantial left of the motorboat. He shivered and indicated to Dominique to heave to and wait for the lifeboat. There was no point in searching any more.

As they reset the sails to ride the waves and wait, the lifeboat could be seen approaching on the crest of a startlingly white bow-wave glinting in the moonlight. It slowed as it approached and came alongside. After a short discussion the lifeboat boson told them continue on their way and took over the search.

The Phalaris continued upstream, lowering the sails as they passed Kingswear and switching to the engine to counter the strong current. They picked up a mooring buoy opposite the Naval College. An hour or so later the lifeboat came alongside again. After a brief exchange they agreed to make their statement to the police and customs the next day. Martin, Dominique and Natalie were left to settle down for the night.

Early the following morning Martin looked out of the porthole across to the quayside. He was in time to see the harbour master's launch cast off and set off on its morning rounds to visit the yachts that had arrived during the night. It turned first towards the Phalaris. Martin tracked its progress, went out into the cockpit and stood waiting for the final approach. Inside, he felt tense and wary, striving to appear relaxed and welcoming to the visitors on the outside. He took the line as they came alongside and helped them across onto the Phalaris.

The customs officer shook hands, introduced himself and then asked:

"Do you mind if these two officers from Interpol observe, sir? There may be a connection here with international smuggling. Commissaire Rousseau and Detective Inspector Antoniarchis."

"No objection at all. Welcome aboard, Commissaire, Detective Inspector," Martin said.

Pierre and Antonia showed him no signs of recognition as they shook hands. Martin was puzzled as to why they had come aboard and quite how he was supposed to react, but took his cue from them.

"I'm not sure we can help you very much officer, except to describe what we saw. It all happened very quickly and we were knocked off our feet by the explosion and the shock wave it caused."

"A description would still be helpful, sir."

Dominique emerged from the cabin and smiled her smile to cover her surprise as she was introduced to the three officers.

"Is there anyone else on board, sir?"

"Yes, a friend of mine," Dominique answered for him. She called down to Natalie, who came out into the cockpit, hair still dishevelled and looking as if she had just woken. She started when she recognised Pierre and Antonia, but quickly hid her reaction by throwing her head back to swing her hair off her face.

"I am sorry to get you up so early, miss, but the matter is quite urgent as I am sure you all understand."

"That's OK, monsieur – how can I help?" Natalie said.

"I'd like to take a statement from each of you as to what happened last night and what you saw."

"Of course. Perhaps you would like to do that in the cabin?" asked Martin.

"That would be fine, sir. Shall we take you first?"

While the two men went below, Natalie and Dominique stayed in the cockpit and talked quietly to Pierre and Antonia.

"Was it Sondheim?" asked Antonia.

"Yes. He threatened us with a gun, but a wave threw him off balance and the next thing we knew his gun went off as he stumbled. The bullet must have hit one the fuel tanks and there was an explosion. The boat just blew apart," Dominique said.

"You had no idea Sondheim would be waiting for you?" asked Antonia.

"Of course not!" Dominique replied. "We thought it was the collector and this was the rendezvous to give him the bloody 'elmet."

She paused, her mind's eye seeing the explosion again and Sondheim silhouetted amidst the flames for a split second before she was thrown backwards in the cockpit when the shock-wave hit the Phalaris. It was an image which would take a long time to fade in her memory. Shaking herself back to the present she added:

"The weird thing was that we received a phone call from the collector immediately afterwards."

"Who took the call?" asked Antonia.

"Martin did – you'd better ask him about it – he seemed unsure afterwards whether it was our collector or not."

Martin came up from the cabin and whispered in Dominique's ear as she passed him to go down into the cabin.

"Tell us about the phone call you received after the explosion, Martin," Pierre said, when Martin had sat down.

"Well, at the time I was sure it was the collector, but I'm beginning to wonder now. It all happened so quickly and my ears were still ringing from the" – he hesitated for a split second – "explosion. Whoever it was knew Sondheim was in the motorboat."

"Did he say what you were to do next?"

"He said to wait until he contacted us again."

Pierre and Antonia looked at each other.

"What is it you're not telling us?" asked Martin.

"Well, we can't be sure," Antonia said slowly "but there is still one tombarolo not accounted for. Possibly the one who murdered Samborini. He may also have been there when your friends were murdered in Bari. He was not picked up in the chapel in Calvi."

"We think he may have been following Sondheim in order to get to the real helmet," Pierre said. "That's why we came down here to warn you it isn't over yet."

"Could the voice have been Italian?" asked Antonia.

"Possibly. He spoke so softly, I can't be sure," replied Martin thinking back.

Dominique came up from the cabin and said something to Natalie as she went below to give her statement. Shortly after the customs officer returned to the cockpit.

"That seems all in order. You may have been mistaken for another yacht. It's not unusual for an incoming boat to be met at the mouth of the estuary at night by fellow smugglers – usually drugs, cigarettes or occasionally diamonds. The goods are transferred and landed in one of the small bays, before being taken up the cliffs to waiting transport. Unusual he was armed though."

"But what about the explosion?" asked Pierre.

"We may never know exactly what caused it – the current is very strong at the mouth of the river and everything will be quickly swept away. It's too dangerous to send divers down at that spot. Mr Handley thought he may have heard a shot just before the explosion. So, if the man was holding a gun and was thrown off balance in the boat and his gun went off, the bullet must have struck the petrol tank. Unlucky for him, but lucky for you." He shrugged his shoulders. "Some of these people know nothing about boats and the sea – they just drive speed boats as if they were sports cars."

Pierre seemed satisfied with the answer and asked no more questions. The customs officer turned to Martin.

"I should ask you whether you have anything to declare, sir, and just check your passports – it will save you all time coming ashore to the office."

"No, nothing, we're just visiting for a few days and will be returning to France for the winter."

"That'll be all then. I have your contact addresses if I should need further details from you. Enjoy your stay in Dartmouth."

He saluted and the boarding party started to leave. Before he stepped onto the customs launch, he turned and asked:

"You didn't hear any other shots I suppose? There were reports ..."

"No, nothing," Martin replied.

"I thought not, Captain. Well, have a good day."

He saluted again.

They watched in silence as the launch drew away. Pierre looked back once and caught their eye.

Chapter 21

"Well, I don't think anyone was fooled. The customs officer wa: clearly under instructions to believe everything we told him!" Martin said, breathing more easily as the launch receded into the distance and reached the shore below the Customs House.

The three of them went back into the cabin. Martin poured everyone coffee and turned to the galley, where the mackerel they had caught on the way over were waiting on the side. Dominique and Natalie sipped their drink and watched him at work.

"We're definitely the *appât* – how do you say? – the bait, but 'ow on earth did Sondheim know where we were?" Dominique said.

"That's a puzzle – I don't know, Dom. He must have tracked our crossing from Paimpol somehow. He's had plenty of time to look for us since his release in London and we were always vulnerable while we were in the Canal du Midi."

"So why not attack us there?"

"He may have thought we'd more chance of getting the helmet to England than he had and so he waited till we'd done the work for him."

"Bastard! Well, now 'e won't be bothering us anyone any more."

Natalie remained silent, still shaken over what she had done the night before. Dominique laid her hand gently on her arm and asked:

"So what will you do now, Natalie? They're not going to investigate this any further whatever they might suspect."

Martin appeared lost in thought as he concentrated on cooking the fish. He turned them over for the final time, added some more butter and sprinkled in some flour.

"I'll go back to La Roquette and try to pick up my life where I left off. Alain and I had planned to set up our own business with the money from this job if we'd been successful." Natalie paused. "But I expect I can go back to my old firm in Nice – I never officially left."

"That might be best," Dominique said.

"I'm not so sure," Martin said, turning towards them, frying pan in hand. "I think it might be better for us all to stick together a bit longer. I don't like what they told us about the remaining Italian still on the run. We won't be able to help you, Natalie, if you're on your own down south."

"I would like to stay with you," Natalie said, smiling for the first time that day. "You have been real friends, especially after how all this started."

Martin refilled the coffee pot and turned out the crisp fried mackerel onto the plates. They continued to discus what to do next.

Their phone went again later that morning.

"We are to take the helmet to the collector in Edinburgh," Martin said. "It was definitely our man this time."

He also knew for certain now that the voice on the phone after the explosion had sounded Italian, but he said nothing to the other two.

*

Dusk was falling when they made their way along the grey streets towards St. Giles' Cathedral. It was cold for the season and they were well wrapped up against the biting wind, which the seasoned Edinburghers seemed not to notice; some not even wearing fleeces or coats as they hurried home after staying late in their offices. The dark shape of the Castle loomed broodingly over them, perched on the edge of the cliff, seemingly ready to throw itself off like many of Edinburgh's citizens had done in the past.

They entered the church and sought the statue of John Knox in the south aisle. He stared coldly, unforgiving, down upon them from his plinth, seeing only their sins, and they felt a million miles from the warmth and easy life-style of the Mediterranean, both physically and mentally. None of them spoke as they looked around them, trying to see into the darker corners of the church. Somewhere, they knew, Rousseau and Antoniarchis would be watching, no doubt with the local police.

An elderly man was approaching. He was not tall, but held himself proudly, perhaps to disguise a certain stockiness natural to his age. He spoke quietly, his Scot's accent softened by years of living south of the border.

"Mr Handley and Mademoiselle Krevine," he hesitated and added "and Mademoiselle Marceau, if I understand correctly. I'm Lord Glenbrae, but please call me James. Charles never said my name? Ever the professional."

They all shook hands as he continued:

"Any friends of Charles and Edward are my friends too. What a terrible business – if I had known ..."

The three of them remained silent and waited while he composed himself.

"Well, to business then. Do ye have the package? You do? Good."

He looked round, eyes piercing the shadows in the church, and slowly turned back to them.

"Just in case we're not on our own here, you understand, I think we'll leave this place to conclude our business elsewhere."

He looked up at John Knox towering above him.

"I never did find auld wee John much fun myself – better than the papists though, mind," he added with a chuckle.

They followed him out of the cathedral. As they were leaving, Martin heard sounds of a scuffle behind and glanced back inside. At the far end of the aisle he could see a group of police surrounding a man who they had wrestled to the floor – the last tombarolo to be rounded up, he was sure. He breathed a sigh of relief and quickly rejoined the others who were already waiting in the car outside. The chauffeur closed the doors and the car swung out into the evening traffic. Lord Glenbrae settled back comfortably in his seat and looked at his three companions.

"Now don't ye go worrying. We have about an hour to go, before we reach the house, so relax and enjoy the ride."

He turned and glanced quickly out of the rear window at the traffic behind.

"Don't you want to see the helmet?" asked Martin, noticing his movement.

"No, no. I've waited this long and can wait a wee while longer. I want to see it first in the right setting, not on my knee in the back of a car."

He looked again through the rear window and turned back to them.

"I want you to tell me all about what happened and how it was that poor Charles and Edward were murdered."

Back inside the cathedral the Chief Constable of Edinburgh was talking to Pierre and Antonia.

"Well, so far so good. We'll take this nasty wee chap away. The sooner we hand him over to the Italians the better. But don't worry we won't lose the others. I've men outside and anyway we know who he is – Lord Glenbrae, a lovely man, well liked here in Scotland. He's a former Secretary of State for Scotland. His family firm makes a lovely single malt – have done for generations."

An hour later Lord Glenbrae's car turned into the drive of a large house set back from the road in its own grounds. The chauffeur opened the car doors for them and Lord Glenbrae strode on ahead. The front door opened as he approached and Martin, Dominique and Natalie followed him inside. He led the way into a library where a wood fire was burning welcomingly in the hearth. He went straight to his desk and handed over a package to Dominique.

"There, that is what I promised Charles and Edward for their work. It's yours now – I'm sure they would find that fair. Well, don't keep me in suspense any longer – show me the helmet."

Martin sat down at the desk and carefully placed the helmet on it. He began to remove the protective packing. There was a knock on the library door and the butler entered.

"The Chief Constable of Edinburgh, My Lord, with Detective Inspector Antoniarchis and Commissaire Rousseau of Interpol."

"Ah! Good evening, Chief Constable, glad you were able to keep up. My chauffeur wasn't breaking the speed limit I hope. Welcome Detective Inspector, Commissaire. Now what can I do for you? "

"Good evening, My Lord. I think you already know why we are here."

He turned towards Martin, Dominique and Natalie.

"Martin Handley, Dominique Krevine, Natalie Marceau, I am arresting you on suspicion of illegally importing stolen artefacts into the United Kingdom and attempting to sell them. You need not say anything, but anything ..."

Antonia had gone straight to the desk and made a show of examining the helmet intently. She swivelled round in her chair and interrupted the Chief Constable.

"I'm not sure a crime has been committed here. This is just a very good replica, Chief Constable. It's not the real thing."

"But you tell to us ..." Dominique started to say, suddenly falling silent.

For a moment no-one said a word; just the sound of the wood crackling in the fire could be heard. Pierre caught Antonia's eye, but both remained impassive. Martin, Dominique and Natalie sat down and looked at each other in puzzlement. Lord Glenbrae looked furious for a moment, but a smile crept slowly across his face.

"Well, Chief Constable, it appears there has been a slight misunderstanding. These young people were just bringing me a lovely wee gift from their holiday in Greece. Surely now, ye didn't think I'd be involved in anything illegal, did ye? It's a wondrous sight nonetheless, don't ye think?"

"Indeed, My Lord. Very impressive. I'm sorry we've interrupted your evening unnecessarily," the Chief Constable said, scarcely managing to keep his fury in check.

"No, don't fret so, Chief Constable. Now you are here and with these distinguished officers from Interpol, ye all must take a wee dram to ward off the cold of the evening, before your return to Edinburgh. Jenkins, bring us a bottle of the '82. No, make that the '45 – the Bonnie Prince Charlie anniversary special."

"Very well, milord."

*

"I still don't understand what happened – was there never a real helmet after all?" asked Natalie.

She and Dominique were sitting by the picture window in La Roquette looking out over the swimming pool down the valley towards the lights of Nice and Cannes.

"We don't know. Either it was all an elaborate sting – or the real helmet was stolen somewhere along the line. Per'aps the Turks still have it."

"Why did so many people have to die, Dominique? The helmet is cursed – I'm sure Achilles thought so too and wished he'd never lent it to Patroclus. Like him, I've lost my best friend."

"We feel the same – I really liked Charlie and *le petit* Edouard. They died a 'orrible death."

Natalie leaned forward and squeezed her hand.

"You're right, Dom, I'm not the only one who has lost someone – I'm sorry."

The door opened and Martin came in. He had just returned from going down to Nice and was carrying some English newspapers.

"Look at this headline – it's a few days old, but I am beginning to understand what happened in Edinburgh."

'Scottish Laird Donates Art Collection To The Nation'

Lord Glenbrae has generously donated his entire art collection to the National Art Gallery of Scotland. Many of the paintings and works of art have not been seen on the open market for decades. Much of the collection was purchased by his father and particularly by his grandfather, the sixth earl.

Lord Glenbrae said: "I would like to donate the family collection as a memorial to two very good friends in the art world: Charles Everidge and Edward Robson. Both recently lost their lives in a tragic incident in Italy when on business for me. I wish to honour their memory in the most fitting way I can think of. I want the public to be able to enjoy these works of art, just as my family has been able to over the centuries.

"He was a nice man, Martin," Dominique said.

"Mm, perhaps." Martin looked thoughtful. "Or he had to do a deal. He knew the police were following us that night, though no-one was expecting the helmet to be a fake, least of all us. Nor was he, though he recovered his composure very quickly."

He looked at Natalie.

"Don't look at me – I was as surprised as you were," she said. "Think back – did the helmet ever leave your sight after Charles and Edward gave it to you?"

"Well, yes, you know it did. You were there."

"Of course! You gave it to Antoniarchis so she could have a replica made," Natalie said.

"So perhaps she had two made and kept the real helmet. She gave one to us to do the deal with Sondheim ..."

"And in Calvi a second one to Dom and me to bring into England, saying it was the real thing!"

"So where is the real one?"

"Good question – we may never know," Martin said. "It's like a sting in reverse."

"At least we got to keep the money – Lord Glenbrae did not want it back – so we got paid twice! Mind you, with a castle like that 'e could afford it. In a funny way I think 'e rather enjoyed the way it ended. Having the real thing would 'ave reminded him of what it cost in lives to get it," Dominique said. "Like us, 'e was beginning to think there was a curse on the real 'elmet and that it should never 'ave been disturbed."

*

Pierre was back in his office in the Sûreté in Paris coping with a mountain of reports and general paperwork. Following the Achilles' Helmet affair, there had been many detailed reports to write and he had neglected the routine paperwork connected to other investigations. Antonia had returned to Athens after the business in Edinburgh and he was forced to admit to himself he missed her. He had a lot of leave to take and was vainly trying to clear his desk before setting off for Athens himself to spend a month with her there. He had a feeling there were things he had still not understood about what happened in Edinburgh.

He got up, stretched, went downstairs and out of the building. It was a crisp late autumn day, but people were still sitting outside on the *terrasses* of the cafés. He went to his usual place at the Café L'imprévu.

The waiter looked up from behind the bar and brought him his coffee and a copy of *Le Monde* without being asked. He turned the pages to the arts section and the name Lord Glenbrae caught his attention. As he read the article a smile crept across his face.

"Ah! Now I'm beginning to understand," he murmured.
"Commissaire?"
The waiter was hovering at his table.
"Excusez-moi, Claude. Je parlais tout seul!"
"Pas de problème, Commissaire."
Further on there was another announcement.

'The National Archaeological Museum of Athens and the Arkeoloji Müzesi of Istanbul are pleased to announce a major joint Exhibition of the treasures recently discovered in the tomb of Prince Achilles and his childhood friend and kinsman Prince Patroclus near the site of the battle for Troy around 1500BC. The exhibition will be held first in Athens and then move to Istanbul.'

*

Antonia met him at Athens airport and drove him back into the centre of town. Pierre spent most of the journey either looking out of the side window or with his eyes shut. Even for someone used to the traffic in Paris, the experience of traffic in Athens was too much. Antonia drove with one hand on the wheel, the other she used to indicate her feelings towards fellow road users, accompanied by descriptions of their family background, which Pierre did not wish to fully understand. The soft top was down and with the wind in her hair Detective Inspector Antoniarchis was clearly enjoying the drive.

"I will take you first to the Exhibition," she said. "We are very proud of it and we're cooperating wonderfully with the Turks. Colonel Kahn has been here to see it and sends you his greetings. He looks very smart in his new uniform. I've been seconded back to the museum for the whole time of the exhibition, so I am very happy too."

She swerved cross the road in front of three lines of on-coming traffic and turned sharply into the courtyard in front of the museum. When Pierre opened his eyes again, she was pulling up in a reserved parking space.

"Leave your bags in the car," she said. "I want to show you something right away."

Pierre followed her into the museum, managing to keep up along several corridors until they reached the main room of the exhibition. The lighting was soft and the exhibits were all in climatically controlled glass cases. They had to push their way through the press of people and eventually ended up in front of the large glass case. Inside was a suit of body armour. Although much of the iron had corroded, the gold rivets and other decoration were still bright and shining. In another case by the side was a huge ceremonial shield and the wooden case it had been kept in, which was decorated in ivory and gold.

Taking his arm. Antonia guided Pierre into a side room where the lighting was even softer. In the middle, all on its own, was a glass case with a golden helmet inside on a red velvet cushion. Neither of them could speak for a few minutes. Then Pierre moved forward and read the inscription on the plaque.

'Kindly donated by the Earl of Glenbrae in memory of Charles Everidge and Edward Robson.'

He turned towards Antonia who was wreathed in smiles at his astonishment.

"But we gave Handley the second replica to take to him, so how could Glenbrae donate the real thing? He never had it."

Antonia shrugged her shoulders.

"Yes, we did. As you know, I simply couldn't take the risk of the real helmet being damaged or stolen on the way to England, so I had two replicas made. They were both on the plane we met on the island of Pantelleria. I sent the original back on the plane."

Pierre just looked at her still mystified. All this he already knew.

"In Scotland, we did a deal. Lord Glenbrae donated his art collection to the National Gallery of Scotland in return for not being prosecuted for having had some of the collection stolen to order. Some of the items may have to be returned to their owners."

"I still don't follow."

"In return we let him keep the replica," she continued, ignoring his remark. "After all if it hadn't been for him we would not have the real helmet. But we respected the fact he wanted in some way to make up for starting something which had led to the deaths of his friends – and others – so we agreed to put this inscription on the plinth of real helmet here."

"But how did you persuade the authorities to agree ...?"

Antonia just smiled her Delphic smile.

"Never mind, all that matters is that you did. This calls for a celebration."

"Oysters and white wine?"

"*Je ne dirais pas non*! – but do you have such exotic things here in Greece, Detective Inspector?"

Antonia pinched his arm hard and steered him towards the exit.

Printed in Great Britain
by Amazon

45161554R00155